A Duke Makes a Deal

Gambling Peers, Book 1

Matilda Madison

ARE YOU SIGNED UP FOR DRAGONBLADE'S BLOG?

You'll get the latest news and information on exclusive giveaways, exclusive excerpts, coming releases, sales, free books, cover reveals and more.

Check out our complete list of authors, too!

No spam, no junk. That's a promise!

Sign Up Here

www.dragonbladepublishing.com

Dearest Reader;

Thank you for your support of a small press. At Dragonblade Publishing, we strive to bring you the highest quality Historical Romance from some of the best authors in the business. Without your support, there is no 'us', so we sincerely hope you adore these stories and find some new favorite authors along the way.

Happy Reading!

CEO, Dragonblade Publishing

Chapter One

London, 1822

"DO NOT BE anxious, my dear," Joseph Woodvine whispered to his daughter, his white mustache twitching with trepidation. "All will be well."

Clara Woodvine smiled tightly at her papa as she held onto his coat sleeve. She tried her best to appear as if she wasn't nervous, even though there was a slight ringing in her ears as they climbed the stone steps. This was to be the most exciting night of her life. Not only was it her first ball in society, but if everything went according to plan, she would be engaged before the night was over, praised and congratulated by every guest in attendance tonight. This night was meant to be a triumph.

What did she possibly have to be anxious about?

Swallowing hard, Clara ignored the erratic beating of her heart. She felt like she had eaten too many sugary treats. She was jittery and nauseous all at once, and no amount of steady breathing seemed to calm her nerves. She wasn't usually prone to worrying. She had always had a healthy dose of self-assurance, but this was well outside her usual realm of experience.

They entered the foyer of the Earl of Trembley's Mayfair home as a footman directed them to a queue that led into the ballroom. Clara turned to face her mother, Mary, who tried to give her an encouraging nod but appeared rather pale herself. They walked through the bright, vaulted entranceway where hundreds, if not thousands, of white flowers decorated every spare inch. It was the definition of elegance, Clara mused as they were shepherded to the front of a receiving line.

"I'm not sure if this was the right gown to wear," Clara whispered to her mother as she tried tugging up the neckline.

Her mother had insisted that she wear the latest fashion London had to offer. While Clara quite liked the pale green color of the fabric, which brought out the green in her eyes, she hadn't been sure the low, square neckline her mother had chosen was appropriate. Nor was she particularly pleased with all the embellishments the seamstress had insisted upon. As Clara glanced around the room, she half suspected her dressmaker had added the extra beading simply for cost's sake rather than fashion. While all the other ladies in attendance wore gowns adorned with satin braided piping or silk laces, Clara's dress was heavily decorated with gold-colored glass beads, stitched in tiny, individual star-like patterns that covered the gown from hem to hem. On a figure like hers, which was far rounder and plumper compared to the narrow hips that were so popular among young ladies these days, she was sure she stuck out like a particularly gaudy sore thumb.

"It's divine, dear. Now stop tugging at it," her mother whispered back, her hand coming up to tuck a flyaway strand of Clara's frizzy ash blonde hair behind her ear. "We should have used oil of neroli on your hair to keep it tamed."

Clara gently batted her mother's hand away.

"I'm quite happy without it. I don't like smelling like an orange grove."

"Yes, but it would have made it smoother. More pleasant to look at."

Clara did her very best not to roll her eyes. She knew her mother was only trying to help and that her hair was unfashionable. Unmanageable even, but it wasn't as if she could do anything about it. It had been that way all her life, and she had long since come to terms with it, and with the other so-called flaws in her appearance. Unusual though it was, she had always liked her countenance and had never wished to change it. It was only now, with the pressures of their family coming out in proper society, that she was becoming aware of how unsatisfactory she appeared, at least compared to the fashion pamphlets. Part of her wanted to fit in, wanted to be accepted, but at the same time, she didn't particularly care for the way that the need to be fashionable was making her doubt herself.

Clara and her mother had spent hours preparing themselves for the Earl of Trembley's ball. While Clara had initially been happy at their invitation, believing it would be similar to the country dances she had attended before coming to London, she soon learned the soirées of first society were vastly different from the ones she was used to. While Clara had always believed herself a brave person, she found that joining the ranks of the peerage unsettled her greatly.

She inhaled and exhaled slowly, noting the scent of roses and wisteria in the air. This was the first formal ball that any of the Woodvines had ever attended, and it certainly wouldn't be the last, so she needed to get a handle on her emotions. Clara's cheek muscles stiffly pulled up as she tried to smile. Had she forgotten how to smile? Bringing up her free hand, she pressed her gloved fingers into her cheek as a footman approached to announce their arrival.

"Mr. and Mrs. Joseph Woodvine and Miss Clara Woodvine," the footman's voice boomed as they came into the ballroom.

Few heads turned, and only one or two ladies' eyebrows raised in vague curiosity, barely sparing Clara an up-and-down glance. For the most part, no one seemed particularly interested in Clara or her parents. For that, she was grateful. Although they were wealthy, nearly obscenely so due to her father's latest invention—a self-raking reaping machine that was set to revolutionize how grain was harvested—the Woodvines were commoners and relatively unknown in first society. There were only a handful of progressive peers who invested their monies in new technologies and who kept track of who was making waves. It had been enough to score Clara some invitations upon their arrival in London—but only a very few. Socially, they were largely overlooked, though that particular tide seemed to be turning.

It remained to be seen whether becoming known would make them *accepted*. After all, monied or not, Clara's mother, Mary, had even been a maid in her youth for a wealthy, titled family. There were sure to be some in the upper echelon who would baulk at the idea of welcoming her as an equal. Clara could only hope that her own marriage would help cement her family's position. It was why she was so eager to find Hubert. The expected proposal could not come soon enough.

Craning her neck as they walked, arm in arm as if they were entering a battlefield, Clara watched for Viscount Dilworth, Hubert Jenkins. In truth, they had only met a handful of times, but for Clara's part, that had been enough. She was sure they would be a love match, and, tonight, he would make their engagement official.

It had been a serendipitous meeting the day she and Hubert had come together. She had been invited to a salon held by Lady Kelsey, wife of banker Sir Alfred Kelsey. It had been a somewhat scandalous topic, considering Lady Kelsey had rounded up several professional men to speak about financial independence and the need for heiresses to protect their fortunes. Clara's father, a practical man at heart, had encouraged his daughter to accept Lady Kelsey's invitation and attend since she was the sole heir and set to inherit the family fortune one day. Clara's mother had thought the entire thing was macabre and, being a conservative woman, hoped that her daughter would find a good husband who would manage the family finances for her.

As it turned out, the viscount had arrived just as the salon was ending and Lady Kelsey had seemed somewhat annoyed by the young lord's unannounced arrival. There seemed to be some disagreement between Lady Kelsey and the viscount about a lost invitation, but as they were both too well-mannered to cause a scene, Lady Kelsey graciously allowed Dilworth to stay. Soon enough, his charisma soon had many of the ladies in attendance smiling. Clara herself had found his quick wit charming, not to mention how attractive his mouth appeared when he would grin at her. She felt herself blush just thinking about his smile. His light brown eyes shined with friendly acceptance, and Clara had found it difficult not to be instantly smitten with the handsome young lord.

It had happened so fast, Clara remembered fondly as she moved through the ballroom. She had only met him for a moment's introduction, but he had called on her twice the following week and three times after that before he had finally declared his undying love for her. Clara had been surprised and somewhat taken aback by his eagerness. She had never been the object of a declaration of undying love before, and while it was rather startling, it was also flattering. At twenty-four years old, she had started to believe that perhaps she just wasn't destined to fall in love. Until she met Hubert. He had seemed to be just the sort of man a lady should fall in love with. She wasn't *quite* there yet, but surely she would be soon. She had no objection to marrying first and falling in love with her husband afterward. After all, they had a whole lifetime ahead of them to spend together—and there was nothing to be gained by waiting.

She was several years older than most debutantes, and Clara understood her chances at marriage were growing smaller every year. The shift in their family's social-economical standing in recent years had been a bit of a whirlwind, and Clara barely had time to maintain her friendships, let alone explore her marital options. It was rather lucky for her to have met Hubert when she did. Her mother could barely contain her excitement at the prospect of her daughter becoming a viscountess. Her father, on the other hand, had been the one whose opinion seemed the most steadfast.

"I must confess, I don't believe this courtship of yours has lasted long enough for you to be certain in your choice," her father said as he led Clara and his wife through the crush.

"Papa, it has been several weeks, and I've learned quite a lot about his lordship," Clara said, her tone hushed so that others could not overhear them, even if no one seemed particularly interested.

"Yes, well, if you are certain that you wish to marry the viscount, my dear, I shan't stand in your way," he said, as his hand came up to his face and he twirled his whiskers with his forefinger, something he only did so when he was uneasy about something. "I would never wish to be an obstacle to your happiness."

"Oh!" her mother whispered-exclaimed. "What greater happiness could there be than a wedding? This is wonderful! Imagine. My daughter! A viscountess!"

"Mother, please. Someone might hear you," Clara said, keeping her voice low. "And thank you, Father."

"Although, one wonders about his intentions," her father said, causing Mary's steps to falter.

"Oh, Joseph, do not dare try to paint their courtship in a poor light. The viscount is simply in love. What's wrong with that?"

"Nothing, my dear. But I won't pretend that it isn't at least curious that the young lord happened upon our daughter when he did." He faced Clara. "Of course, I would never find it strange in the slightest that any man under the sun would fall in love with you, dear daughter, as soon as they became aware of your merits. You are quite perfect in my eyes. But then I'm not an impartial judge, nor am I a disinterested party. As your father, it is my duty to see you well settled. I would be failing in my responsibility if I didn't at least express my concerns about Lord Dilworth."

"Hush, Joseph. Someone will hear and think you're disparaging the viscount," Mary said, peering over her shoulder as they walked.

"Settle down, dearest. I only wish to approach it from a logical point of view," he countered before turning back to Clara. "Now I know it isn't unheard of to fall in love with members outside one's social circle. But let us recount the last, oh, five marriage announcements written in the *Times* about peers who marry wealthy heiresses. And should we not also take into consideration his presence at the salon? It was a discussion on financial literacy for heiresses. His attendance was suspicious, to say the least."

"I'm well aware that without my inheritance, the viscount would probably never look twice at me," Clara said calmly. "But I hardly think a man's lack of funding can determine his character. Perhaps he inherited his debt and is no more responsible for it than I am."

Mary nodded furiously at her daughter's words.

"If anything, the viscount is very astute and enterprising to have attended such an event," Clara continued. "And if the result of a practical act is an acquaintanceship, which led to love, which will result in a happy marriage, well, it's hardly an issue, is it?"

Joseph shook his head and smiled at his daughter, his deep-set eyes shining slightly.

"Dear daughter, how can I possibly be happy to see you married off when I will have no one to argue with when you are gone?"

Clara smiled and hugged her father.

"Mama will argue with you."

"I shall do no such thing," Mary interrupted. "Your father enjoys talking circles around everyone. Only you enjoy entertaining his dizzying speech."

Clara tried ignoring her sadness at the prospect of moving out of her parents' house. She so enjoyed her discussions with Papa. They would spend hours trying to convince the other to change their mind. Then, having done so, they would proceed to argue the opposite point, just to see if they could get the other to change their mind once more. It was a game that she would miss dreadfully upon her marriage to the viscount. There would be letters and visits, of course, but it wouldn't be the same.

However, everything changed, she reminded herself as she set her shoulders back a fraction. She would meet her new life with determination and an open mind, just as her papa had always taught her.

Clara always hoped to make a match like her parents. They had such an easy and compatible marriage and had always been good helpmates to one another. While they hadn't been a love match at first, it had grown into one. That was perhaps the most charming thing about their story. They had married out of practicality and love had bloomed all on its own. Her mother had often said that her father's respect towards her had been the deciding factor that made her say yes when he proposed, and it was that consideration that Clara longed for most. Respect from one's spouse was a rare and precious gift. She had witnessed so many of her friends marry men who didn't seem very interested in their wives' opinions.

But Clara's father had always supported his daughter's analytical thoughts and Clara only hoped to find someone who was equally curious. Dilworth had been terribly curious about her ever since their first meeting and as a gentleman, he displayed the utmost respect towards her. Clara was very pleased about it indeed. And if she wasn't in love yet, surely she would fall in love soon, and with who better than a handsome, young viscount who already avowed to love her devotedly?

As her papa recognized several older gentlemen who were gathered around the refreshments table, he took Clara's hand from the crook of his arm, squeezed her fingers, and headed over to meet his associates. Meanwhile, Clara and her mother were approached by a short, plump woman with refined features and kind eyes. She was dressed in a deep, ambiguine colored gown, with glittering jewels wrapped around her neck and set in her dark curls.

"Welcome to Elswick Terrace, Mrs. Woodvine, Miss

Woodvine," the woman said as Clara curtsied deeply, just as her mother had taught her. Though she didn't know who this woman was, she could tell by the gems that adorned her neck that she was a lady of importance. "My son informed me that he extended an invitation to you and your family tonight. Evidently congratulations are in order to you and Lord Dilworth. However," she said, looking around, "as neither my son or Lord Dilworth is present, I shall have to introduce myself. I am Lady Trembley."

"Oh, my lady," Mary said, curtseying again. "It is an honor to make your acquaintance. But the engagement is not quite official. The viscount has not yet asked my daughter."

"Oh, no?" the countess said, turning to Clara. "I was under the impression Dilworth had plans to announce his engagement tonight."

Mary couldn't help but smile widely at her daughter, who felt rather silly for being the center of both women's attention. Clara wasn't sure why, but she felt unsure all of a sudden. Shaking her head, she tried to brush off her feelings and gave the women a small smile.

"I should be fortunate indeed if the viscount should bestow such an honor on me," she said demurely.

The countess's eyes narrowed slightly as she scrutinized Clara.

"My dear, it will be he who is lucky," she said quietly. "Never forget that."

Clara could tell that Mary was shocked by the countess's words, but all she could do was grin.

"Yes, my lady," she said before another guest distracted the countess.

She left Clara and Mary as she glided away, but they were not alone long. In the next moment, Hubert was upon them.

Clara's stomach seemed to buzz at the sight of him. Though there was not anything exceptionally striking in his fair complexion, regular features, and light hair, Clara thought he was quite dashing, especially once one had to chance to get to know him. He was always smiling and impeccably dressed, and Clara doubted there was a man anywhere in the world that was a more perfect example of what a gentleman should be. While he was slight in the shoulders, he appeared relatively fit and she had come to like that they were the same height, feeling that it gave her equality to him.

"Mrs. Woodvine," the viscount said with a nod before turning to speak to Clara, his round, blue eyes shined with eagerness. "My dearest," he said. "I'm sorry I could not escort you and your family to tonight's ball. I had a previous engagement I could not avoid."

"It's quite all right," Clara said. "We just were introduced to the dowager countess."

"Ah, yes, the old bird is making her rounds," the viscount said, glancing around. Upon seeing the shock and discomfort on Clara's face at this show of disrespect toward their hostess, he quickly turned contrite. "My apologies, dearest. The dowager countess and I have never gotten on for some reason."

"It is her loss to be sure," Mary started.

The viscount gave her his most charming grin as thanks. He always flirted just a bit with her mother—indeed, with most women they encountered. It was a curious thing to witness, but she supposed that was how fashionable people behaved. She told herself it didn't bother her, even if it seemed a bit insincere.

"Are you all right, my heart?" he asked sweetly.

Clara gazed at him and instantly allowed herself to be swayed by his smile. She shook her head.

"It's only nerves, I suppose," she lied smoothly. "I've never attended such a formal ball."

He peered around the room, looking more bored than impressed.

"Yes, Elswick Terrace is an impressive home," he said dismissively before turning back to her. "But it pales compared to my country estate, Emerson Abbey."

Clara gazed tenderly at the viscount.

"Where is it?"

"In Devon," he replied. "You will adore it, I'm sure."

Clara smiled, though she felt a strange sense of unease. It seemed the viscount had forgotten to ask her to marry him and assumed she would say yes.

Of course, she would say yes. He was a viscount, for heaven's sake. An eligible, handsome, charming viscount who was close to her own age. He had all of his hair, his teeth were straight, he didn't seem moody or ill-tempered, and while she suspected that he was in desperate need of funds, her dowry should be more than enough to smooth that trouble away, and then there would be nothing to stand in the way of their happiness. A marriage to him would elevate her beyond all her wildest dreams, and wasn't that the greatest thing she could do? Elevate her status as well as her family's.

An inkling of doubt seemed to settle in Clara's stomach. While she appreciated that she should want to marry as far up the social ladder as she could, she couldn't quite stifle the nagging sense that told her she didn't quite belong with Dilworth. Even her friend Bettina Moppet, whom she had befriended when she first came to London, had not spoken very highly of Dilworth, but she was careful never to say anything reproachful about the viscount.

Perhaps these bursts of doubt were simply the result of nerves. Surely there was no reason for her to question what anyone would view as a brilliant match for a girl of her background.

"If you'll excuse me, dearest," the viscount said as he stared into the corner of the ballroom. "I see someone I have business with, and I can't lose sight of him."

"Oh," Clara said, just as the orchestra started to pluck and play at their strings as they warmed up their instruments. "I thought we might dance."

"Darling, it isn't quite right to ask a gentleman to dance," he said as if speaking to a child. "I'd refrain from doing so while I'm gone."

"I didn't mean it that way," she miffed. "I only meant that—"

"To be sure, to be sure," he said quickly. "I'll only be a moment."

The viscount disappeared into the crowd, leaving Clara and her mother alone.

"Really, dear, you shouldn't have asked him that," her mother admonished beneath her breath. "You know better."

"I wasn't asking him to dance," Clara countered. "I just assumed he might wish to ask me since we are to announce our engagement this evening," she said, glancing around the room. "I'll admit, I thought that dancing might help me feel more at ease. I've never been to a ball like this. I suppose I was expecting something smaller, more like our country soirees."

"Yes, it's certainly very different—very grand," her mother agreed. "But you will grow accustomed to it. We shall wait amongst the wall over there, by all the chairs, and when the viscount returns, I'm sure he will make you the center of his attention."

Clara nodded in agreement but had the strangest feeling that the viscount wouldn't make a speedy return. Hubert seemed distracted this evening, almost as if something was commanding his attention. She was curious about what might affect him so. She would ask her mother's opinion, but Clara often sensed that her mother was too stuck in her below-the-stairs mentality to ever question the behaviors of titled men. Perhaps she should write her friend Holly Smyth when she returned home that evening.

Clara had written her friend every detail of her courtship with the viscount so far, and where her mother was wildly impressed with the upper crust, Holly was the granddaughter of a Marquis and far more critical of her social class. She had congratulated Clara on finding a beau but expressed her worry about such a quick courtship. Clara had waved off Holly's warnings, quite sure that she was being overly cautious. But Holly had grown up in their world and was, therefore, Clara's most reliable source of reference.

Clara sighed at the idea of her friend and the quiet little village where she and her parents had lived before their financial windfall. It was a darling town with country lanes, stone cottages, and a river that cut directly through town. As the daughter of the primary landowner, Holly had been stationed much higher than her in society, of course, but in the countryside, those divisions were not as rigorously maintained, and a strong friendship had developed between them from a young age. She had spent her entire childhood running around the village with Holly. Though Clara knew it was ridiculous to be nostalgic for a time when her family had less, she couldn't help but remember the simplicity of their lives before money and the pressures of the ton had changed everything.

Clara followed her mother to the far side of the ballroom. The crush of the crowd had grown since their arrival, and it wasn't easy to make their way through the throng of guests. Her mother moved ahead, slipping between people before several bodies moved behind her. Clara halted just as another group of visitors stepped in front of her. Sighing in a very unladylike manner that earned her several contemptuous stares, Clara sidestepped the group and continued to the outskirts of the room. Another halt in walking caused her to become somewhat annoyed. There were far more people in attendance than she'd expected, and before she was caught in the crowd, she moved quickly between a pair of gentlemen who had allowed a narrow space to come between them. Clara escaped the ballroom within minutes. She was rather proud of herself for evading so many people when a sudden force knocked into her shoulder, pushing her forward.

Throwing her hands up to brace herself for a fall, Clara was surprised when she felt large, warm hands quickly grab her by her shoulders, pulling her back before she could tumble to the floor.

"Oh my," she said as she caught her footing. She turned to see her savior. "Thank you. I didn't see…"

As Clara's eyes lifted to see the man whose hands were still on her, the words on her lips died away. He stood a whole foot taller, effectively towering over her. His black, wavy hair was pushed up in a fashionable, lazy style that most gentlemen tried to accomplish these days. His stormy blue eyes glared at her; his full mouth, set beneath a large nose in a stern face, was set in a scowl.

Clara swallowed hard as she stared at him, convinced that he was the most attractive man she had ever seen. Of course, Clara doubted he felt the same as he was staring at her as if she had just morally offended him.

"I-I'm sorry," she whispered.

For a fraction of a second, the man's eyes flashed with something dangerous, and Clara felt the pulse in her neck begin to flutter. His attractive face and imposing manner made her want to squirm. As his eyes drifted down her face to her chest, she felt exposed and slightly excited. She was sure she should be offended by his open stare, given that it felt as if he could see right through her, but she couldn't manage to muster any offense.

Her cheeks burned with embarrassment as he looked into her eyes.

"The fault was mine." His deep, cultured voice curled around his words.

He bowed slightly and turned quickly, leaving Clara slack-jawed, watching him as he disappeared down the long hallway of Elswick Terrace. What a terrifying man. She exhaled slowly, finally realizing that she had been holding her breath in his presence. Clara had never seen a man so commanding in all her life.

"Was that the Duke of Combe I just saw?" a feminine voice said behind her, causing her to be pulled from her private thoughts. She turned to see a very petite woman with dark hair peering down the hallway. She leaned towards her taller, redheaded friend. "I wasn't aware he had rejoined society."

"I'm surprised he had the audacity to come," the redhead answered.

"But he and the earl are such good friends," the other lady said. "Of course, he would come to Trembley's first ball since the earl inherited his title."

"Still, it's astonishing that he would dare to show his face given all that's been printed in the *Times* about how he treated his poor wife," the redhead said, shaking her head. "Do you know, I heard he nearly killed the poor woman before divorcing her." She made a *tsk tsk tsk* sound as she shook her head. "Supposedly, his temper is just as wicked as his dalliances. I wonder if he's come here for one of Trembley's famous card games."

"To be sure. All men are affected by gambling. It seems the duke is no different."

"I can only hope he'll have the decency to confine himself to the card game and avoid the rest of the ball. After all, there are innocent ladies here."

"Do you think his mere presence here might sully them?"

"Lord knows, but I wouldn't let my daughter anywhere near a divorced man," the redhead said as her eyes fell on Clara, who turned her head quickly and walked away.

Her cheeks warmed with embarrassment for eavesdropping so brazenly. But at the same time, she felt as if the ladies themselves should be at least a little ashamed of gossiping, especially about a man neither of them seemed to know personally. She didn't think the divorced duke deserved such belittling.

Clara made her way back into the ballroom. She had read a bit about him in the gossip pages. When a story was large enough or wicked enough, it would always make its way around, and Clara vaguely remembered hearing about the duke and his unfortunate divorce sometime last year.

The papers had labeled him the Divorced Duke, and they had been brutal in detailing most of the ordeal. The Duchess of

Combe had supposedly suffered greatly in her marriage with him until she'd fled to another man for protection, leading the duke to divorce her only three years after the two had wed. Rumors had persisted that the duke had wicked tastes and had forced the duchess into depraved situations of the carnal variety.

It seemed a large part of refined people's day was spent gossiping, and Bettina had been particularly interested in anything scandalous. Only a week prior, while having tea at Bettina's home during her mother's weekly social gathering, Clara had overheard the Novak sisters being reprimanded by their mother for discussing an article about the former duchess's new life in France. Mrs. Novak had pointed out that gossip wasn't the best form of getting information, but her daughters had countered that it was best to pay attention to rumors, insisting that they always carried a grain of truth. Bettina had listened to the exchange with rapt attention. It was a shame that Bettina was away currently, visiting the country for the week. No doubt she would be astonished to hear that Clara had actually encountered the scandalous duke. Clara would have to be certain to tell her friend all about it when they met the next day, since Bettina and her family were travelling back to London sometime later that night.

The duke's divorce had only been recently finalized as both the House of Lords and the House of Commons were required to grant it. It should have taken longer, but the duke was well connected and seemed to have rushed the matter through.

"I cannot believe it! I just saw the Duke of Combe," someone to her left said as Clara sought her mother, who was sitting against the wall, dutifully waiting for the viscount return.

His attendance was not only interesting to see but to most of the guests. Within minutes of reaching her mother, Clara had overheard at least three other people talking about the duke.

Clara couldn't understand it. It seemed relatively trivial to constantly talk about a man who had suffered a divorce. Divorce was a scandal in and of itself and quite rare, but it hardly seemed an interesting enough topic. And while everyone claimed that the duke's behavior within the marriage had been quite shocking, no one seemed to know any specifics. All Clara had been able to gather from it was that she should be wary about marrying a man with a poor temper. She would not like to be indefinitely linked to a man who would raise a hand to her. Perhaps the duke was violent, and his wife had been lucky to escape him. And yet, having met him, she found it hard to believe. His touch had been tender, if not gentle.

What a silly thing to think. How could she be aware of what sort of man he was from an interaction that lasted for less than a minute? She had no way of knowing anything about him and would do well to push him entirely out of her mind.

And yet, as she watched the ladies and gentlemen pair off to start the dancing, wishing to join the happy couples, she found herself wondering about the duke. Her skin seemed to tingle where their bodies had crashed together, and she unwittily raised her hand to her shoulder and rubbed the spot where they had met. She wondered what it would be like to feel the duke's arms around her as they danced across the crowded ballroom.

But those were foolish thoughts. She shook her head, trying to fight off her curiosity. She was nearly engaged after all, if only Hubert would come back from wherever he went and propose…

Chapter Two

SILAS WINTERS, DUKE of Combe, was trying very hard to quell the rising apprehension he felt at his core. *Damn it.* He shouldn't have come tonight. His nerves were raw simply from accepting the Earl of Trembley's invitation, and while he had convinced himself that he wouldn't let his foolish anxieties ruin yet another evening, he was finding it difficult to follow through. He was so preoccupied with his troubles that he had nearly run over a lady.

Silas fought the urge to peer over his shoulder, wondering if the blonde woman in the overly beaded jade color gown who he had knocked over was staring after him. A miserable reminder bubbled up in his mind. Of course she was. Every guest in attendance tonight would stare at him. He could see the shocked glances and hand-covered mouths as he walked deeper into the house. Could practically hear the disdain in their whispered voices. Curious stares from the men and frightened glares from the matron attendees made him second-guess his coming here tonight.

The Divorced Duke had finally emerged from his hiding, and everyone was eager to see how broken he was.

He gritted his teeth as he made his way to the library, where the card game was being held. It grated him to know that once upon a time, he hadn't cared a bit what everyone believed of him.

He wished he still felt that way, but an awful, paralyzing feeling had slowly crept into his bones since his divorce. Silas had become accustomed to a crippling, debilitating sensation that suffocated him every time he tried to leave the house. Thankfully, it hadn't hindered him from venturing to his gentlemen's club, White's, but he often kept his head down and hardly spoke to anyone when he was there.

This infernal handicap was more than embarrassing. It was devastating. His doctor hadn't been able to help. He had likened Silas's feeling to panophobia, a discovery by French physician Boissier de Sauvages, but it wasn't brought on by darkness. Terror only seemed to encroach on him when he was in large groups.

Like tonight.

But Trembley had found a way to work past Silas's crushing issue. The earl was notorious throughout the ton for holding not-so-secret card games, where any and all bets were viable if everyone agreed. Though Silas always played with money, he had taken a horse and, in one instance, a trunk full of silk during the games. His mother and younger sister Violet had profited the most from that wager as he had sent the fabric directly to their modiste.

When he reached the private library, he felt his jagged breathing even out. It wasn't nearly as crowded as the ballroom. And thankfully, none of the gentlemen here seemed to notice his discomposure at all. They were utterly focused on what they hoped to win. As Silas moved between the tables, he found a small card with his name. Reading the placement card to the left, he saw Lord Fishbourne sitting next to him. Silas was pleased enough with that. Fishbourne was a direct, quiet man. He moved around the table, reading the names on the cards. As he reached the opposite side of the table, he frowned.

He was in no mood to be seated across the pharos table from Hubert Jenkins, Viscount Dilworth. The man was widely recognized as one of the worst gambling addicts in all of London, typically spending much of his yearly income within the first few months of the year. The young man had shifting eyes and though he appeared far more confident than the last time Silas had seen him, Silas understood what addiction looked like. It wouldn't matter if the viscount won every hand all night. He would eventually lose, as did everyone who had no control over their compulsion to gamble.

Silas scanned the room and saw Derek, the Earl of Trembley, conversing with his brothers. While Trembley was Silas's oldest friend, he knew that he took his gaming tables seriously and Silas being paired with the viscount was just bad luck. But he needed to try. It was Derek's first time hosting a ball since the family came out of mourning, and he had specifically requested that Silas attend. The inheritance of Derek's title had been a bitter experience, as all the Trembley brothers had been quite devoted to their father and had believed he was in fine health.

Moving around the tables, Silas made his way toward the brothers. All three were tall, with broad shoulders, but that was where their similarities ended. Derek's reddish-brown hair and dark eyes set him apart from his younger siblings. He was quick with a smile to those he was acquainted with and was grinning widely as Silas approached.

"Combe," he said, patting the duke on the shoulder in a friendly, familiar gesture. "I'm happy you came."

"Yes, it's nice to see you out at an actual ball as opposed to some dark corner of White's," Trembley's middle brother, Fredrick, said with a grin that matched his brother's.

"Yes, well, here I am," Silas said.

"Excuse me. I think I see someone," the youngest brother, Alfred, said before skirting away.

Silas watched him leave before turning back to Derek.

"I'm assuming it was his doing that I'm seated with Dilworth?" Silas said, becoming annoyed at how visibly amused the other Trembley brothers were.

"Come now," Fredrick said. "Dilworth's not that bad. I heard him telling Lord Bromley that it isn't gambling if it's a sure thing."

Fredrick winked, and Derek chuckled at the foolhardy statement.

"Bloody idiot," Silas said under his breath. "What was Alfred thinking?"

"He didn't do it on purpose, Combe. It was the luck of the draw," Derek said. "Besides, Dilworth won't be able to play long. He doesn't have the copper."

"Which makes me curious as to why he was invited at all," Silas replied.

"Ah, that was my fault," Fredrick admitted. "I had overheard him talking to Lord Hampton at the races. He told the old codger that he was good for something because he was set to marry an heiress."

"How fortunate for Dilworth," Silas said. "And how miserable for his fiancée."

"Come now. Just because your marriage didn't turn out well doesn't mean the institution is without merit."

Silas made an expression of disgust.

"Spoken by someone who was never married."

"Well, that's true, but I'm not against it. It is the way of the world, as you know." He paused then, and a flicker in Derek's gaze to his brother told Silas they were being cautious around him.

He sighed, trying to beat down the growing feeling of agitation. He shouldn't have come here tonight. He wasn't ready. But all the same, he couldn't ignore the request of a friend.

Silas turned back to Fredrick, eager to distract himself from his thoughts.

"Did you say Dilworth was set to marry an heiress?" he asked. "What foolhardy family would tie themselves to Dilworth?"

"New money," Fredrick said. "Some inventor. Woodvine, I believe, is the name."

Silas had heard the name before. He had been wrapped up in

a three-way investing situation with a business associate some years ago. He had been allowed to invest and had very nearly committed himself before he changed his mind. It wasn't that he didn't believe in the product. A chaff cutter was an important invention for the agricultural community, particularly horses. It cut hay into smaller pieces to be mixed with forage, leading to healthier and better animals. But he had been unsure when he was new to making investments. He had come to regret it. The Woodvine investment had returned five-fold for its investors. Silas had learned the lesson that if he believed in a product, he should put his weight behind it.

"I've heard of Woodvine," Silas said. "He has a daughter?"

"He does," Derek said. "And Fredrick invited him and his fiancée here tonight as a congratulatory gesture." Derek gave his brother a pointed glance. "Without thinking."

"He's not a bad man," Fredrick tried, eager to defend himself. "He's quite good company, and he's always up for a fencing match at the club."

"He's an addict," Silas said. "He shouldn't be here."

"He's his own man," Derek said. "If he chooses to put himself in this situation, then it's hardly our place to stop him. To toss him out would be an insult at this point."

Silas exhaled, conceding the point. Dilworth was his own man, and even if Silas was aware of the signs of addiction, he could not and would not intervene. The viscount would hardly welcome a stranger telling him how to conduct himself. Besides, Dilworth was not his concern.

"Very well," Silas said. "But he should have to prove his coin. He's been denied entry at White's several times due to unpaid bets."

"He eventually pays," Fredrick tried.

"I've little interest in being paid several months from now," Silas countered.

Fredrick appeared irritated but nodded.

"Very well," he said, going over to Dilworth.

Derek poured Silas a glass of scotch and handed it to him. Silas took it and sipped the amber liquid slowly as he looked over the gentlemen taking their seats.

"Thank you for coming tonight," Derek said after downing his drink.

Silas only nodded.

"I understand it's difficult for you to attend these sorts of things these days. Balls and soirées, I mean."

"It's of little consequence," Silas said, shaking his head, uncomfortable with the entire conversation.

He took another sip of his scotch, put down the crystal glass, and headed back to his table without another word. Silas had become a recluse since his divorce, and while Derek was one of the few people in the world to understand his anxiety, Silas still didn't like to talk about it. Just as he didn't like to discuss the divorce that had triggered his anxiety—or the woman who had been his wife.

The image of Cynthia's lithe body and cold brown eyes sent his body on edge. As if thinking of her name could conjure her, Silas dug his fingernails into his palms to distract himself from his memories.

Though he had been convinced they had been a love match, three years of marriage had proven to him that no such thing existed. He and Cynthia had a tumultuous relationship, one revolved around arguments, jealousy, and power over the other person. It had been an exhausting marriage. They had been hostile towards one another, like oil and water, yet had always reconciled passionately, making the riotous angst of their arguments seem almost worth it. That was, until Cynthia had gone too far.

Silas clenched his jaw as he took his seat. The game was set to begin with Dilworth, Lord Fishburne, Mr. Grant, and the dealer.

"Combe," Dilworth said, an eager smile on his face. "It's good to see you out and about."

"Dilworth."

"Have you come to lose your coin?" Dilworth tried to tease.

"I doubt it will be you whom I lose to."

"Come now, I have a good luck charm, now."

"Is that so?"

"It is," Dilworth pulled out a velvet box and opened it to reveal a large, oval amethyst stone on a gold band, surrounded by tiny opals. "Here it is."

Silas glanced up from the ring. He was only six years older than the viscount; Silas felt an eternity older.

"Is that it?"

"Brilliant, isn't it?" Dilworth said, closing the tiny velvet box. "I bought it for my fiancée. Miss Clara Woodvine. Do you know her?"

"I do not," Silas said.

"Remarkable woman. Well, rather unrefined and a bit old, but remarkable nonetheless."

"What lavish praise," Silas said sarcastically. "Can we play?"

"Of course, I'm just making small talk," Dilworth said, smirking as he laid down his cards. "Dealer, I'll take two."

Silas, Fishburne, Grant, and Dilworth played for the next hour, and Silas had to admit that Dilworth had played soundly for the first half hour. The viscount was talkative, chatting away with Grant, who was close to folding for good. Fishburne had already bowed out, having little care to lose more than a couple hundred pounds. Dilworth, on the other hand, seemed determined to win. Unfortunately for him, Silas wasn't one for losing. At least, not at cards.

After Grant dropped his cards, Silas and Dilworth played another twenty minutes before Dilworth's obvious tells started to annoy Silas. He would chew at his thumbnail whenever he drew a high card, or he would click his tongue when he got a three of a kind or lower. His eyes were constantly darting from his cards to Silas's face, as if trying to gauge his opponent's reaction. But Silas stayed perfectly motionless, like a jungle cat waiting to pounce until finally, they showed their hands for the last hand, the one on which Dilworth had staked all his remaining cash.

"His Grace wins," the dealer said as Derek came up behind Silas, patting him on the back in a congratulatory way.

"Good game, Dilworth," Silas said as he went to stand up, glad that the game was finally over.

"Wait," Dilworth said desperately. "Let me use this," he pulled out his ring. "As collateral."

A few heads turned to watch as a small group came around their table.

"Dilworth, you don't want to do this," Silas said quietly.

"Why?" he asked abrasively. "Afraid?"

So much for being a good sport. Silas was well aware that the young man was trying to bait him, but he couldn't help but want to teach him a lesson. Deep down, he knew that it had something to do with his baser urges to control and dominate. Instead, he told himself he was doing it for Dilworth's unlucky fiancée. If Silas won, Dilworth wouldn't have anything to propose with, and she might break free from her unfortunate engagement.

"Very well," Silas said, sitting back down. "Play."

Of course, Dilworth lost the ring in three rounds while becoming increasingly sweaty and frantic. Soon, all Dilworth had come with belonged to Silas. He stood up at the end of the hand and motioned for one of the footmen to collect his things. Ignoring Dilworth's pleas, he moved around his chair.

Only then did he hear something that froze him in his tracks. He shook his head, wanting to believe that he must have imagined it, but from the stillness of the room around him, Silas hadn't been the only one to hear it. Turning around slowly, he glared at the viscount.

"What did you just say?"

"Let me bet my fiancée's dowry," he begged, sweat trickling down his temple, his expression pleading.

Silas stared blankly at the man. A mixture of pity and disgust bubbled beneath the surface, but he felt no desire to accept the man's vile offer. Dilworth was desperate, and Silas did not engage with his sort.

"Absolutely not."

"Please, Combe!"

"It's not your money, Dilworth," Silas bit out. "She's not even married to you."

"Then I bet *her*."

The words fell from the man's lips like coins on a table. The room became deadly silent. Everyone had heard Dilworth's wager. There could be no denying what he had just said, even though it was entirely unbelievable. That Dilworth would bet his soon-to-be wife was beyond ghastly, beyond inhumane. It was the act of a frantic man. A sick man, which was precisely what Dilworth was.

Dilworth brought his fingers to his temple, wiping away the sweat droplets that beaded down his face.

"You'd bet your fiancée as collateral?" Silas asked. "Have you no concept of propriety? Or pride? What right do you even have to make that offer? You don't actually have any claim to the poor girl."

"This from a man who let his wife leave him?" Dilworth baited.

Though Silas didn't make a move, Derek's hand flew up to his chest to hold him back as the crowd of men collectively held their breaths. Dilworth was beyond the ability to think clearly, and Silas was aware of it. Still, he could not allow him any leeway. Not when he'd insulted Silas in front of so many people. It was an offense, a challenge that needed to be answered immediately. The others in the room likely expected him to challenge Dilworth to a duel.

But Silas had another idea.

"Very well," he said, sitting back down. "One hand. If you win, you take everything I've won tonight." Dilworth's eyes flashed with greed and want. "If I win, I get your fiancée."

"Done."

Silas had hoped the man would at least pause and think about what he meant to do—that the words would shock some sense into him. But that hadn't happened. At this point, Silas knew there was nothing he could do.

It seemed the other men were holding their breath as the croupier shuffled and cut the deck before dealing out the cards. Silas picked up the edge of his hand, seeing that he only had a pair of threes. It wasn't a good draw, but then it wasn't terrible either. He'd managed to win before from a worse starting position—and if he lost, it would hardly be a tragedy. He would only lose money, of which he had plenty.

His eyes landed on Dilworth, who sat a little straighter with his shoulders pressed back as if he were pleased with his hand, even as the light from the oil lamps made the perspiration on his forehead glisten, betraying his anxiety. He handed in two cards and received his new ones, while Silas threw his three spare cards on the table for the dealer to retrieve and was handed three more. Silas pulled the edges of his cards up and was somewhat surprised to see that he had recovered the other two threes. A four-of-a-kind was a good hand, but was it good enough? The viscount puffed out his chest like a preening peacock, blatantly satisfied with his cards. Dilworth tapped the table to signify that he would bet.

"Let's not go round and round then," Silas said. "You've only one thing to bet. Or rather, one person," he said pointedly. "Show your hand."

Dilworth smirked as he laid down his cards. Five cards, all clubs, gave Silas a moment's pause until he realized that being the same suit was the only organization they had. It was a flush, but not in any order, which meant his four-of-a-kind was the superior hand.

Silas laid down *his* cards and watched the man before him shatter. Dilworth's eyes bulged out of his head, staring at the hand. He seemed frozen, unable to comprehend that he had lost. As the others came up to pat him on the back and say poor luck, Dilworth did not acknowledge anyone. Silas nearly felt pity for the man, but in the end, there was no room for it. Dilworth had done this to himself.

Silas had just begun to stand, with intentions to leave the table and partake in a cigar, when Dilworth finally spoke.

"Again," he said desperately. "Please. You must let me try again."

Silas's jaw clenched as he attempted to swallow down his growing anger. After betting and losing everything, including his fiancée, had the man truly not had enough? He turned on the young lord and was about to dress him down when he spoke.

"I'm begging you, Combe, please. You must play me again."

"You've nothing left to bet with, Dilworth," Silas said, his tone rough, his patience coming to an end. He wasn't sure if it was his anxiety or this man's audacity, but Silas was losing his calm façade. "Go home and lick your wounds."

"I have money. It's coming, I just have to—"

"You've already lost a dowry and a wife, Dilworth. Now I'm losing my patience, and unless you want to witness the full extent of my temper, I suggest you leave now."

Dilworth seemed to snap out of his trance when he heard the word "wife." He shook his head slightly in disbelief.

"Surely you don't mean to take Miss Woodvine from me? She's nothing to you."

"Nor you, apparently."

"But if I don't marry her, I can't pay you her dowry."

"A dowry I can collect myself now that you've lost her," Silas said.

The intention of his words was clear, much to the surprise of several gentlemen in attendance. Dilworth gawked incredulously. A murmur broke out among the men around them, and Silas made the mistake of turning around.

The familiar thread of panic threatened to take hold of him as his eyes took in the scene around him. These were men he had known all his life, friends, and acquaintances but with all of their attention focused on him—many of them pressing in close so as not to miss a word of the exchange between him and the viscount—their presence unnerved him. The hot hands of dread seemed to reach over his shoulders and wrap its fingers around his neck, constricting his airway. He swallowed uncomfortably as he shifted, turning back to face Dilworth.

Not now, for God's sake. He couldn't have an attack here, in front of all these people.

"You don't mean to marry the girl," Dilworth said in disbelief. "She's practically an old maid."

"Combe," Derek said, coming towards him as his voice dropped. "You can't want the girl. Let Dilworth keep her and take what he has offered."

Silas squinted at his friend, close to telling him that Dilworth didn't own the girl and therefore had no right to keep her, when a strained, feminine voice suddenly sounded from above.

"I'm afraid that won't work," the voice said, loud and clear from the second story.

All the men in the room's heads snapped up, startled. Silas felt hostile at the idea of being spied on. Still, when the same frizzy-haired, curvaceous woman he had bumped into earlier that night came down the secret spiral staircase that led to the main floor, he felt something else stir within him, beneath the crippling panic that had tried to settle around him.

Was this Miss Woodvine?

Chapter Three

THE SPARKLING LUSTER of the ballroom had certainly kept Clara distracted for a time, and while she had hoped to be asked by at least one gentleman while waiting for her dear Dilworth to return, none had approached her. But as melody after melody played, Clara grew tired as boredom settled into her restless heart. Where had Dilworth gone to, and why hadn't he returned? She had moved throughout the manse with her mother for the better part of half an hour, hoping to find him, but they hadn't had any luck.

"Ah, there are my loves," her father's voice sounded from behind Clara and her mother, causing them to turn. He frowned upon seeing their faces. "What's wrong, my dears?"

"Lord Dilworth has gone missing," Mary said, her brow knitted together in worry.

"Missing?"

"I'm sure there were some gentlemanly pursuits he needed to attend to before he could give us his full attention," Clara said with a bleak smile, not really believing her own words. "I'm sure he will appear momentarily."

"Yes, of course," her father agreed with a nod, though from the way his face scrunched up, it was evident that he believed otherwise. "Would either of you care for a refreshment?"

"No, thank you," Clara said.

"Yes, please," Mary said, turning to her daughter. "Stay here, dear, in case Dilworth comes back. It is the best spot in the ballroom to catch his eye should he come searching for you."

"Yes, Mama."

Her parents headed towards the refreshments table and Clara's shoulders dropped. She was trying hard not to feel sorry for herself, but it wasn't easy. She had expected this night to be magical. Tonight, she would be getting engaged. She was supposed to be dancing and smiling and being congratulated by people, for goodness' sake. And yet so far, she had been utterly ignored.

Feeling rather glum, she took the very unladylike position of leaning against one of the marble pillars that lined the ballroom as she scanned the room once again. After confirming that there was neither hide nor hair of Dilworth in sight, she sighed. Her head gently tilted against the cool pillar and her eyes drifted to the ceiling above. A very detailed mural of celestial beings had been painted above the ballroom, and Clara found herself staring at the elaborate artwork.

It was a beautiful scene from Greek mythology, but one Clara didn't immediately recognize. A bearded god who held a lute and was dressed in dark robes had his hand outstretched to a beautiful woman set before a starry sky. It was unusual, considering most murals painted skies set during the day, but it was enchanting nonetheless. She was somewhat mesmerized by the visual when she heard the dowager countess's distinct voice from behind the pillar.

"Where are your brothers, Alfred?" she asked, her tone annoyed. Clara turned slightly so that her ear was turned to hear better. Surely the viscount was with the other brothers—the answer to the dowager countess's question might lead her to find her erstwhile fiancé at last. "Derek has been missing for nearly an hour, and I haven't seen Fredrick since the first of our guests arrived."

"It's the game," the young lord said as if that was all he needed to speak to explain.

"That foolish game," the countess said with an exaggerated huff. "When will Derek learn that life is not all fun and games?"

"It was at your hand that we first learned to gamble, Mother," her son replied with faux chastising.

"Oh, hush," the countess replied without making the slightest attempt to deny it. "I never taught you such bad manners as to hold a tournament in the middle of the ball."

Clara couldn't help but smile.

"No, you didn't. And Father certainly wouldn't have approved, but then he never reined in Derek's behaviors, did he?"

"No," the countess said, her voice suddenly soft and wistful. "Your father always rather enjoyed you and your brothers' antics. He always said there was plenty of time to… To…"

A stilted silence followed while a mixture of guilt and sadness crept into Clara's heart. She began to regret her eavesdropping. She'd had no intention of intruding on this family's grief.

"Yes, well," her son said, his tone uncomfortable. "I wouldn't fret about it. Derek is aware that he can't continue with his card games during events, particularly now that he has to take on the duties of the earldom and host these parties himself. He just wanted one more—and it has been interesting, to say the least."

"There's always an interesting match, Alfred. But we must remember there is a time and a place for such things. Can you please tell both of your brothers that they must come host to our guests?"

"They will very shortly, I'm sure. By the time I exited, there were only two gentlemen left playing."

"Who?"

"Dilworth."

Clara's ears pricked up at the mention of her would-be fiancé. While she felt some relief to know where he had been, she felt a healthy dose of indignation as well. Had he been playing cards this entire time?

"That does not surprise me," the countess said. "Heaven help the poor woman who marries him the way he loses." Clara felt her heart drop and barely caught the woman's next words. "Who else?"

"Combe."

"*Combe*? I wouldn't have thought he'd have any patience for a man like the viscount. Why on earth are they playing together?"

"The tables were assigned randomly, I assure you," he said, sounding miffed. "Though next time, I will be sure to draw again, given how much grief I've been given over the grouping."

"It's fine, dear," the countess said. "Now, be quick and gather your brothers. I want them marching out here the moment the hand ends."

"Yes, Mother," he replied.

Seconds later, the countess passed by Clara, who pivoted quickly around the pillar so the lady would not see her. So that's where Dilworth had been this entire time! The indignation she'd felt at first was swelling into full, unchecked anger. He had decided that some foolish card game was more important than spending time with her. And what was all this about him having a gambling problem? To be sure, she had known that his finances were somewhat strained, but she had assumed that was because of a bad investment, or debt that had been inherited from prior generations. From the way the dowager countess spoke, though, it sounded as if his gambling was enough of a serious, persistent problem for his losses to be common knowledge.

Clara didn't know which bothered her more, his lack of manners or his lack of self-control. It had been at his request that they attend this ball together but he had abandoned her to gamble. It wasn't polite at best, and she shouldn't allow such behavior. What would he be like if they married? Would he try to gamble away her inheritance? He'd seemed so refined, so well kept. She'd never pictured him as a gambler. But now she had a new perspective on him, and she did not like the look of it at all.

A heavy dose of worry slid down the back of her throat. She needed to talk to Hubert to get to the bottom of this. If he wouldn't come to her, she would go to him.

Clara peered down the hallway to where a man was striding away. Intrigued to see if she could follow this Alfred to find her soon-to-be fiancé, Clara hurried down the hallway after him.

Large numbers of guests wandered throughout the main hallway, making it difficult to keep track of the gentleman. But the crowds worked in her favor in other ways. In the bustling rush of dozens of people seeking to find their friends, or reach the refreshments, or locate the powder room, no one paid any mind to her as she darted around, trying to keep the younger Trembley in her sights.

At the end of another long hallway, they had distanced themselves enough from the crush that Clara could see him lift the edge of a great tapestry hanging on the wall and slide behind it. The tapestry rippled gently before settling back into place. There must be an entrance or passageway of some sort behind it—she could think of no other explanation.

Clara quickly moved towards the tapestry. Hands flat against the rough fabric, she felt all around it until she discovered a bump against the wall. Moving her fingers behind it, she pushed the tapestry back to find a small wooden door with a cold metal latch. After a quick glance down the hallway, she pulled back the latch, pushed the door open, and hastened inside.

It took a few moments for her eyes to adjust to the darkness. She stood at the foot of a cramped staircase that led to a sliver of light at the top. Intrigued, Clara's hands went to the walls in search of a handrail, but when she found none, she skimmed her fingertips along the wood paneling.

Step by step she went, her heart thudded loudly in her chest. What a marvelous thing to have a secret passageway in one's house! Clara loved clever hiding places and wondered where this one led to as she climbed.

When she reached the top, she realized the sliver of light came from the other side of a heavy, velvet drape. Her fingers curled around the fabric as she gently pushed it aside and peered out cautiously, uncertain what she would find. The number of books on the far wall could only mean she had arrived at a library, or at least on a balcony in a library. There was no one up here. Besides a chair and some oil lamp sconces, it seemed rather a tight area, and she doubted more than two bodies could stand up here comfortably.

Coming out from behind the drape, Clara saw a small landing to her left that led down a tight spiral staircase. Clara noted that this room smelled heavily of cigars and books as her hand settled on the top of the railing. She was tempted to go down it when she heard voices from the room below.

"I suggest you leave now." A strong, masculine voice caught her ears.

She gingerly peered over the railing, making sure not to lean too far forward in case someone saw her. But no one seemed to be looking in her direction at all. Everyone's attention was focused on the center of the room where a number of gentlemen were standing around a table. The tall, dark-haired duke she had bumped into earlier that evening was staring daggers at Dilworth.

Her breath caught in her throat.

Dilworth moved, coming around the table.

"Surely you don't mean to take Miss Woodvine from me? She's nothing to you."

"Nor you, apparently."

Goodness, they were talking about her. But why? What was happening? Why would Dilworth be conversing about her with a man she had never met before?

"But if I don't marry her, I can't pay you her dowry."

Oh dear, they *were* referring to her. But it had to be a jest…Surely Dilworth hadn't…*bet* her dowry? What right had he to do such a thing? They weren't even engaged!

"You don't mean to marry the girl," she heard Dilworth say. "She's practically an old maid."

Clara's mouth fell open as her cheeks grew hot with embarrassment. Old maid? Was that what he thought of her? After all his flowery declarations of how he adored her, was this the truth? Here she had believed they would make a fine match—that they had a good foundation to build a real and genuine love. Apparently she had been wrong.

Stupid, stupid girl. She scowled as tears came to her eyes. No, no, she couldn't cry. Not here, not now. It was mortifying to be the object of a bet, and she would surely die of shame later that night when she returned home, but she wouldn't give any of these vile men the satisfaction of seeing her shamed. Not after they had stood by and allowed such a disgraceful bet to be made in the first place. No one had interfered, and even now, no one spoke in her defense. It was indeed a mystery why anyone outside of the ton would wish to marry into the peerage.

Well, she had something to say about it. Taking a deep breath and feeling somewhat numb, she found the spiral staircase that led down to the room's main floor.

"Combe," the earl was saying. "You can't want the girl. Let Dilworth keep her and take what he has offered."

"I'm afraid that won't work." Clara's voice came out far louder and calmer than she felt.

She descended the staircase slowly, shaking with fury as she steadied her raging heartbeat with stable breath. Though these men were supposedly descendants of honorable men, she glared at them without any respect.

"Miss Woodvine," Hubert said, taking a step towards her, but she held up her hand, stopping him.

"Remain there if you would," she said coolly as her brow arched. "I've no wish for you to come any closer."

"Miss Woodvine—"

"And I would greatly appreciate it if you refrained from speaking to me. Ever again, if you can manage." She turned to see the Duke of Combe, whose dark hair and heated stare bore into her with unreadable scrutiny. "I'm sorry to inform you, your grace, but this man is a fraud. He does not have any claim to me or my dowry. And he never will."

Dilworth said, "But—"

"The lady told you to stop speaking," Combe growled.

Clara's eyes caught the duke's, and she felt her racing heartbeat to a different feeling. Was she grateful? Scared? *Aroused?*

Yes, to all those, but she couldn't let herself acknowledge any of those feelings. Not now, and certainly not in front of any of these men, particularly the duke.

She moved away from him to face the earl.

"I was unaware that the Trembley house held such vile games. Wagering away people as if they were cattle. Had I known, I would have refused your invitation a thousand times over."

"Miss Woodvine. You must allow me to apologize."

"Must I? Very well, then. Apologize, if you find it so necessary. But know that I do not accept." She stuck out her chin. She knew what she was about to say was social suicide, but she'd rather be dead to these sorts of people anyway. "Every man in this room is a dishonorable cad."

Her hands were shaking uncontrollably now as she took on their offending stares. Clearly, they didn't like to be called to task for their behavior. Well, she didn't like being wagered away, so it seemed that no one in the room had reason to be happy.

She tucked her hands behind her back so they would not see and clutched her gloved fingers together as tight as she could. She swallowed hard as she eyed every one of them, her eyes settling on Combe for some reason. She wouldn't give Dilworth the satisfaction of looking him in the eye, and while the others all appeared too stunned to know how to respond to the situation, Combe seemed, well, steady. There was a fire in his eyes that had no right being there, but she found herself focusing solely on him.

"I am ashamed to have come to this house," she said. "If any of you feel an ounce of remorse for watching this disgusting act play out, I ask that you show your repentance by forgetting my family and me indefinitely. I shan't acknowledge any of you ever again. But I won't tell anyone about this either. It is my hope that it will be forgotten and that no one outside of this room will ever learn what has taken place," she said, barely noticing out of the corner of her eye as Dilworth grabbed something off the table and stuffed it into his pocket. She couldn't muster any curiosity over what he had swiped. Whatever he did was none of her business anymore. Her gaze stayed fixed on Combe. "I wish to be left alone," she said. "Forever."

When no one spoke, she nodded and turned to leave the way she came. She wondered if she had shocked them into a stupor, for she was up the stairs, down the hidden staircase, and in the hallway in a matter of minutes without anyone saying a word or making the slightest move to stop her.

Clara was eager to find her father and mother, and when she did, she told them that she had come down with a terrible headache and wished to leave immediately. Concerned for their daughter, the Woodvines said their goodbye and were soon on their way home, away from the glitz and glamour of Mayfair and back to their respectable neighborhood of Paddington.

Of course, after Clara's maids helped her undress and closed her door, Clara couldn't hold in the emotions any longer. Crouching down against the base of her bedroom door, pathetic tears streamed down her cheeks as her arms wrapped tightly around her bent knees.

How absolutely humiliating the entire evening had been! She had never been so furious before, and the shame of it all seemed to consume her. What an awful combination. When her anger eventually subsided, she was left with a terrible pain in her heart that she hadn't ever experienced before.

If Clara had ever doubted her place in society, tonight's events confirmed it. She had no business mingling and attempting to become friendly with the ton. No business aspiring to marry into their ranks. To be used as she had been, to be bet on and traded for...well, it had been far worse than any heartache that might have come from learning that the man she had hoped to be a help mate to had lost her in a gamble.

Clara squeezed her eyes shut tightly as tears gently fell down the sides of her face. Her hand came up to her forehead, and she tried to rub away the now genuine headache she felt. Miserable, she stood, made her way to her bed, and laid down with a thud. Surrounded in darkness, she wondered about Dilworth. He was not worth the aggravation, but she had pinned many of her hopes on him. Although she was sure she wasn't actually in love with him, she'd had hope of love growing between them once they were wed. She'd spent many hours picturing their happy future together.

But it was not to be.

Feeling dejected, Clara rolled to her side and gazed at the window. It was a clear night, and feeling restless, she pushed herself up and swung her legs off the bed.

Her bedroom commanded a view of the courtyard at the back of their house, and she made her way to it. A circular pond sat in the center of the green, with the square garden separated by four boxwood-lined yards, each with a pear tree planted in the middle. As she wiped away her tears, she saw the reflection of the stars in the water and lifted her eyes upward.

How fitting, she mused as she gazed up at the night sky. The stars had seemed so close, almost within reach, when it had only ever been an illusion. Just like she had had the illusion that there was a place for her among the glittering throngs of the ton. It had been not very reasonable to think that she might find her happily ever after so quickly but she had stubbornly believed it. Why shouldn't she find happiness and love? Her parents had been happily married for decades after having accidentally met in an apple orchard.

Now, though, she wondered if she was doomed to marry a fortune chaser just because she was wealthy. Even if she did marry someone who claimed not to care about her fortune, how could she ever trust her future husband's honesty? Her dowry seemed the most attractive thing about her, and she hated it. Perhaps she should run away and develop a new identity where she didn't have any money. Then she could see who was truly worth investing her time with.

Just then, a star shot across the sky, its shimmering tail disappearing just as quickly as it had appeared. For a brief moment, she contemplated making a wish, but then she didn't want to be the kind of foolish girl who believed in such nonsense anymore.

Looking back down at the reflecting pool, she frowned. Her breath fogged the window before her. She traced her index finger against the condensation, making a circle as she sighed.

"I wish someone *would* love me."

Chapter Four

S EVERAL BLOCKS AWAY, on the eastern side of Hyde Park, in a mansion not unlike the Earl of Trembley's, Silas laid in bed, his hands cradled behind the back of his skull. He stared up at the canopy of his four-poster bed, concentrated on the thumping of his heartbeat that rang in his ears. *What a bloody mess of a night.* He closed his eyes tightly and tried to force himself to sleep, fighting off the consuming panic that flooded his veins.

It had been a mistake going to Trembley's home. Not just because of the anxiety that he had fought against daily since his divorce, but because of the guilt he had felt the moment he realized that the poor Miss Woodvine had witnessed the unscrupulous affair of being used as collateral.

It seemed he would have no peace tonight. After wrestling with the decision to remain in bed or get up, he finally tore the sheets from his body and grabbed a dressing robe. Tying the belt at his waist, he found his slippers and found a cheroot cigar on the nightstand.

Unwilling to fill his bedroom with smoke, Silas walked to the window, opened it and sat partially on the frame as he struck a match to light his cigar. His bedroom window sat at the front of the house, overlooking a small public park, but it was too late for anyone to be scandalized by a duke in a dressing robe, hanging partially out of his second story bedroom window.

Taking a long, smooth pull off the cheroot, Silas exhaled slowly and leaned back to see the night sky. It was an ugly habit, smoking, one he had picked up almost immediately after his divorce when he'd been desperate to find something to soothe his frazzled nerves. He had tried several times to quit, but there never seemed to be a good enough reason to do so.

He inhaled the sharp flavored taste of smoke as he replayed the events in his mind. He should have refused to participate in the card game the moment Dilworth started betting things he had no governance over. The man had obviously been out of his depths in that room and while Silas recognized that it wasn't his fault, he couldn't help but feel shame for letting it go on as it did. Not to mention the odd mixture of guilt and curiosity he'd felt when Miss Woodvine appeared.

The frizzy, ash blonde beauty was taller than most women, and she had an arresting presence. She was strangely attractive, with a wide, full mouth, strong nose and grey-green eyes that had glowed with indignant fury when she discovered their wicked game. The overly bejeweled gown she wore, particularly in the bust area, had been hard to miss, but while it was unfashionably gaudy, it had certainly caught his attention. It was almost as if her dressmaker had been trying to signal to everyone that she didn't quite fit in, that she didn't belong. Silas rather liked that about her.

Of course, Silas couldn't afford to be interested in anyone. He had promised himself after his last debacle of a marriage that he would never again marry, let alone feel for another woman. It didn't matter that he found Miss Woodvine attractive or that he had felt a primitive claim to her when she appeared in all her disgruntled glory in Trembley's library.

Cynthia had made sure that Silas would never love again.

His fingers snaked through his dark hair as he inhaled his cheroot. Cynthia had left her mark on him and he had been a ruined man ever since.

They had been mad about each other in the beginning. Surely, no one had fallen more swiftly or deeply in love as Silas and Cynthia. Their relationship had burnt brightly, like a shooting star and had fizzled just as quickly, leaving scars on them both.

Silas was stone still as the memories came rushing back to him. Pain in the dark, pain in the day. It had been the only way to have her, the only way to please her—and for a time it had been how he found his own pleasure. In the early days, it had seemed as if their desires blended effortlessly, but where Silas had firmly set limits, Cynthia was boundless.

It had been innocent enough in the beginning, starting with biting, pinching, and the like. A bit unusual, to be sure, but nothing he had been unwilling to provide, if that was what his beloved craved. But soon Silas had learned the true depths of her depravity. Her pain tolerance was unlike anyone he had ever met and Silas still wasn't sure if he'd genuinely enjoyed inflicting so much on her, even when she begged for it. It wasn't that she couldn't handle it, but Silas had always felt as if he went too far.

Maybe if it had been only an occasional indulgence, he could have dealt with it more calmly, but she craved pain and was soon insisting on it every time they laid together. It was obvious that neither his opinion nor his own pleasure mattered to her. And while he was the one to apply physical force, Cynthia was anything but passive in return. But the pain that she chose to inflict was psychological in nature. Nothing gave her more satisfaction than hurting Silas in the way only she was able to. The constant games and lies had soured their relationship, though it had taken a long time before Silas had been willing to admit that to himself. He'd loved her so passionately that he hadn't been able to imagine giving her up, even when being with her brought him torment rather than happiness.

Silas took another drag from his cheroot, remembering the agony he had felt when Cynthia tried to use his heart against him. He had finally accepted that they were doomed when he'd walked in on Cynthia with the Marquis of Winston, at Trembley's country estate during a weekend house party. She had demanded a divorce soon after and Silas, disgusted with her actions and himself, had given it to her.

He was told it would be humiliating, that he would be a laughingstock of London and that he couldn't let his wife get away with embarrassing him like that, but Silas hadn't cared. He felt as though his heart had crumbled and ceased to exist. What did he care what the public thought of him? Nothing they could say mattered to him when he'd already been brought as low as it was possible to be.

The sight of Miss Woodvine that night, in all her rageful indignity had caused a stirring within him that made him feel like he'd woken from a long sleep. She had been so beautifully furious, so justly irate that it was as if her passion had sparked something back to life in him—most notably, the first embers of desire he had felt in quite some time. For the first time since Cynthia, he had wanted to bed a woman and the realization made him wary.

He glanced up at the sky, wondering what it would be like to touch Miss Woodvine. She was so unlike Cynthia in every way. Honestly, she was not the sort of woman he had ever given much notice to but, he could not shake her from his mind. She was an inventor's daughter, an heiress from a world he understood very little about. There was something honest about her, something wholesome that he couldn't quite understand. She seemed uninterested in the ton's opinions of her, as opposed to Cynthia who had lived for gossip.

It was clear Miss Woodvine had a very low opinion about him as well as his peers. But a part of him wondered what she would say if he tried to claim his winnings…

He shook his head and grinned, imagining her becoming red in the face and cutting him to ribbons with her words. Silas had no intention of making any claim to her, and he certainly had no intentions of marrying her, but he let himself imagine what that might be like for a moment. Miss Woodvine would prove to be a lively wife; of that, he had no doubt. He wouldn't fit into her life any more than she would fit into his, but then his world hadn't been quite right for a long time.

Taking a final pull from his cheroot, he decided the least he could do was to apologize to Miss Woodvine in person. While he was sure she wouldn't be happy to receive him, let alone accept his apology, it was his responsibility to hold himself accountable for his actions, and as a gentleman he planned to do just that.

Standing up, he stretched as he saw a shooting star streaked across the sky. He had often compared his relationship with Cynthia to shooting stars. He couldn't help but appreciate the fanciful notion that they could make dreams come true. It sat in the same theory as luck when it came to gambling.

Only fools relied on such things as luck and wishes. If it were possible, he would wish to be whole again, to cease having the crippling anxiety that had been left in the wake of his broken marriage. All he truly wanted was peace.

Once more, the image of Miss Woodvine flashed in his mind as he removed his robe and slipped into bed. He closed his eyes and saw her bright eyes, her full lips and the curve of her body. He was annoyed to feel himself harden. Clearly it had been far too long since bedding someone if the thought of Miss Woodvine could make his blood run hot.

SILAS HAD DECIDED it would be best to apologize first thing in the morning. He waited until a quarter past nine, far earlier than what was socially acceptable, but Silas preferred going out before the fashionable hours as to avoid the crowds. He rode to Paddington where he had learned, through a series of personal inquiries, that the Woodvines had taken lodgings. It wasn't polite to turn up without notifying the family, but he assumed it was his best chance at actually being seen by Miss Woodvine, who had explicitly told him and the rest of Trembley's players that she never wished to be approached by any of them.

He knocked on the black lacquer door of the handsome brick building and waited for it to open. When it did, an ancient butler answered the door. His white hair stuck out from the sides of his head and he seemed slightly unfocused. He stared at Silas with confusion.

"Sir?" he asked.

"The Duke of Combe," Silas said. "I've come to see Mr. Woodvine."

"Eh?" the old man said, leaning forward, obviously hard of hearing.

"Mr. Woodvine," Silas repeated, louder.

"Aye, what about him?" the butler asked, his hazy eyes squinting suspiciously.

"I'm here to see him."

"And who are you?" the butler asked, closing one eye as if that would help with his hearing.

"The Duke of Combe," Silas repeated, slowly.

"Who?" the butler asked again.

"The Duke of," Silas said, practically shouting, before stopping himself. Reaching into the pocket of his coat, he pulled out his card. "Here."

The old man took it and squinted. Evidently his eyesight was just as bad as his hearing.

"A duke, is it?" the butler said, leaning back to gawk at Silas up and down. After a moment he nodded. "Aye, I suppose you are."

Silas's mouth fell into a hard line and he glared at the old butler. Who would employ such an insolent man?

"Woodvine!" the butler abruptly shouted over his shoulder, startling Silas as well as a couple who were walking on the street behind him. "A duke is come!" He turned back and nodded at Silas. "Right this way."

The sheer unprofessionalism this ancient butler showed made Silas a little wary of entering, concerned about what he would find, but he was on a mission and he wouldn't let a little peculiarity deter him. He followed the man into the house and into a large, empty parlor.

"He'll be done in a minute," the old man said before disappearing.

Silas stared after him, bewildered that he had just had such a strange introduction. Looking around the room, he noticed that it was rather sparsely decorated. There was only one landscape painting hanging on the far wall and there was hardly any furniture, save a very old, over stuffed settee and two wooden chairs. It was strange. Usually London homes were overtly decorated, especially by those with wealth like the Woodvines.

The soft echo of footfall sounded behind him and he turned around half expecting Mr. Woodvine. He was surprised then to see Miss Woodvine, dressed in a pale-yellow morning dress, her frizzy blonde hair wrapped with a matching ribbon. She gave the impression of innocence incarnate, especially when she noticed him.

Her grey-blue eyes were wide with recognition and she instantly frowned.

"Oh. It's you," she said.

Silas bowed towards her.

"Good morning, Miss Woodvine," he nodded. She curtsied, but just barely as she kept her gaze on him.

"We did not receive your calling card," she said, her tone neutral. "Had you let us know that you intended to call, we could have told you that my father is not at home."

"He's not?"

"No, he's gone to his offices."

"Ah, I see," he said as he held his hands behind his back. "And your butler couldn't inform me of that?"

Clara's eyes softened at the mention of the butler.

"He's rather senile, I'm afraid. He doesn't always know what's happening."

"Then why not release him?"

She glared at Silas.

"Because, my lord, my family prefers to take care of those who take of us."

Aware that the topic seemed a sore subject, Silas held his hands up in surrender, not wishing to offend her further.

"Well, it's no matter. I didn't truly intend to pay a call on your father. I was using him as a decoy."

"A decoy?"

"Yes. I came to see you, actually."

One of her light brown brows arched up in speculation, Silas couldn't help but note that she really was very striking in an unconventional way, even if she didn't appear happy to see him.

"For what purpose?"

He took a step towards her and brought his hands up before him.

"To apologize for my actions last night," he said. "I should not have taken Dilworth's bet. And I know you said you never wished to see any of us again—"

"A request you've ignored outright I see," she said flatly.

He cocked his head. She was going to make this difficult, it seemed.

"My lady, I've come to make amends. There's no point in staying angry. No harm has come to you or your name. If anything, you've been saved from a terrible marriage."

She scoffed. "You know nothing of what I want and you've no right to tell me to stop being angry," she said, before adding, "I was humiliated last night. There's harm in that, isn't there?"

"Yes, and for that I am sorry, but I think you're not appreciating the fact that you were also saved from marrying such a vile man."

"Saved?" she repeated. "By whom? You?" She took a step forward and Silas's brow lifted. Who did she think she was, crowding him? Didn't she know most women avoided him? "I suppose you think I should be grateful to you for using me instead of coinage?"

"Well, considering the type of man Dilworth is, yes actually," he said. "You would have ended up living in a poor house if you married him."

"And pray tell me how that is any of your business?" she asked.

Silas's brow furrowed.

"I'm sorry, did you wish to marry Dilworth?" he asked, confused at her argument. Wasn't she aware that she was saved? "Because from the way you spoke to him last night, I would assume you were quite done with him."

"Who I wish to marry is no concern of yours."

"I think you're being a bit ungrateful," he said, only to see the full fury of her gaze land on him.

"How dare you sir, come into my home, barely apologize for treating me no better than livestock, then expect me to be grateful for interfering in my life? My relationship with Dilworth was not your concern and it certainly didn't require your handling."

He took a step towards her, annoyance breaking into frustration. He stood nearly a foot taller than her and he was willing to use his size to intimidate her and quell her sharp tongue.

"Handling?" he repeated, confused by this woman's reaction. She should be thanking him for his interference. "I didn't bet you away, my lady. It wasn't my idea to involve you at all. I believe your anger is misplaced. The viscount could have attempted to bargain you away to someone who would actually feel entitled to compensation in return for winning. Don't you realize how fortunate you are that when he chose to make that ill-fated wager, I was the gentleman on the receiving end? This way, you were able to find out for yourself the kind of man he truly is without you having to come to harm through the lesson."

"Ha!" she said, raising her hands at him, as if catching him in the act. "The sheer arrogance of your class is astounding, really. How any one person could be so convinced that they are without fault or error and then tell everyone that their actions are for their own good…well, it truly amazes me."

Silas glared at her as he took another step towards her. She hadn't realized it, but her words had struck a chord deep within him and his immediate response was to lash out against her.

"I did not say it was for your own good," he said slowly, so that she might hear his every word. "I simply implied that you were better off."

"The difference being?" she quipped.

Good Lord, what a frightful woman she was. He stared into her grey-green eyes. What a fascinating color. He had never seen eyes quite like hers before and even if she gave the impression that she was poised for battle, he felt an odd sort of need go through him. Her back was pin straight, her shoulders pressed back and her chin jutting out with a sense of superiority, while she was accusing him of such behavior, but he couldn't beat down the want to touch her.

She was a combative, if naive woman, he decided as he eliminated the space between them, hoping to impose a sense of dominance over the situation. She didn't cower, to her credit, but he did notice she swallowed as he crowded her, the small muscles of her neck working. For some reason, he felt satisfaction at the thought that his closeness caused her some discomfort.

Loose strands of her champagne blonde hair that would not be contained framed her face. She looked rather like one of the sirens from mythology he had seen in paintings. Upon closer inspection, Silas realized that her hair was actually curly, but had been brushed out. He fought the urge to touch it, ignoring the sudden twitch of his fingers.

"I've only come to inform you that I have no intention of claiming my winnings from last night's game," he said slowly, trying hard to banish any illicit thoughts from his mind.

"Am I meant to thank you?" she said acerbically. "Or commiserate over all that you have sacrificed in the name of being honorable? My dowry is certainly a substantial amount."

He shook his head.

"I'm not in need of funds. I gamble because I enjoy it. Not because I can't help myself."

"Like Lord Dilworth?" she asked and he nodded. "I don't understand it. Why must he gamble? Especially if he is so inept at it."

"He is an addict," Silas agreed. "Some men cannot help themselves. And as for what you would be worth… Well, at the risk of overstepping, I think you alone would have been prize enough. No matter what your dowry might be, your worth exceeds it."

Her round cheeks turned the palest shade of pink and Silas's body seemed to react. He curled his fingers into his fist, ignoring the desire to reach out and touch said cheek.

"That is kind of you to say," she said after a long moment.

"I do not mean it to be kind," he countered.

"Oh."

He stared at her for a long while. The wild idea of having won her again sounded in his mind, like a drum of war. Why would it not release him? He had no actual claim to her and yet it had felt so real last night, so blatantly genuine. What did that say about him, he wondered? He did not want to know and he opened his mouth to speak when unexpectedly, she began talking.

"I'm sorry you were not compensated for your winnings last night, however," she said, shaking her head. "It wasn't right of Lord Dilworth to bet something he did not have."

"No, it wasn't."

"And it wasn't right for you to take such a bet. It is your own fault for accepting his wager. Shameful, really." Her mouth twisted to the side of her face and her brow furrowed, as if she were deep in contemplation. "What possessed you to take such a bet, if I may ask?"

Silas opened his mouth, but hesitated. She was being rather intrusive with her questioning, but then he felt as if he owed it to her to explain himself. It was, after all, why he had come.

"I'm afraid it won't paint me in a very good light," he admitted.

"I already don't see you in a very good light, your grace," she said evenly and for the first time in a very long time, Silas laughed.

It startled him, just as much as her it seemed, for she jumped a little at the noise. What a surprising woman. He looked at her with confusion, unsure why he found her so amusing—and so intriguing.

"Very well then. Dilworth baited me. Or maybe he just wounded my pride," Silas said, shaking his head, amazed at his own honesty. "Either way, I couldn't allow his challenge to go unanswered."

She shook her head in disappointment.

"What silly creatures men are," she said, almost to herself.

"Are you suggesting that women aren't concerned with their pride?"

She shrugged. "*I'm* certainly not." Silas laughed again. Only this time she scowled at him. "I'm *not*," she insisted.

"So, your pride wasn't hurt when you discovered your soon-to-be fiancé had used you as collateral in a bet?"

"My pride wasn't hurt so much as my sense of decency. I was appalled by his actions," she said. "As well as yours."

Silas bit the inside of his lip as he fought off a sneer. Her gaze dropped to his mouth and while a part of him wondered what she found so interesting, he finally stopped fighting to urge to touch her as his hand came up to push back on her unruly strands of hair.

She inhaled sharply at his touch.

"You compare me too much to Dilworth," he said softly. "I already told you why I took the wager."

"Yes, your pride," she said, her tone slightly condescending. It aggravated him. "How terribly important."

Did she not know who she was talking to? Silas had spent the better part of a year hating himself for having let a woman destroy his pride and everyone in the ton know it. Was Miss

Woodvine unaware of it?

He bent his head slightly and spoke directly in her ear, unable to stave off the desire to take something from her. A kiss perhaps? If not to silence her, then as payment for her disdain.

"You're a rather insolent thing, aren't you? Heaven help the person who ever tried to put you in your place."

Her words stumbled as she swallowed.

"E-excuse me?"

"I believe I am owed a debt, Miss Woodvine."

"What do you mean?"

But Silas would not explain. That nagging sense of desire he had had since last night reemerged, stronger now that it had been embroiled by her own words. A single kiss could not hurt anyone and he *had* been cheated out of his winnings after all.

When she didn't move away, Silas pulled his head back and watched her round grey-green eyes. She seemed both worried and curious as she stared at him. As much as Silas knew it was a poor idea, he gathered her into his arms as he pressed his mouth to her.

Electricity seemed to snap between them from the moment their lips touched. Silas felt as if he had been starved for far too long and a feast had been laid before him, overwhelming him with bounty. His hands roamed over her body, dipping and feeling the soft flare of her hip, the curve of her waist, the weight of her breast.

He had been a man in the desert without water, suddenly plunged in a springtime pool. His hands gripped her tightly, pressing with a power he could barely restrain until he heard a soft whimper escape her lips.

He stopped abruptly, releasing her as if he had just touched the sun. What had come over him? He curled his hands into fists as he turned back to look at her.

Miss Woodvine stood, looking slightly disheveled, her mouth red and swollen from his kisses. Her hand crossed her torso and gently pressed against her belly. Shame and desire slammed into him. But what was oddest was what he *didn't* feel. The constant thread of anxiety that haunted him night and day seemed to have temporarily left his body…though the longer he stared at her, the more he felt its return.

"Your grace—"

"Good day Miss Woodvine," he said stiffly, and left without another word.

Chapter Five

CLARA WATCHED IN a daze as the duke left the receiving parlor without so much as a backwards glance. She had been rather shocked by her own boldness when she hadn't stepped away from him or pushed his hand to the side when he'd touched a strand of her hair, but Clara's bizarre desire to feel the duke's hands on her body had stopped her from retreating from his advance. And then there had been that kiss.

That. Kiss.

Clara's hand came up from her midriff to her throat. Never in her life had she been kissed with such possession. Dilworth had kissed her once or twice when they had been able to steal a moment away from her mother's chaperonage, but those had always been gentle, placid kisses. Clara had found them pleasant enough, but she had never felt the complete, untethered yearning she had when the duke had held her.

Every inch of her skin seemed to tingle with warning. The duke was a dangerous man, one who had run off his own wife with depravities that were rumored to be too scandalous to be mentioned in print. If that kiss was any indication, Clara knew the rumors about him must be true. She tried to focus on the audacity of his actions, while also trying to ignore the heat that had pooled low in her belly.

Men like Combe were never deprived of anything. He had

probably spent a lifetime indulging in all sorts of wicked pleasures and Clara felt a pang of shame at having been his latest indulgence. She had no doubt that he considered any woman—herself included—to be nothing more than just another conquest. Even though her ideas of propriety were less rigid than those of the ton—life in the country having supplied her with a healthy bit of knowledge about where babies came from—she still felt discomfited by the idea that the duke felt so entitled that he would claim her lips like that as if they were his for the taking, whenever he pleased.

She was even more uncomfortable with the fact that she had liked it.

No doubt the duke thought kissing her was some sort of game. It was a brazen thing to have done. And then to act as though that kiss was compensation for the duke's lost winnings. It was downright insulting and if Clara hadn't been so intrigued, she might have said so.

Combe had been surprisingly gentle as well as intense. From the stories Clara had heard, the duke was a wicked man, yet Clara couldn't quite see the dissolute figure from the gossip pages in the man she had just kissed. Despite his reputation, he hardly seemed like the type of man to force any woman to do something she didn't want. He had refused to claim his winnings from his bet with Dilworth after all and even though he had kissed her, she was sure he would have stopped if she had protested.

Why *hadn't* she protested? That was a question she couldn't seem to answer. She didn't like the duke, or at least, she knew that she shouldn't—even if she did find him remarkably attractive, in a dangerous sort of way. While she always believed that a person's character was the most important thing, Clara couldn't deny that the duke's striking, dark features, formidable size, and underlying arrogance made her body react in ways that she would rather not say.

Clara touched her hair absentmindedly, wondering if her gentle frizz had been to the duke's dislike and if he found her as attractive as she found him. Probably not. She wished her hair would either be tightly curled or smooth, unhappy that it should settle in between. The ashy blonde coloring was decidedly not in fashion at the moment and she was aware that her appearance was rather underwhelming.

Clara was a bit of a beauty conundrum. Not a single one of her attributes could be considered attractive on their own, but she had been put together in a way that all the unassuming features complimented each other. She always believed of herself as pleasantly plain and she supposed everyone saw her as she saw herself. Was that how the duke saw her? She found herself wishing she could view herself through his eyes. Maybe then she would understand why he had kissed her—and why, immediately afterward, he had rushed away.

She stood for a moment, staring at the doorway the duke had practically run out of, wishing she could make sense of the whole encounter…but then she shook her head, unwilling to stand around to try and decipher it. She was to meet Bettina Moppet in the park this morning along the Serpentine and she would not be late.

Just then her mother entered the parlor, her brow creased with concern.

"Dear, Trevor just came out to inform me that the Duke of Combe was here?" her mother asked, smiling gently at the ridiculous idea that the duke had been there. "I told him he must be imagining things again, but he insisted."

"Yes, the duke was here. He just left," Clara said, as she straightened the cuff of her sleeve at the wrist. "He came to see Papa."

"Whatever for?"

"To invest with him, I am sure," she lied. She hadn't told her parents what had happened the previous evening, deciding that neither needed to know what had happened. "Shall we go?"

"In a moment dear," her mother said, coming up to her. "Do you mean the duke spoke to you about investments?"

"Of course not, Mama. He simply stated that he hoped to talk to Papa about business—and I explained that he wasn't home, so he would have to pay his call another time," she said, putting her hand through her mother's arm. "Now can we please go? I promised Bettina that we would be the first ladies on the bridge today."

Her mother sighed loudly, obviously deciding that the duke's visit was of no consequence as they moved out of the room.

"Very well."

Clara had often found herself rather lonely since coming to live in town. Most of the ladies she had met did not seem to know quite what to do with her. While she had attended a number of salons and luncheons, she had struggled to form a real connection with the others she encountered. Bettina was the rare exception who had seemed to truly welcome her friendship, which had made it all the more upsetting when Bettina and her family had traveled to the countryside to visit friends for the whole of the past week. There was a great deal she wished to discuss with her friend, which was why Clara was eager to get to the park where she knew Bettina would be waiting.

The road along Hyde Park was already filled with carriages by the time Clara and her mother made their way through town. The fashionable hour was upon them and Clara was hardly surprised that it was so busy. She and her mother quickly exited their carriage and brushed out their skirts as they began their walk.

They had only been in London for a month, but Clara always found that she missed the country whenever they came to the park. It was well manicured and always had a lovely, curtailed set of flowering plants, Clara often longed for the wide-open spaces and wild flowers of the countryside. Still, the park was lovely. She didn't like how slow she was expecting to walk, but she would still be able to reach her friends in a timely manner.

"There's Bettina," she said to her mother, nodding at the bridge. "I should like to go over there for a moment, Mama."

"Go on, dear," her mother said, patting her on the hand that she held in the crook of her arm. "I see Lady Berry over there."

Clara nodded and headed towards the bridge where Bettina stood with several other young ladies, bent slightly forward as they discussed some topic Clara was sure to find interesting. She reached them quickly, moving into an opening of their circle with ease.

"I'm sorry I'm late," Clara said, smiling at the girls who all stared at her with surprise. "We had a bit of a delayed start this morning."

The ladies did not speak however. Instead, they all shared peculiar stares with one another, before glancing at Bettina. Clara tilted her head, confused, before turning to see Bettina as well. The ice blonde beauty had a small sneer on her lips as she looked back to Clara.

"Miss Woodvine. To what do we owe the pleasure of your company?"

Clara frowned, confused.

"We made plans to meet here," she said, her eyes scanning the others again. "Did we not?"

"We did," Bettina said with a demure smile that rankled Clara's nerves. "But I don't recall extending the invitation to you."

One girl, a redhead named Janet Clovers, covered her mouth, trying to hide a chuckling noise while another all but glared at Clara, as if she'd committed some terrible faux pas. But she couldn't imagine what she could have done to cause offense.

"I'm sorry, is there something amiss?" she asked.

"Not at all," Bettina said. "It's only that, well, we think it would be uncouth to associate with my fiancé's former paramour," she said, nodding knowingly at the others. "It seems rather bourgeois to do so."

"It's a divine ring," one of the girls cooed.

"So romantic," another said.

Clara stared at Bettina, uncertain what she was talking about.

"You're engaged?" she asked. Clara's eyes dropped to Bettina's hand. A purple amethyst sat on her fourth finger; a ring that had been described to her at length. It was the ring that Dilworth had told her about. Realization dawned on her as her blood ran cold. "To Dilworth?"

"Lord Dilworth, Miss Woodvine," Bettina said haughtily, her chin ticked up with arrogance. "He is a viscount and should be addressed with some respect."

"Country folk have such a lacking appreciation for society," Janet said, ignoring Clara completely.

"So do inventors daughters it seems," another girl, Winnifred, said.

Clara frowned as the coldness she felt was replaced with a miserable heat that crept up her neck. What was going on?

"I don't understand," she said, trying to ignore the queasy feeling that was settling in her stomach. "Dilworth only last night—"

"Yes, dear Hubert told me about last night," Bettina said, batting her eyes as she retold her friends the story. "He was all set to propose to you, but at the last minute couldn't dream of not spending the rest of his life with me."

Clara's brows lifted.

"How romantic," Janet gushed.

"He told you that?" Clara asked, her hands curling into fists.

"He did. He came over first thing this morning to tell me and profess his love. Papa tried to say no, but as I'm sure I've been in love with my dear Hubert for months now—"

"Months?" Clara repeated incredulously. "You said a week ago that it was unfortunate that I should have to marry someone so soon, because it wouldn't be any fun to attend next season alone."

Bettina's cheeks burned bright red with embarrassment as one of the girls snickered, hiding behind her fan.

"I said no such thing."

"You did too."

"It doesn't matter," Bettina said loudly, causing some passersby to watch their group. "Hubert and I are going to be married in a month and then I'll be Viscountess Dilworth."

"And you'll be paying for all his debts," Clara said hotly.

That had been the wrong thing to say. The collective gasp from the others told Clara that she had gone too far, but really how could Bettina not realize that Dilworth was only marrying her for her money? It had been a painful thing to admit herself, but then it was hardly something she could ignore. The fact of the matter was Dilworth was a villain, despite his title.

Bettina pulled her shoulders all the way back and spoke loudly.

"I wouldn't expect a country mouse like you to understand. Dilworth has thrown you over for someone of his own class, which really is the way it should be," she said, scowling at Clara. "I mean, it's painfully obvious you've tried to elbow your way into society. Just because you're rich doesn't mean you belong."

"Don't be a poor sport about it, Miss Woodvine," Janet said. "Dilworth simply wanted someone of his own class. I'm sure there are plenty of..." she paused, her mouth hanging open for a moment, before her eyes lit up. "...merchants and the like who would be happy to take you on as a wife."

Clara's eyes went wide. To be used by Dilworth had been one thing, but to discover that her friends weren't really her friends at all and had tossed her over in the blink of an eye, well, it was all too much. True, she had only known them for a matter of weeks, not really long enough to develop the kind of closeness that she shared with Holly, but she had thought that they at least *liked* her. Where was all this scorn coming from? What had she done to deserve it? Did she really no longer have any value to them at all now that she wasn't on the verge of marrying a member of the aristocracy? She tried to think of something brutal and biting to say, to put them all in their place, but she couldn't think of anything.

Her mouth hung open, as they waited for her retort. What a

silly, stupid woman she was, believing that she would be accepted by these people. Her hand went up to tuck a phantom strand of hair behind her ear as the humiliation of the situation washed over her. She wanted to turn and run and nearly did so, when she remembered the words the duke had said to her that morning.

Heaven help the person who ever tried to put you in your place.

It had been intended as an insult, she was sure. But it made her feel rather proud for some reason. Then he had kissed her and all her good sense had left her.

The recollection of his hands on her body came crashing over her. The taste of his mouth, the scent of mint and cigars on his clothes as he held her flashed in her mind as she blinked several times, trying to dislodge the memory.

Oh, don't think about that now! Why would that of all memories pop into her head at this moment?

"You really must close your mouth, Miss Woodvine," Winnifred said, a smirk on her face. "You look like a fish."

All the other girls tittered and laughed as Clara snapped her mouth shut as she felt something within her break. Heart racing, she took a step forward, crowding Bettina.

"Take Dilworth," she heard herself say. She glared at the rest of the girls. "He's hardly worth the ground he walks on. If you're so inclined, you should know that I overthrew him. He's nothing but a fortune-seeking blackguard."

Bettina's face contorted with fury.

"You're lying."

"I should thank you, for releasing me of him," she said quickly. "I'd hate for him to come snooping about me again should you come to your senses and realize what a ghastly man he truly is."

The others' eyes went wide as a small crowd formed around them.

"How dare you?" Bettina spouted. "You're just mad that despite your monies, you can't keep a fiancé." Bettina pouted exaggeratedly. "How sad it is you've taken to insulting a gentleman, simply because he threw you over."

"He did not throw me over," Clara said, her temper rising.

"He did though. He told me all about it," she said taking a step forward. "He said that he couldn't bear to marry someone so far beneath him—"

"He did not."

"He said he was ashamed every moment he was in your presence. That you were so obvious in your social climbing that you never cared to learn proper manners or decorum," she accused.

Clara's ears began to ring.

"He said it was appalling that your mother had been a maid and that your father was an embarrassment," Bettina dug in. "He said he wouldn't marry you if you were the richest girl in the entire world."

Fury bubbled within Clara as Bettina's words cut into her. Was everyone in the ton an absolute monster? She could barely control her breathing as she began speaking, words flowing from her mouth without registration.

"He's just mad he lost his bet!" Clara lashed out.

The words fell from her mouth too quickly, before she could weigh the wisdom of letting them slip. Several pairs of stunned eyes stared back at her.

"Clara?" Her mother's voice sounded from somewhere behind her.

Turning, Clara saw a sizeable crowd had formed. People were watching her, speaking behind their hands as they glared at her. She could feel herself turning red.

"What bet?" she heard Bettina ask behind her.

"Clara dear, I think it's time to go," her mother said, cutting through the crowd as she reached her daughter.

Clara felt sick to her stomach as her mother pulled her away, hearing more and more people behind her echoing the question *what bet,* and speculating that it was likely that Dilworth had made some grievous gamble.

"Oh no," Clara said as they hurried to their carriage. Her

gloved hand curled into a fist and she pounded it gently against her forehead. "Foolish, foolish idiot."

She had just caused a scene in front of half of London. Surely she was ruined and any chance of making a future match had gone up in smoke the moment she let her temper get the better of her. How could she have let herself become so unrestrained in front of so many people?

She sighed. Maybe she was being too dramatic. Maybe there wouldn't be too much hullabaloo about what had just happened in the park and it would all blow over?

Clara tapped her forehead with her fist again, knowing that it wasn't likely.

"I'm such a fool."

"Easy dear, what's all this about?" her mother asked, pulling her hand away. "What bet? And did I actually overhear something about Dilworth proposing to that Bettina girl?"

Clara shook her head as she climbed into the carriage, plopping herself on the bench seat. She was quiet until the carriage pulled away and only spoke when her mother's hand reached for hers. Turning, she saw the concern in her mother's eyes.

"Dilworth is a gambler—and not a very good one. After losing all of the money he had brought with him to the ball last night, he proceeded to bet me and my dowry in a card game," she said sadly. "A game that he lost. After witnessing such a thing, I can no longer feel any respect for the viscount. It's why I've not made any attempt to see or speak about him."

"A card game?" her mother repeated. As the words settled around them Mary's eyes went wide with horror as she realized what Clara was saying. She grabbed her daughter's hand and squeezed. "Oh, no, Clara. That can't be true. That's despicable!"

"It is true. Once he realized that he'd ruined his chances with me, he must have rushed to the next heiress he could find. He proposed to Bettina Moppet last night, right after her family returned to London," Clara said as her gaze dropped down to her knotted hands.

"Oh darling, I'm so sorry," her mother's grip tightened. "Oh, what your father will say."

"Must we tell him?" she asked, feeling ashamed. Her father had had his suspicions of the viscount from the beginning, but she hadn't wanted to listen. It was embarrassing to have been proved so entirely wrong. "I can't bear to discuss it anymore."

"I'll inform him myself," her mother said, before sighing. "We should have never come to London. I knew what these people were like but I thought it wouldn't matter—that our wealth would make us belong. How wrong I was."

"I just want to go home," Clara said as the pain of her betrayals bubbled up. "I just want to leave and never come back."

Her mother's grip tightened on her fingers again and for a while neither spoke. When the carriage reached their home and they were about to climb out, her mother spoke.

"My dear, to whom did Dilworth lose his bet?"

"The Duke of Combe," Clara said.

"Goodness gracious. Is that why the duke came to visit this morning?" her mother asked. The fine lines on her drawn face made her appear older and Clara hated to see her so distraught. "To…to claim his unscrupulous winnings?"

Clara glanced at her mother in shock.

"Goodness no, Mama. He came to apologize for putting me in such a position."

"Oh, thank heavens," her mother said, breathing a sigh of relief as her eyes rolled up. "You can never be too sure with these people, my dear. They've absolutely no morals. I should know. I used to work for them." Her mother shook her head. "Still, it is rather remarkable that the duke would come to offer his apologies."

"I suppose," Clara said, not seeing why it should be remarkable that a man who was in the wrong would apologize for it. "But it hardly matters."

"Why is that?"

"Because I don't plan on ever seeing the Duke of Combe again."

Chapter Six

A NEWSPAPER DROPPED unceremoniously on the table beside the leather club chair Silas occupied in the far back corner of his club, White's. Gavin Winscombe, Silas's oldest confidant and friend, sat next to him, his dark auburn hair falling over his forehead as he loomed over a map, studying it.

Silas, Gavin, and Derek had all attended Eton together, though the start of their friendship had been unusual. Gavin was an orphan, raised by an ancient aunt in Scotland who had brought him up alone after the tragic loss of his parents to a bout of scarlet fever. Gavin had taken ill as well, but he had survived, even though it had left him with weak lungs. When he reached school age, the other boys at Eton had singled him out for being different as children so often do.

Silas and Derek had happened upon Gavin and another student in an all-out brawl and had tried to separate them, when Gavin turned his frustrations on them. Soon the other student had disappeared, leaving the three fighting each other until they were eventually sent to the headmaster's office, where he had demanded to know who had started the fight. None of them had been willing to inform against the others and thus had been compelled to suffer their punishments together. A bond had been formed then and for the remainder of their school years, the three had been inseparable.

Gavin was set to leave in a few weeks for a six-month tour of the continent and had made a point of meeting Silas that afternoon to discuss routes and people to visit while on his journey. He had just decided on stopping on the Greek island of Skopelos when the newspaper landed with a flourish on the table. Several men seated at tables nearby turned their heads to see who had tossed the publication.

Silas looked up and saw Derek Trembley's serious face, standing over him. He was obviously waiting for Silas to react.

"Uh-oh," Gavin said leaning back, a concerned look on his face. "What's wrong?"

"Have you read this?" Derek asked, nodding to the newspaper.

Sighing, Silas leaned over the table and saw that it was folded open to display a gossip column, which held little interest for him. Leaning back, he glanced back at his friend.

"I see nothing worth discussing," he said.

"'Divorced Duke's Deal,'" Derek said, taking a seat opposite of Silas and Gavin. "It's all anyone is talking about."

Silas peered past Derek to a group of young men that were speaking animatedly across the room. There was one man standing in front of a group of four others, using his hands to describe something or other. Another man with light hair and an easy smile turned just then and caught Silas's eye. His grin instantly faded.

Clearing his throat, Silas turned away, trying to push down the beginning of his irrational panic. He knew logically that there was nothing to be anxious about, but his body reacted of its own accord. It seemed that even at White's he couldn't fully control his problem.

"What?" Gavin said, leaning forward to pick up the paper, reading the title. "They're talking about the writer's ghastly use of alliteration?"

"Yes, Winscombe, that," Derek said sarcastically. "Not about the egregious bet placed at my home—"

"Your own fault for inviting Dilworth," Gavin interrupted.

"—and the consequences thereafter," he continued, appearing annoyed. He turned to Silas. "Now that poor Woodvine girl is getting raked over the coals for it."

Silas glanced up, irritated.

"Why? She was the victim in all of it. I'd say she's the only one in the whole mess who can claim to be blameless."

"Perhaps, but it seems she had a bit of a falling out with Dilworth's new fiancée."

"His what?" Silas asked, picking the paper out of Gavin's hand.

He read the horrendous article, detailing a very public scene that took place a few days earlier in Hyde Park. Miss Woodvine and some girl named Bettina Moppet had argued publicly while others watched. Supposedly, Miss Woodvine cried loudly and stomped her feet while Miss Moppet fainted from the entire ordeal.

Silas was suspicious. The entire article made Clara out to be some sort of wild, hysterical creature, even going so far as to call out her humble beginnings as the reason for her graceless outburst.

Silas didn't think she was graceless. She could be somewhat proud and a bit annoying, but she hadn't been hysterical. Hell, she had witnessed her fiancé use her as collateral and then had calmly told an entire room of peers that they should be ashamed of themselves before leaving without so much as a whimper.

Whoever the author of this article was, they obviously did not know Clara Woodvine. Silas suspected that someone had paid off the reporter to paint Clara in a bad light. But then why had the Divorced Duke title been used?

Reading further, the article went on to detail how Lord Dilworth had been bullied into making a deal with the devil himself, Combe, who had demanded Dilworth use his own fiancée to pay his gambling debts. Silas rolled his eyes. It was certain that this writer was in debt to Dilworth somehow, as it went on and on about Combe's rumored treacherousness.

He tossed the paper back on the table, where Gavin quickly snatched it back up.

"It's a crock and you know it," Silas said, his voice strained. "You saw her at that card table. She wasn't some shrill banshee. She was calm and collected. Furious too, as she had every right to be, but she wasn't hysterical." He nodded his head towards the paper in Gavin's hand. "Dilworth must have paid for this article. Or perhaps his new fiancée footed the bill, knowing he doesn't have two pence to rub together."

"Perhaps the writer owed Dilworth a favor. Either way, it was a shame I couldn't make it to that card game," Gavin said, his eyes scanning the paper as he spoke. "I should have very much liked to witness Miss Woodvine's speech."

"Yes, why didn't you make it?" Silas asked, ignoring Derek's disgruntled face. "You never miss a Trembley ball."

"I had to visit my uncle," Gavin said, shaking his head as he looked down. "The old fool wanted me to attend some dreary house party this summer, but I informed him that I was going to be away." He waved his hand in the air. "It doesn't matter."

Silas eyed Gavin for a moment, wondering if he was being vague on purpose when he turned to see Derek glaring.

"You told him what Miss Woodvine said?"

"He was going to find out anyway apparently," Silas said, nodding to the newspaper. "That article is rubbish. You know as well as I Dilworth is to blame. This writer is compromised."

"It doesn't matter. This is now what everyone will see as the truth. What does it matter that a dozen or so people witnessed something else? Now hundreds of thousands of people have read what they will take to be the real story," the earl said, shaking his head. "What are you going to do?"

Silas frowned.

"About what?"

"About all of it," Derek said, gesturing to the paper. "Your honor is in question."

"That is certainly true," Gavin said, returning his attention to his map.

"My honor was signed away with my divorce, if you recall," he said, exasperation boiling up. "I've no say of how people think of me, and I do not care."

"That is certainly not true," Gavin added.

"Don't you have a boat to catch?" Silas snapped at Gavin.

"Not until the end of the month," he answered, his white teeth flashing.

"So that's it?" Derek asked. "Dilworth wins?"

"Wins what?" Silas asked honestly. "Some second-rate wife who will soon find out that the only reason the blackguard married her was because of her money? Why should I care about that?"

"You cared when Miss Woodvine was Dilworth's victim."

Silas stilled. Derek had him there. He *had* cared when Clara had been involved, but for the life of him, he couldn't understand why. The mention of her set Silas's extremities tingling. The kiss they had shared had set his blood on fire and he had been hard pressed to remember a time when he had felt such need. He had thought of little else since then and now that it seemed she was in a bit of a public scandal, he had to beat down the masculine urge to come to her rescue.

"And see what trouble it's brought me. Believe me, I will not repeat my mistake," he said coolly. "Let these fools cry foul and be entertainment to the masses. I will not participate."

It was Silas's greatest aggravation to be written about, but he had learned the last time that the more he protested, the more the gossip came. He knew now that it was wisest to ignore such fodder.

Silas could feel both men watching him and while it aggravated him greatly, he remained quiet until Gavin spoke.

"A shame about poor Miss Woodvine. She'll likely not have any peace now."

A moment of silence followed before he spoke.

"Why not?" he asked in spite of himself.

"Well, she's an heiress and a poor judge of character it seems." Gavin shook his head as he leaned forward. He picked up a crystal glass, half full of amber liquid and took a sip before continuing. "She'll likely be sought after by ever indebted man in England now that Dilworth doesn't have a claim to her."

"Her family should take her out of London then," Derek said. That earned the earl a contemptuous glare from Silas. "She obviously doesn't fit in to town life. She'd probably be better suited as the wife to some country squire or a vicar."

"With her coin?" Gavin said, disbelieving. "Not likely. No, she'll probably be married within the month to some poor, enterprising peer. He'll find her, comfort her, tell her that she has been wronged—"

"She *has* been wronged," Silas interrupted.

"—and since she seems to lack the insight to determine between friend and foe, I have no doubt that Miss Woodvine will end up shackled to some spendthrift before the season ends."

Gavin shrugged his shoulders as if expressing that it made little difference to him while Silas seethed at his words. She didn't lack insight. She had merely trusted the wrong people at the wrong time. Anyone who had been thrust into a new world might have made the same mistake. Hell, *he* had made that mistake and he had far more experience than Clara.

It shouldn't matter to him if one poor man or another bothered her, but it did make him feel uncomfortably protective. Perhaps he should do something, to stave off the penniless peers who would undoubtedly harass her over the coming weeks. Besides, she was technically already spoken for.

"What did you say?" Derek said, his brow raising.

Silas's gaze lifted at the question, unaware that he had mumbled his last thought out loud. When he realized what he had said, he coughed.

"Nothing," he insisted, shaking his head, but Gavin was staring at him with a curious glint in his eye. He squinted at his friend.

"You think she belongs to you, don't you?" Gavin said slowly, more like a statement than a question. "Because of the bet."

Silas felt his skin grow warm at the accusation.

"That's absurd. I do not."

"But you do," he said, leaning forward. "You think because you won her—"

"I didn't win her—"

"—that you have some sort of claim to her."

"Surely not, Combe," Derek said, appearing alarmed. "The girl is not suitable. She was made for the country life and nothing more. Her mother was a maid, for heaven's sake. You wouldn't suit."

"You sound like a pretentious ass," Silas said.

"I'm merely pointing out that it would be illogical. Whether you appreciate it or not, you have to see that she isn't suitable."

"Why? Because the ladies of our social standings are such prizes?"

Derek's eyes went wide at his words.

"At the risk of sounding arrogant, yes."

"Really?" Silas asked, letting his temper finally flare. "And I suppose a well-bred lady, one born into privilege and stature would benefit me. The daughter of an earl perhaps, who had been coached and practiced in polite society her entire life. Someone whose performance at the pianoforte was once described as perfection? Who spoke French and German without a hint of an accent? Who was deemed the jewel of the season during her coming out? Perhaps someone like that would suit me better?" he said, describing in detail his previous wife.

Both Derek and Gavin shared an uneasy glance with one another, aware of who Silas was talking about. They obviously did not expect that reaction—and neither did Silas, who hadn't even planned on offering for anyone until that very moment.

What was wrong with him? He didn't care one ounce about Clara Woodvine and he had sworn to never marry again. Yes, there was some small, spiteful part of him that wondered about courting her, if only because she was the exact opposite of Cynthia, but he was hardly going to pursue such insanity.

"No, perhaps not that sort," Derek said slowly, his eyes cautiously on Silas. "But you have to know that you don't actually have a legitimate claim to the Woodvine girl, Silas. The bet does not hold up."

"Doesn't he?" Gavin chimed in, standing up all of a sudden. "Dilworth did ask to use her as collateral and no objections were made."

"*I* objected," Silas said.

Gavin shook his head.

"But you relented."

"She wasn't Dilworth's to bet," Derek argued. "He had no legitimate claim to her."

"Except that he did," Gavin tried. "He was set to announce their engagement that very night, wasn't he? It was the entire reason he had been invited by your brother." Gavin turned to Silas. "If he won, how much would you have owed him?"

"Several thousand pounds," Silas answered.

"And would you have paid him if you lost?"

"Of course."

"Then as far as wagers go, it sounds like if anyone has a claim on Miss Woodvine, it would be you, Combe."

"This is preposterous," Derek said. "You can't bet people."

"No," Silas agreed. "You can't."

"And you can't court a woman so very obvious your opposite."

Silas turned to his friend and let out a huff.

"What a hypocrite you are."

Derek's eyes rounded.

"I beg your pardon?"

"You just said that it was preposterous to use people yet in the same breath state that Miss Woodvine isn't worthy of being pursued."

"Yes, and?"

"Well, what is it? Is she a person of worth or not?"

"I…" Derek began before his mouth closed. Silas and Gavin waited for a moment before Derek clucked his teeth. "Very well. I see your point. But what do you even know about her besides her father's business dealings?"

Silas considered that. The truth was that he didn't know very much about Clara Woodvine, only that she seemed to be the mirror opposite of his ex-wife. She was forward and spoke with a refreshing practicality that made him curious to know more of her opinions. She didn't cower, but then she hadn't seemed particularly cruel either, much unlike his last wife.

Silas had no wish to ever be connected to another female again, but the idea of Clara being insulted irritated him beyond reasonability. He should do something. Her image had plagued his mind for days and the more he thought about her, the more he wondered if he might be able to perhaps alleviate some of the unwanted attention she was getting.

"She is attractive," he said lowly, to no one in particular. "Her wit is sharper than most."

"A strangely beautiful creature, from what I hear," Gavin said, pressing the issue.

"Why are you so interested in Combe's love life?" Derek asked Gavin suspiciously.

"Why aren't you?" Gavin countered. "He's been through hell, hasn't he?"

"Yes but—"

"And he's been locked away for the better part of a year dealing with, well," Gavin said, avoiding Silas's eyes. "Whatever it is that he's been dealing with."

Silas snorted humorlessly. He had confided in both Derek and Gavin the panic he felt at the idea of being in public places other than White's. Derek flexed his fists, obviously uncomfortable with Gavin's mentioning it.

"To be honest, I find her rather frustrating, but my… problem… Well, it seems to fade when I'm in her presence."

Though he kept his eyes on the corner of the table in front of him, he sensed both men were staring at him.

"Is that so?" Derek said after a long pause.

"Yes. I'm sure it's because she's more annoying than anything, but I did notice that I didn't have any trouble when I went to her home to offer my apologies."

Gavin's hands shot up.

"Well now, that seems reason enough to, at the very least, investigate this woman. Besides, you've been badgering him to make a return to society, Derek. Knowing how difficult it is for a divorced person to traverse through life, I see no reason why he shouldn't at least get to know this Woodvine woman," Gavin concluded as he sat back down, leaning into his chair. "Combe won her, after all."

Derek gawked between the two men, appearing utterly confused.

"You cannot seriously be considering this, Silas."

"Calm down, no one is getting betrothed," he said. "Gavin's just trying to annoy you."

Gavin grinned and while Derek did seem to settle after that, Silas couldn't shake a budding idea from his mind. Perhaps he could use Miss Woodvine and her distracting personality to better his own situation. If he could spend some time with her, he would have the opportunity to perhaps see if her presence could somewhat deafen his anxieties. It would certainly be worth investigating. Maybe he could finally bring some amount of peace to his life once more. And it wouldn't hurt her reputation if it was reported that she had caught the attention of a duke. Scandal-ridden though he was, his title still carried weight. It could provide her with some protection.

Perhaps they could help each other? He needed to speak with Clara again and soon.

Chapter Seven

CLARA HAD SPENT the better part of the week locked in her room, unwilling to see or speak to anyone, even her parents. She knew she was behaving like one of the spoiled ladies she had viewed with disdain since arriving in London, but she couldn't help herself. She had been humiliated by Bettina Moppet and Dilworth and now she was the laughingstock of all of London. All she wished was to disappear.

Of course, that was an impossibility. With Papa's business dealings, they were compelled to stay in London until Parliament let out, which meant they would likely stay for several more months, much to Clara's horror. Well, at least they wouldn't be invited to many balls. The invitations had decidedly diminished since her argument with Bettina in the park. However, a growing number of calling cards were coming in daily from suitors. Clara had refused them all, wary of anyone now that her faith in her ability to judge people had been so utterly shaken. She had no wish to make any new acquaintances. It was best to stay firmly out of society, where she could do no more damage to her reputation.

The last caller she'd actually spoken with had been the Duke of Combe. Oddly enough, the kiss they had shared had been the only thing she had experienced in the past week that had offered her a pleasurable solace away from intrusive thoughts and terrible gossip. She found herself thinking about it often—and then scolding herself for dwelling on it when it was all too likely that he had already forgotten about it. It was probably for the best. She needed to stay away from members of the ton.

She had written her friend Holly about all her troubles and had not received a reply. When her maid had begun to knock frantically at her door, she hoped that it was because she had finally received a letter. But Clara only found her maid, Elizabeth, staring wide eyes as she opened the door.

"Elizabeth," she said with concern. "What is it?"

"There are a great many things happening downstairs, miss," Elizabeth said, hurrying inside. "You must dress for dinner."

"I don't feel like going down tonight," Clara said, turning to follow her maid towards the wardrobe. "Maybe a tray can be sent up, like last night?"

"No, no, no," Elizabeth said, pulling out her finest dresses. "You must dress."

"Not in a ball gown, surely?" she said. She put her hand on Elizabeth's wrist, stopping her. "Is there something wrong? What's going on?"

"The Duke of Combe has arrived and requested an audience with your father," Elizabeth said with a hushed tone, as if saying it too loud would cause the duke to leave. "He was very insistent."

Panic set in as Clara's heart started to race wildly. What on earth was the duke doing here and why did he wish to speak with her father? She had planned never to see him again.

"What does he want?" she asked as she quickly undressed. She nodded to the icy blue gown that had a lace detail along the hem and bodice. "When did he arrive?"

"A quarter of an hour ago, miss," she said as she helped Clara dress. "He seemed rather determined."

"Determined? What does that mean?"

"Well," Elizabeth said as she laced Clara up. "He walked with purpose."

"Did he? Hmm. None of these fine gentlemen ever walk with purpose," she said. "But surely he only came to discuss some sort of investment with Papa. That's the whole reason why we're in town after all."

"Perhaps, miss," Elizabeth said, sounding unconvinced.

The maid forcibly pushed Clara onto a plush bench that sat before her vanity and quickly brushed out her hair. She applied some rose water to smooth the most aggravating waves and then pulled it all back into a simple psyche knot style that allowed Clara's natural hair to appear simple yet regal in a Grecian sort of way.

She hurriedly put on her slippers and her maid all but pushed her out the door. She raced towards the top of the stairs and took a deep breath before descending with her best attempt at a calm façade. Why she felt so excited made no sense to her. Clara was not particularly interested in the duke, but the idea of seeing him again made her uncharacteristically eager.

Upon reaching the landing, she was unsure if she should go to her father's office or search for her mother. The grumbling of her stomach made the decision for her and she went to the dining room, hoping to find a morsel or two to eat before the duke appeared.

Unfortunately, she would have no such luck. Entering the dining room, she saw her father, mother, and the duke, discussing something at the far end of the table. They instantly stopped talking when Clara appeared and she felt suddenly uneasy.

"Good evening," she said, curtsying as the duke bowed. "Forgive me, your grace, I was unaware that you were joining us tonight."

"I hadn't planned on it. In fact I'm late for another appointment," he said, his dark eyes on her. "But I had wished to discuss something with your father and it could not wait."

"Ah," she said with apprehension as a footman pulled out her chair. She sat down as did her mother. "A business venture, I presume?"

"No," her father said. "Not quite."

Clara looked at her father and then the duke. She waited but when her father didn't say anything, the duke did.

"I asked your father if he would allow me to court you," the duke said, his eyes on Clara.

Terror mixed with arousal coursed through her blood at hearing his words. Her eyes went wide and for a moment no one spoke.

Had this man lost his mind?

"My dear?" her father said.

Clara shot up.

"Papa, may I speak with the duke privately for a moment?"

"I don't think that would be the best idea, Clara," her mother said warily.

"It will be fine," Clara said over her shoulder as she was already leaving the room. "The parlor door shall remain open."

Although Clara was usually a dutiful daughter, the audacity of the duke had shattered her sensibility. She was not going to be courted by him and she planned on telling him so in so many words.

Clara heard his heavy footfall behind her as she came into the parlor, turning on him the moment she was halfway into the room.

"Why are you here?" she asked him pointedly, not bothering with any pretense of politeness.

The duke's dark hair fell over his brow as he tilted his head.

"To court you," he answered, peering over his shoulder. He turned back to face her. "Do you often dictate your house like this?"

"What I do in my own home is none of your business," she said quickly. "And don't lie to me. I want to know why you are here."

"I don't lie," he said, his tone dangerous as he turned on her.

"Well, you can't make me believe you're here to actually court me," she said quickly. "You're plotting something, I've no doubt."

"What something?" he asked.

"I don't know! Some more humiliation," she said putting her hand to her forehead. She squeezed the bridge of her nose. "Why won't your kind leave me in peace?"

"My kind?"

"Yes, the peerage," she dropped her hand. "I've done nothing to invite this sort of torture but you all seem hellbent on ruining me for no reason."

In an instant, he was before her, towering over her like some fallen angel. Surprised that he was so close, she saw a wash of pain sweep over his face before melting into a concealed mask.

"I'm not trying to torture you," he said slowly, almost more to himself than to her. "I only wish to help."

She stared at him with unabashed confusion.

"Help? How?" she asked.

"By spending time with you."

"And why would you want to do something like that?"

"Because I find you..." He hesitated, before landing on a word. "Peculiar."

Her brows lifted.

"Peculiar?"

"Yes."

Clara tilted her head, debating whether she should be insulted or worried. He was acting strangely.

"Are you feeling unwell, your grace?" she asked, deciding to give him the benefit of the doubt.

"No," he ground out. "And I don't like being treated as if I'm some sort of madman."

"There are quite literally hundreds of other women who would better suit you."

"What makes you so sure about that?" He asked.

"Because there are," she said, gesturing her hand around the room as if every eligible lady in London stood along the parlor wall. "There were dozens of ladies at Trembley's ball the other night, each one finer than I with proper pedigrees who would suit you much better than I."

"Why would you say that?"

"Because we are from two different worlds. I would think you would prefer to spend your time with ladies who share your tastes, your upbringing—

He put his hand up and she stifled her words. He seemed eager to say something, but also hesitant. Deciding to wait, she folded her arms across her chest to see what he had to say.

Taking a deep breath, the duke spoke.

"I've had my fair share of fine ladies. That said, I don't think pedigree makes the woman and I find myself intrigued by you."

"But I am not intrigued by you."

He had the gall to smirk and Clara had to beat down the unwanted excitement she felt surge through her.

"Not yet."

Insolent man.

"Not ever. I have no wish to have any more relations with members of the peerage," she said, her chin raised. "Furthermore, I have no desire to be courted by anyone. Especially you."

"I'm not leaving until you agree."

"Absolutely not."

His brow cinched together and he shook his head. "Are you unaware of what I'm offering? The entire city thinks you're a madwoman for verbally attacking Dilworth's new fiancé."

"I didn't attack her," Clara said furiously. "That article purposely tried to murder my character."

"Regardless, it's all anyone is talking about. Now, I feel obligated to assist you, considering my part in all of this. Since Dilworth, the sniveling worm, is only working to protect his own skin, I thought I could offer to court you, as a gesture of good faith, to possibly fend off any unwanted suitors that are undoubtedly on their way here."

Clara frowned. She *had* already been inundated with several dozen calling cards, all from men she didn't know. She had no doubt they were only after her fortune.

"And what concern is it of yours if I'm set upon by fortune hunters?"

"I feel some sense of responsibility because I had a hand in ruining your would-be engagement with Dilworth."

"I was under the impression that you believe you saved me."

The duke did not answer right away and Clara saw something dark pass over her eyes. He stared at her like she belonged to him and for a moment she felt as if she did. It was ridiculous of course, but then she had never felt something so undeniable.

"I do," he said quietly, staring at her. "But I shouldn't go about saving those who don't wish to be saved."

Though she knew he was talking about her, Clara couldn't help but see a deeper meaning to his words. Had he tried to save someone before her? Had something happened between him and his wife? She was desperate to know. An eager wish to know everything about him bloomed in her chest but, she had no right to any of his history. At least, not yet.

"I still don't see how this would benefit you."

"It would benefit us both. If we were seen together, my position would undoubtedly squelch any rumors about your, well, provincial upbringing."

"Provincial upbringing?" she repeated, annoyed. The duke nodded. "That still doesn't tell me how you would benefit from this arrangement."

A shadow passed over his face and Clara was curious as to why he seemed to hesitate.

"I believe you would be helpful to me," he said slowly, his eyes dropping for a moment.

"In what way?"

He became shuttered as he turned away from her, his hands clasped tightly behind his back.

"Does it matter? I wish to help alleviate some of the damage my wager with Dilworth has caused you." He turned back to see her and Clara felt her heart jump slightly at the unmistakable discomfort she saw in his eyes. "Will you accept my help?"

Curious as to why he should be in any sort of pain, Clara tilted her head in consideration.

"You wish to form a partnership then? To bring up both our stocks in the eyes of the ton?"

"In a way, yes."

There was something in his eyes that made the hairs on the back of her neck stand up. It was a clever plan, Clara had to admit but she couldn't shake the feeling that there was something else he wasn't telling her.

"So, this is your olive branch then? To help smooth over my reputation, while fixing yours as well?"

"Yes."

It was a stretch, but if it meant she could escape the number of suitors who were already beginning to line up at her doorstep, she thought it was worth it. She held out her hand.

"Very well, I accept," she said quickly. "You may court me."

The duke's brow lifted in surprise. His eyes dropped to her outstretched hand before taking it. Clara ignored the shiver that shot down her spine as his large hand enclosed around her gloved fingers.

"Just like that?" he asked, his tone oddly low.

"It is a smart plan and I don't find you objectionable. Besides, you said you wouldn't leave until I agreed. I agree, which means you may leave."

He smiled and the crinkle at the corner of his dark eyes caused a strange sort of flutter in her stomach. He pulled her towards him.

"Are you only agreeing to get rid of me?"

She pulled her hand out of his grasp, ignoring the spark she felt. She was wary of how he made her feel both giddy and irritated at the same time.

"Possibly."

"Fair enough," he said, taking a step away from her. For a moment she was afraid he might leave, but then he turned around and she noticed a sheepish expression on his face. "I hope being linked to me won't cause you more trouble."

"What trouble?" she asked.

"My history," he said slowly. "There are people who don't particularly care to associate with a divorced duke."

She had overheard as much the night they met, but surely not everyone in society would think like that. Although, knowing the ton as she did now, she wouldn't be surprised if they shunned even a duke.

"Your divorce is not a problem for me," she said honestly, although she did intend to learn more about it now that they were linked. "Nor am I concerned with the opinions of others."

The duke gazed at her with an intensity that made her catch her breath. What an odd feeling it was to be the center of his attention. She felt as though he was staring right through her. Was this what it was like to be courted, truly, by someone who wasn't simply after her fortune? She felt her cheek warm beneath his gaze and saw his eyes light with fire.

"Then I will call on you tomorrow," he said.

"Very well," she said with a nod. He turned to leave when she spoke. "Should we go for a promenade? Maybe around the park?"

The duke's back became stiff and Clara noted the rigidness of his body. Slowly he turned back to face her.

"A walk?"

She tilted her head.

"Why not? I think it would be the perfect setting for people to see us together. Not to mention it is where my last humiliation took place. I think returning there will be the quickest way to overcome all those rumors about me."

His mouth set in a hard line and his whole face seemed suddenly drawn. It made her uneasy. What was wrong?

"Very well, then," he said, taking her hand as he bent over it. He pressed his mouth to the back of her knuckles before standing up. "Until tomorrow then. It has been a pleasure, Miss

Woodvine," he said.

"Clara," she said softly. "You may call me Clara."

He nodded.

"Silas," he said before turning away.

Clara watched for a second time as the duke left her parlor, only this time she followed and went to the dining room where her parents had been anxiously waiting.

"Well, my dear?" her mother asked. "What did he say?"

"He asked to court me and I accepted," she answered truthfully.

"It's not just because he's a duke is it, my dear?" her father asked, his brow knit with worry. "I hope you do not feel that we would push you to make such an advantageous match, simply because you can. Especially after what transpired between you and the viscount."

"No, I told him that being a duke was rather a mark against him."

"Oh dear," her mother exclaimed.

"But it is neither here nor there. We are to go for a promenade tomorrow, Mama. You'll need to chaperone."

"Oh, well then," she said, looking at her husband. "Very well."

Very well indeed. Clara spooned her ham and pea soup. She would be courted by the duke. Even though he only seemed interested in boosting her persona, she couldn't help but feel wildly giddy over the fact that the dark and dangerous duke would be accompanying her around the park.

Chapter Eight

SILAS WASN'T SURE if he should have explained his problem to Clara before agreeing to escort her on a walk through Hyde Park. What had seemed like a mostly plausible idea yesterday now seemed impossible. Yes, when she had first brought up the notion, he had feared that it might be difficult for him, but being in Clara's presence had given him a false sense of security and he had foolishly believed he could handle the crowds at Hyde Park. But since he had risen this morning, the thought of what he was about to face had weighed heavier and heavier on him, and all his confidence had slowly ebbed away.

He stuck his fingers into his vest pocket and fished out a watch as he waited in the Woodvine foyer. A quarter past ten. He had purposely come early, before the fashionable hour so that he could avoid the largest of the crowds. But even the prospect of a smaller number still had his pulse racing and his panic rising. Would he be able to hide it? Perhaps Clara wouldn't mind if he remained quiet during their outing. He would need to concentrate on his breathing to stop himself from experiencing the full force of the panic that often settled in when he was in public.

Just then, voices sounded from the top of the stairs. Turning, he saw Clara, dressed in an overly embellished maroon and crème striped walking gown, followed by her mother who wore a similarly styled dress.

Who in the world was their seamstress, he wondered as his face remained blank upon their descent.

"Your grace," Mrs. Woodvine said, coming up to him. "We are so grateful to be in your company this morning."

"The pleasure is all mine," he said, his eyes fixed on Clara. "Shall we?"

"Yes," the ladies said in unison as they moved around him.

They were out of the house and into the carriage in a matter of minutes. Silas tried to make small talk with the mother, but the closer they got to the park, the warmer his body became. His clothing seemed stifling and too tight, becoming more confining with each moment that passed as his gaze drifted out the window. Good lord. Why were their so many people here?

The sidewalks and roads seemed to be overrun with people. Did people really come to gather at the same exact time as each other simply to gossip or whatever it was people did?

"Your grace?"

"Mm-hmm?" he said, turning back to his companions. The mother had an expectant expression on her face, while Clara tilted her head, her eyes seemingly going right through him. He shook his head. "I beg your pardon, Mrs. Woodvine?"

"I was wondering if you were attending the races next week?" she asked, evidently repeating herself. "Mr. Woodvine and I have never actually been and we had planned on going, until, well…"

Mrs. Woodvine glanced at her daughter and Silas saw Clara flush with displeasure.

"She means, until I caused a scene and made our family the target of gossip," Clara said honestly.

"That's not what I meant, dear," her mother said.

"It's quite all right, Mother. His grace happens to be on our side." Her eyes flickered to Silas's face. "Aren't you?"

"I am," he said, his tone deep and honest, before turning to face Mrs. Woodvine. "I actually don't believe a word of what was written about Miss Woodvine."

The older woman sighed with relief.

"Well, that is good to hear," she said, her shoulders dropping a fraction as she watched her daughter. "I don't know why they wrote those lies. Clara did speak somewhat loudly, but she certainly didn't scream and no one fainted."

"Thank you, Mother," Clara said, slightly embarrassed.

The corner of Silas's mouth turned up at her discomfort. Evidently, she wasn't quite as calm and collected as she appeared.

Turning to peer back out the window, Silas's good humor vanished as the carriage came to a stop. The door was opened by the footman. When Silas didn't move to exit, he felt the Woodvines' eyes on him.

"Silas?" Clara whispered, low enough that her mother couldn't hear, but it seemed to echo in his ears.

He watched her steadfast eyes and he felt the erratic speed of his heartbeat begin to slow. Clearing his throat, he shook his head and climbed out of the carriage. He did not turn around, though he was sure a number of people were watching him as he waited, first to help Mrs. Woodvine out of the carriage and then to help Clara. When they were all out, he took a deep breath and offered his arm to Clara. She slowly slid her gloved hand into the crook of his arm and they turned to follow the wide stretch of path that led into the overcrowded park.

Silas felt his mouth dry as he kept his eyes on the tree line. His legs felt stiff and jell-like at the same time, and he knew that in a matter of moments, he would be awash with the terror that gripped him every time he came out in public. Only this time, as he felt the panic rising, the small, warm grip of Clara's hand held onto him, tethering him.

"Are you all right?" she whispered, leaning ever so slightly towards him as they walked.

"Yes," he lied gruffly.

"Are you quite sure? You seem unwell."

Unwell was an understatement. He felt as if a stone was pressed against his chest, making it hard to breathe.

"I'm fine."

"It would be all right if you were unwell," she continued and his panic began to give way to irritation. "I would understand if you wished to turn back."

"We're not turning back," he bit out in a harsh whisper.

Hopefully his tone had scared her off from asking any more—

"I wonder if you are coming down with something then?" she continued. He looked at her out of the corner of his eye and noticed that she was facing straight ahead. His eyes darted around them and he realized that nearly everyone they passed was staring at them, all while Clara prattled off about illness.

Was she worried about him? Surely not and yet her voice seemed so concerned. He found himself wondering if he could tell her about his damned anxiety. Would she be understanding? Or would she politely smile and nod at his confession, while plotting a way to escape their arrangement?

He turned his head and attempted to listen as she chattered about this and that. To his surprise, his own anxiety seemed to dim as he recognized the tension in her voice. He gently squeezed his arm around her hand.

"You're nervous," he said lowly as he bent down to her ear.

Clara turned to face him, her bright clear eyes catching his as he felt a drop in his stomach. What was the matter with him?

"If I admit I am, will you tell me what's wrong?"

He didn't wish to tell her, but then something in her steady gaze gave him confidence. He exhaled slowly as they walked.

"I have an issue, being out in crowds like this," he said so quietly he doubted she could hear him over the conversations around them. He bit his tongue before continuing, suddenly bitter at his own weaknesses. "It makes me uncomfortable."

When Clara didn't answer he was sure she believed he was some kind of pitiful fool. How could a man of his size be made to feel uncomfortable in crowds? What danger did his addled mind expect to find in this pleasant public park? Her fingers squeezed against his bicep and he felt the strangest of surges go through him. It was a small reassurance, he knew, but it had surprised him.

"Is that why you've not attended any social events for the past year?" she asked.

"Yes," he answered.

She was quiet for a moment, before turning her face to his.

"Well, if you stay close to me, I'll keep you safe."

Silas let out a gentle huff of laughter. What a ridiculous thing to say. She was markedly shorter than him and while he did not think she was weak, the differences in their physical powers were evident. It was preposterous to think that this woman could keep him safe from anything. Surely she had to be joking. But Clara did not join him in his laughter.

His brow creased.

"You're serious?"

"Very much so."

"And how would you be able to keep me safe?"

"Distraction," she said as they slowed their steps, coming to a particularly crowded section of the crushed stone path. "If you feel wary about crowds, you might focus your attention on me and in doing so, forget that there are people around."

"And you think that would work?"

"It's working now, isn't it?" she asked.

Silas wasn't able to argue with her. The misery he had felt along their ride to the park had certainly subsided far more than he ever could have expected. Maybe she was on to something.

"I suppose I should keep you near me then."

Clara smiled at him, but seemed oblivious to his meaning.

"I wouldn't mind," she said. "But if I'm ever not close by and you find yourself experiencing the same feeling, remember that it will pass. Let it be."

He scoffed.

"Easy for you to say. You've obviously never experienced it."

"No," she admitted. "But a friend of mine's mother was a nervous sort of woman." Silas glared down at her and she blanched. "Not that I'm calling you nervous. Or a woman."

Clara bit her lip, obviously worried that she had offended him. Silas breathed deeply.

"This woman," he said, ignoring her apology. "Who was she?"

Clara smiled wistfully.

"My dear friend Holly Smyth's mother, Lady Eloise Smyth. Perhaps you knew her? She passed away about five years ago now, but I remember her quite well. She was always very kind to me."

Silas shook his head. "I did not know her, no."

"Oh," Clara said, her shoulders dropping a bit. "Well, she was a fine lady. But she often suffered a certain sort of attack, as she put it. Sometimes, when it would happen, her face would become drawn and her eyes would appear distant. I am not certain what precisely triggered them, but I remember she would experience them from time to time when I visited.

"Her eyes would close and she would breathe deeply for several moments before regaining herself. When I asked if she was all right, she told me that she often experienced a terrible bout of anxiety and that she had suffered from that malady for many years."

Silas was skeptical, but curious.

"And she just closed her eyes to dissuade it from overcoming her?" he asked, unbelieving.

"No, not exactly. When I asked if her closing her eyes helped, she told me that once when she was caring for Holly's younger siblings, their twins, not long after their birth she had felt the beginnings of one of her bouts, but the timing was quite bad for it happening on a day when she was rather busy. Well, dreadfully busy from what she explained. The twins had been crying nonstop, the entire household staff had come down with a sickness, and she had been so tired from the demanding workload that when she felt her attack come on, she got angry."

"Angry?"

"Yes. Apparently, she had been so upset that she decided to

drop everything and let the bout happen, in an effort to be done with it as soon as possible so she could get back to work. But the moment she decided to let it happen, it faded away."

Silas's feet slowed.

"It faded away?"

"Yes."

"You're not serious."

"I am," Clara said. "That's what she told me and that ever since that day, instead of dreading or fighting the feeling, she simply let it be. She would wait for it to come, accepting it. She said they were never as bad as they had been before that day."

"But she still suffered from them?"

"I suppose, but she said they were far easier to manage after that," Clara said.

Silas wondered if such a thing were possible. It seemed the opposite of what he wanted to do. When the choking anxiety would fester in his chest, he wanted to beat it down, to strangle it away. To simply let it wash over him sounded like poor advice, but then he hadn't been able to find any doctor that could explain to him what he was experiencing, nor did he know of any other way to stop it.

He turned his head and watched Clara's profile as they continued their walk, rather in awe that this person would have such information and he wondered what else he might learn from her.

OVER THE NEXT several weeks Silas escorted Clara to three different social events and each time he focused solely on Clara in an effort to stall his anxiety. Remarkable, it seemed to work. Whenever he felt particularly overwhelmed, he remembered what she said and allowed it to happen. Only it never seemed to come on as strongly as before.

Clara's technique hadn't completely rid him of his problem,

but his anxiety had seemed smaller, almost manageable by the time they had visited the newly built National Gallery Museum.

Clara was bright and articulate, having been schooled by her father during her formative years when the family had lacked the means to provide for a proper tutor. Mr. Woodvine was a staunch believer in the higher learning and had provided Clara with a diligent education, particularly in the subject of philosophy, where she had been a very eager student. Silas knew that many would consider her unrefined, for her manner lacked the polish that he was accustomed to, but no one could claim she was unintelligent, and he admired how settled and certain she was in her thoughts and opinions. He was accustomed to fashionable ladies who shifted their tastes to match whatever was in vogue. Clara, on the other hand, was firmly fixed in her likes and dislikes.

She was free with her opinions as they wandered through the gallery, forming critiques and drawing comparisons with displays she had seen elsewhere. Every story she told him was humorous, engaging and charming and he was soon unaware at how others glanced at them as they walked about. He was simply enjoying her in the most basic way and he had been surprised to discover that the ease and pleasure he felt around her made it simple for him to open up and share his own past with her.

She had been delighted to discover that he had a younger sister who currently lived with his mother in Bedfordshire at his estate and conveyed her wish to meet them, which had warmed his heart for some reason. While he was particularly close with his mother, his relationship with his sister Violet, was one he hoped to mend soon. She had been devastated by his divorce and though she had eventually accepted it, he doubted Violet had fully forgiven him yet.

Clara was curious about his other relationships and he told her about his friendships with the Earl of Trembley, discovering that her friend Holly lived next to Gavin's uncle, the baron who Gavin was heir to.

The walk in Hyde Park with Clara and her mother had become front page news and soon the papers were writing about their journeys about town as though it were a matter of some sort of national importance that every Londoner should know about. Silas had forgotten what it was like to be the center of attention, but since he was now technically courting someone as a divorced man, it seemed his relationship with Clara was the only thing anyone wanted to write about. While Clara had initially been flabbergasted by all the attention, she eventually accepted it—or at least, learned to ignore it, keeping her attention fixed on him and paying little heed to those around them.

She was surprisingly well-read. Silas realized as much when he had offered her and her parents his box at the opera to see Jean-Jacques Rousseau's play, *Le devin du village*. She and her father had discussed the philosophies of the playwright afterwards in the carriage ride home.

"Rousseau believed that human beings, by nature, are capable of knowing goodness," Clara said as the carriage pulled away from the steps of the opera house. "I think the fact that Colin and Colette came back together showed his optimism in the human condition."

"Ah, but did not their human condition lead to their distrust of one another in the first place?" her father pointed out.

"But trust isn't a guarantee. One must earn it." She turned to Silas. "Don't you agree, your grace?"

Silas had quickly become used to hearing the elder Woodvine and Clara discuss all sorts of philosophies. He had even found himself tempted to brush up on his reading, if only to keep up with the two.

"I do, though I'm inclined to point out Rousseau's main belief was that of self-preservation. I think it's human nature to protect one's self from harm."

"But Rousseau's other belief is empathy for one's fellow man," Clara added. "Colin and Colette were bound to reunite because of their love for one another."

"But that isn't always the way of things."

"If it meant to be, there is no reason why two people shouldn't be together."

Silas tilted his head.

"Are you really saying that things like circumstance and condition have no impact on a relationship?"

"Not at all," she said and he nodded. "However, I believe that human factors only provide obstacles. They cannot truly keep two people apart."

He let a bark of a laugh. Obviously, she had not experienced enough of life if she still believed that.

"So, you believe in fate, is that it?"

"Clara dear," her mother said with a small shake of her head, obviously trying to dissuade her daughter from arguing with Silas.

"I believe in the good of humanity and even the good that comes from learning from our mistakes. It's set us forward, regardless of how painful those lessons may be at the time."

Silas looked at her with disbelief. It was strange to believe one thing and have the opposite so plainly explained to him.

"Clara, there's no need to argue with his grace."

"It's quite all right, Mrs. Woodvine. I find Miss Woodvine's staunch views rather refreshing," he said as he watched her. Turning, he faced a concerned looking Mr. Woodvine. "However, seeing as Rousseau also didn't believe people should own property, I'm liable not to follow him so devotedly."

"No, of course not," Mr. Woodvine said as Silas turned back to Clara.

Was she smirking at him? That was curious. Perhaps she simply enjoyed arguing for argument's sake.

The ease with which he was able to talk to Clara was the most surprising part of their partnership, as she had come to call it. Without the pressures of a proper courting, both he and Clara seemed far more at ease with each other than anyone else.

Silas was fascinated by her patience and understanding. Whenever he spoke, her brow would lift and she would tilt ever so slightly towards him, giving him her undivided attention. It unnerved him slightly, but then everything about Clara was starting to affect him in a way he hadn't believed possible.

Not after Cynthia.

He had accidentally broached the subject of her with Clara one afternoon. He had come to call with the intention of them taking a walk, but a storm had interrupted their plans. Mrs. Woodvine had decided to busy herself with needlework in the corner of the room. However, after only twenty minutes, she nodded off. Her hand dropped to her lap as her embroidery frame fell to the floor, landing silently on the carpet. The gentle snore from her mother made Clara smirk.

Clara moved around the room and picked up the frame. She placed it on top of her mother's sewing basket before returning to the settee.

"I was wondering if you and your parents would like to go to Vauxhall tomorrow evening," he said to her as she seated herself again.

"Are you sure?" Clara asked. "I would think the crowds would be uncomfortable for you."

"I would agree, but I've found your technique helpful and I should like to see how I fare in a large setting."

Clara smiled brightly at him and the oddest pinch gathered in his chest.

"That's wonderful. I'd be happy to go with you," she said, her smile deepening. "Poor mother. She'll be thrilled to be sure, but I'm afraid of what we're doing to her," she said, dropping the book she was reading to her lap as Silas took a seat in the chair opposite of the settee. "She is torn in two, you know."

"How so?" he asked, leaning forward to take a teacake from the three-tiered plate stand.

"Well, she is very hopeful that this courtship of ours will lead to a wedding and is trying her best to help things along," Clara said. "On the other hand, she doesn't trust you."

Silas frowned.

"Why not?"

"Because you are a duke and dukes are not to be trusted."

"You and your family are terribly prejudiced, you know," he said, his eyes on her as she leaned forward to fix her tea. She was wearing a tangerine-colored gown today that was so trimmed with frills and ribbons, she looked like the contents of a sewing basket. He really must find out what seamstress they patronized. "It's not my fault I was born with a title."

"But you weren't born with it, were you?" she asked. "You inherited it from your father."

"Yes, and when I was seventeen, he passed away and it fell to me. Hardly my fault really."

Clara gave him a sad smile.

"I'm sorry you lost your father. That must have been difficult when you were so young."

Silas shrugged, shaking his head.

"We weren't close. Even when I returned from school during holidays, he was always too busy to bother with me."

Clara's eyes went round as her smile vanished.

"That's terrible."

Silas wasn't sure how to respond. In his experience, it was common for men of great position to be busy. He knew of dozens of men who had little to no relationships with their fathers. It was probably difficult for Clara, whose family was terribly close, to understand.

"It wasn't. Not truly." Clara's brow puckered with concern as if she didn't believe him. Lifting her teacup to her mouth, she blew on the hot liquid before taking a sip. Silas watched her intently, unsure why such a task should be so interesting to him. "I promise," he said, his voice inexplicably husky. "I did not suffer much from his passing."

"But you lost the one person who had held your position. The person you were meant to learn from, not only about your position, but about all of life's nuances."

"Such as?"

"I don't know. How to go about in life. What sort of friends to choose, what sort of woman to mar—"

Clara's mouth snapped shut and her eyes dropped. A faint blush touched her cheeks and though Silas was aware that he should be annoyed, he also felt the sudden urge to touch her cheek.

Concerned with that thought, he frowned as she looked up and upon seeing his face, she blanched.

"I'm so sorry—"

"There's no need to apologize," he said, shaking his head. "You're right. Perhaps if my father had been alive when I met Cynthia, he would have been able to warn me."

Clara was quiet, staring at him and he could have sworn he felt her willing him to continue. Remarkably, he did, ignoring the discomfort he felt when he discussed Cynthia.

"What was she like?" Clara asked softly after a long moment.

Silas's eyes met Clara's and an unfamiliar need to unburden himself suddenly came over him.

"She was beautiful. Or rather, she still is I suppose," he said, trying not to sound defeated as he usually did when he spoke of her. "I believed she was perfect in nearly every way."

"Oh," Clara replied.

The expression on her face made Silas curse himself for his tactlessness.

"That is to say, she seemed perfect, but…"

"What?"

"I'm sorry," he said, shaking his head. "I don't much like to discuss her."

"Because you loved her so much?" Clara asked as Silas's gaze met hers.

The forwardness of her question made him feel hostile and he opened his mouth to deny it, but the words wouldn't come. He hated that he couldn't control his emotions when Cynthia was brought up, but he had no right to snap at Clara. He took a deep breath and shook his head.

"I did," he finally admitted. "More than I should have."

"How could loving someone so much be a bad thing?"

Silas wanted to tell her, but it was difficult to explain. He had loved Cynthia with every part of his heart, accepting things only a fool in love would accept. He had been dedicated to her, but in loving her so openly, so completely, he had left himself vulnerable to her torment. It was why he had vowed never to love someone so deeply ever again.

But he couldn't tell Clara that.

"I was too jealous, I suppose."

"One can only be jealous if there's a reason to be," she said smartly. "If there isn't any doubt between two people, then jealousy does not…" She stopped talking, seemingly aware that she was overstepping. Turning to face Silas, he saw the apology in her grey-green eyes. "Oh dear. I've gone off again, haven't I?"

"I don't mind."

"But it's rude, especially when I'm talking in theory and you're talking about reality."

"But you are correct," he offered, hoping to ease her concerns. "There was doubt. I doubted her."

"And she could not forgive you?" Clara asked after a long pause.

"She could not live with me and my fears," he said slowly before adding. "And I could not live with her rules."

Clara's brow knit together and she had opened her mouth to speak, when her mother startled awake.

"I was just resting my eyes for a moment," she said loudly, breaking the tension that had settled around Silas and Clara. He stood up and Mrs. Woodvine's eyes went wide. "Oh, you are not leaving so soon, your grace?"

"I'm afraid I must," he said, both eager to be away from this conversation, yet disappointed that he had to leave Clara. She stared at him with question. "But I hope you all will join me at Vauxhall Gardens tomorrow evening."

"Oh, yes of course!" Mrs. Woodvine said, while he kept his

gaze on Clara. "That would be splendid."

"Splendid indeed," Clara said as she stood. "Good-bye, your grace."

She curtsied at his bow and he left without a backward glance. He hadn't wanted to discuss Cynthia with her or anyone for that matter, but as he exited the house, he felt as though a weight had shifted off his chest.

It was the strangest sensation and yet, for the rest of the day Silas felt lighter than he had in months. He had expected to feel hostile and miserable after talking about Cynthia, but Clara had been surprisingly easy to talk to and he was eager to see her the following evening, though he reasoned it was because he wished to see how he would react to the crowds of Vauxhall.

Vauxhall Gardens was going to be a true test of his ability to manage his anxiety.

A part of him felt guilty for using her to stem off his own anxiety, but she hadn't seemed to mind.

As long as they were arm in arm, it seemed his anxiety could never fully form. Of course, their touching had led to him feeling a whole slew of other things, and it was difficult to be close enough to touch constantly.

The next evening, during the fireworks display near Vauxhall, while in the company of her parents, Silas and Clara had put enough distance between themselves and the elder Woodvines to speak with some privacy.

"You must let me apologize for yesterday," Clara said as they walked along. "I was too forward."

"No," he stopped her, unwilling to accept her contrition when he knew she had done nothing wrong. "It was good for me to talk about. I've kept that part of my life quiet for so long, I thought talking about it would make me angry, but the opposite happened."

Clara's brow lifted as she turned to face him, a loose strand of blonde hair laying across her cheek.

"Really?"

"Yes."

"Then may I ask you something?"

"I don't see why not."

"What did you mean, what you said you couldn't live by her rules?"

Silas's steps slowed as did Clara's. Turning to see where her parents stood, he found that they had stopped several yards away to watch a pantomime show. Looking back at Clara, he wondered how much he could tell her, without terrifying her.

"I'm not sure I can explain it," he said, debating on telling her anything at all.

"Please," she said. "It's vexed me all day."

"Has it?"

"Yes."

Silas took a deep breath, convinced that he was losing his mind for even considering talking about such a topic with an innocent young woman. But a long-forgotten desire to tease came floating up with in him, like the smoke over a fire. Her intent gaze, so ready to learn, made him feel things he hadn't felt in a long time.

"Cynthia enjoyed experiencing pain. In all aspects. It didn't matter what sort, physical or emotional. She fed off it and for a time I gave it to her. But it wasn't something I could tolerate. I wanted to control her, to force her desires away because they hurt, but our vices never matched up quite the right way."

After a moment of quiet, Silas wondered if he had gone too far, but then Clara spoke.

"Control," she said softly, more to herself than to him. Silas opened his mouth to try to explain more, but then she continued. "What do you mean, she fed off the pain?"

"Just that. It was as if she could only find joy in misery."

"And you would attempt to help her by controlling her? How did that work?"

Silas felt warm. How could he explain it to her without sending her running for the hills?

"Why are you so interested?"

"Because I'm always interested," she countered and Silas smiled.

"Yes, I suppose you are. Very well. In our moments of intimacy, she would want me to hurt her, physically. I believed that what she truly needed was something to...to take her out of herself. To make her focus on sensation so that she could lay aside whatever turmoil lived in her heart. I would attempt to provide that in ways that didn't hurt. Sometimes, I would restrain her. Sometimes, I would give her commands to follow, in the hopes that focusing on those would free her from the weight of other burdens."

"What sort of commands?" Clara asked in a low whisper.

"Without scandalizing you, I'll try to give you an example," he said as they stopped before a large stage, where a play was being performed. Clara turned her head to see the performance. Silas lifted his hand to the back of her head and pulled on one of the dozens of blue ribbons that had been piled on and weaved into her hairstyle. Thankfully, it came out with ease, though Clara whipped around, her own hand going to the back of her head.

"What are you doing?"

"You always seem to be hiding behind all these sorts of things," he said holding up the ribbon. "You needn't, you know."

"I..." she started, seemingly uncomfortable. She held out her hand. "May I have it back?"

"I thought you were curious as to how this game was played?"

"I am," she said, her hand lowering as fraction.

"Then pay attention," he said, his eyes intently on hers as he leaned forward, his voice dropping as his mouth hovered above her ear. "You may have this ribbon back, but I want you to tie it around your thigh, just above your knee, every day for the next seven days." He pulled back and saw Clara's bottom lip drop open as a deep blush stained her cheeks, but to Silas's surprise she didn't baulk or pull away. She seemed frozen and he realized that she wasn't going to slap him, or storm away. A familiar pang hit him square in the heart as he exhaled. "Do you understand?"

He only meant to show her by example, but the teasing he had initially desired had melted away and another feeling replaced it.

"Y-yes," she said softly.

Her eyes lifted to his and a surge of longing slammed into Silas's chest. Damn it. She was too keen to please and he was shocked to find that he was just as eager to press on, but he knew he shouldn't.

He handed her the ribbon and she took it, seemingly conflicted and he worried it had been too much. "I hope I didn't offend you."

"No," she said quickly as they continued their walk. After a long moment she looked up at him. "Do you… Are you…"

"Yes?"

"I have several questions, but I'm not sure how to ask any of them," she said honestly. "I'm afraid I'll say something foolish and you'll laugh."

"I would never laugh at you, Clara," he said earnestly.

Clara looked up at him and he thought he could see something akin to desire in her expression. But he was too fond of her and of their friendship. He decided to shake his head and dissuade her.

"Come," he said, holding out his arm to her.

Clara's hand came to the crook of his arm but neither one moved as a spark shocked both of them. It was dark out and even though there was a sense of relaxation that made Vauxhall Gardens an enjoyable place, neither seemed particularly sure of what to do next.

Thankfully, Mr. Woodvine appeared then his wife.

Thankfully indeed.

Chapter Nine

BY THE END of the month, Silas and Clara were being regaled in the papers as the most popular people in London, much to Clara's satisfaction and Silas's displeasure. He loathed gossip, but his little game with Clara to rehabilitate her reputation had worked, it seemed, and he was happy that she was content with the results. Why, just the other morning there had been an article that had practically named them engaged.

Divorced Duke's Devotion

It has come as a surprise to myself as well as most of my readers that the Duke of Combe, otherwise noted as the divorced duke, should find himself enamoured with none other than heiress and inventor's daughter, Miss Clara Woodvine. The unlikely pairing, while shocking, has really become something of a treat to witness. It seems the duke has been captivated by this provincial princess, having saved her from a potentially harmful fall down the steps at the opera two nights ago. It seems that while Miss Woodvine's antics from a month ago should have ended her social climb, her clumsiness has only charmed her would-be suitor.

He would have preferred the article to refrain from calling her clumsy, but it was certainly an improvement over the insults that were showered upon her only a few weeks earlier.

Still, by the time he arrived at Wincombe Terrace that evening for Gavin's going away dinner, he found that the latest article had seemingly turned on him.

"Well, if it isn't the divorced duke himself," Gavin said, smiling as Silas arrived at Wincombe Terrace. He peered over his shoulder. "You've not come alone, have you? I've been reading all about you and Miss Woodvine and had hoped to finally meet the woman who, how did the *Times* put it… Swept you off your feet?"

Silas scowled at his friend, fighting the urge to strangle him. There were going to be no more than fifty people attending the farewell soirée for Gavin that night and while Silas had been sure he would have fared fine without Clara, she had insisted that she attend in order to be there for him in case he needed her, though they had decided not to come together. Clara had begun to worry that their partnership had reached its peak and if they weren't careful about their inevitable separation, her reputation would be worse off than after her break off with Dilworth.

"The Woodvines will be arriving later," he grounded out. "And shut your mouth about those damn articles."

"Why should I? There all anyone's been talking about," Gavin replied, waving to Derek from across the room. "I should think you would be happy to receive some good press. Seeing as how your name is so often dragged through the mud."

"I don't know why they insist on writing about us," he grumbled. "A few walks here and there hardly seem news worthy."

"Ah, well, the subject matter is rather interesting, I'm afraid. Divorced Duke's Dire Dilemma was the title from today's paper. It seems the author is worried about your intentions."

Silas made a face.

"Intentions regarding what?"

"Miss Woodvine, of course. It seems her star is on the rise and there are rumors she may have a slew of other suitors soon enough, if you keep dragging your feet."

Silas didn't reply to Gavin as Derek finally reached them.

Even though his relationship with Clara was supposed to be a ploy to better both of their reputations, Silas had begun to wonder what it would be like to actually offer for her.

It was ridiculous, he knew, particularly because of how they met, but something had shifted between them during the past few weeks.

A strange sort of friendship had bloomed between he and Clara.

There was a level of ease and comfort between them that Silas had never known with a woman he was supposed to be courting. Clara was patient and helpful—and he couldn't deny that he was powerfully attracted to her. While their touching one another had started as a distraction to his anxiety, it had become important to him in many different ways. He found a surprising number of excuses to touch her, from escorting her during walks, to brushing a frizzy strand of hair off her face when it became loose. Clara in turn had been just as diligent in her effort to pluck pieces of invisible lint off his jacket. Each brush, each touch seemed heavier—at least, to him. Perhaps he was simply reading too much into it. He had considered broaching the topic once or twice, but when her amicable voice had echoed in his ears, he stopped himself.

Silas had quite forgotten how to approach a woman.

"Continuing to play this game of mock courtship, I see," Derek asked under his breath, as another couple was announced to the drawing room. "You're going to ruin that girl, you know."

As the days in Clara's company had unfolded, Silas had begun to give his feelings some proper consideration. She was so unlike Cynthia and while he knew she wouldn't appreciate being compared to his previous wife, Silas couldn't help but note the difference between the two. Almost to a fault.

"If I am, I don't see how it's any concern of yours."

"Come now, Derek. They're only having a bit of a lark," Gavin said as a butler came towards them. Each man took a brandy and Gavin sipped his before continuing. "Silas isn't serious. And Miss Woodvine is in on it. Isn't she, Silas?"

"Yes," he said stiffly.

"I hope so. Because it would be a mistake to create an expectation of serious intentions if you have none," Derek said.

"So you keep saying," Silas said, taking a sip of his brandy.

"I just don't want you to make the same mistake as before," Derek said. "You went through hell after Cynthia left you."

Feeling agitated, Silas downed his brandy completely.

"I quite remember, thank you," he said, placing his glass on the table as he turned to leave.

"Where are you going?"

"To get some air."

Silas exited the room, passing the dining room where the table was set for an elaborate feast of roasted quail, steamed vegetables, creamy soups and copious amounts of wine to take place in the coming hour. For now, the early guests were still in the parlor.

Silas was sure he would be able to take a moment alone. He walked swiftly towards the back of the house where a terrace sat before the garden. He pulled out a cheroot and a match, lighting it quickly and inhaling in a startled rush when he realized he wasn't alone.

Exhaling, he turned and saw Clara, back pressed up against the wall that separated a set of doors. Her ice blue gown seemed to glow in the moonlight and those damn beads that seemed to decorate her bust in each of her hideous dresses sparkled like crystal. He watched her chest rise and fall as she inhaled deeply, her eyes on the sky above.

He moved towards her and leaned his back against the wall right next to her. Tilting his head back to see what she saw, he spoke.

"I didn't know you'd arrived."

"Mama's dress caught on the carriage door when we exited and it caused a tear. She was so embarrassed; she asked the footman to see us in quietly so that she might bother one of the maids for a needle and thread."

"So, you snuck in?"

Her head rolled against the house to look at him and he felt his heart pound.

"Yes."

"And what are you doing out here?"

"Gathering myself before the rest of the evening. I know we've been out publicly together, but a party like this reminds me of Trembley's ball and, well…I'm a bit nervous I suppose," she said, her eyes shining in the moonlight. "What are you doing out here?"

"The same," he said. After a moment he pushed off the wall and went to lean against the baluster. "People talk too much."

"They do," she agreed. "I didn't know you smoked cheroots." He shrugged, but made no move to speak. "I always believed it was an unhealthy habit. Breathing in smoke seems unwise."

"Then you shouldn't do it," he said, smirking.

She squinted her eyes at him. "You shouldn't either."

"Why not?" he asked, feeling rather maudlin. "It's not like anyone cares."

"I do," she said.

The honesty in her tone made something in him react. It felt as if she had simultaneously kicked him in the stomach and kissed him on the mouth. *What a bizarre feeling,* he mused as he stared at her.

"Do you?" he asked and she nodded.

"Of course," she said, taking a step towards him. "We are friends, are we not?"

Friends. What a glorious and hateful word. To be honest he had wanted to be her friend, but there was something unmistakable about Clara Woodvine, something he couldn't articulate that made him want to be so much more.

Lost in thought, Silas flicked his cheroot too zealously as the tiny ember end caught the knuckle of his left ring finger. It didn't hurt, but the surprise of the burn caught him off guard and he dropped the burning cylinder.

"Damn it," he said, pulling his hand up to his mouth.

"Oh dear," Clara said, coming toward him. She reached for his hand. "Here, let me see."

Clara's gentle fingers pulled his close to inspect his injury.

"It's nothing," he insisted.

"It's a burn. It's already turning," she said. "I once burnt my finger on the French toaster that sat in our hearth when I was younger." She held up her pointer finger for him to see. Though it was dark, he could make out a tiny, white slash across her fingerprint. "I howled like a baby when it happened."

"I assure you; I won't do that."

She smiled.

"You may if you'd like, I won't tell," she teased. She turned her finger around so that she could see her old injury. "I was very little and I would not stop crying until I received three kisses, one from each person in our household. Papa, Mama, and my great Aunt Laney."

Silas stared at her with a strange fascination. It seemed every time she opened her mouth, a jewel of a story would fall out and he found himself eager to collect all of them. A tiny smile pulled at the corner of her mouth, almost as if she were thinking about something amusing.

"What?" he asked, his voice rough.

Her eyes flickered up.

"It's a silly custom. A kiss can't take any sort of pain away."

"Can't it?" he asked.

The look in her eye was one of daring, but Silas couldn't understand until the next moment, when she brought his hand to her lips and pressed her soft mouth to the red, raw skin. She stayed there only a moment, but it was an image Silas would always remember.

"See?" she said, her cheeks covered in a blush. "It doesn't work."

Perhaps it hadn't taken the sting of his burn away, but it had elicited another feeling elsewhere on his body that distracted him from everything else. As he stared at her, he wondered if he might explore the feeling.

"Clara," he said, his tone low.

"Yes?"

"If I did try and claim my winnings from that bet with Dilworth," he said slowly. "What would you do?"

She watched him with wide eyes.

"You mean, collect my dowry?"

"No," he said as his hand came up to her face. What was possessing him to do this? It seemed entirely mad…and yet, he didn't want to stop. "I mean, if I wanted to claim you as my prize. Would you consent?"

She didn't move, but her eyes widened with surprise.

"As what? Your mistress? Your wife?" The corner of her mouth pulled up in a sarcastic half smile. She shook her head. "Does it matter? There is hardly a difference."

"There is a difference," he said, his thumb following the edge of her jaw. "One would make you a duchess."

"I wish you wouldn't jest, Silas," she said, seemingly holding her breath as she gazed at him. "It's not a very sporting thing to joke about."

"I'm not joking."

"Then you're going mad," she countered. "We've hardly known each other a month."

"It's been five weeks, technically."

"Don't you think that's a short amount of time to decide whether to spend the rest of your life with someone?"

"No longer than you knew Dilworth."

Her mouth opened to argue as her eyes flashed with challenge, but no words came. Then, she let out a defeated laugh and nodded.

"I suppose that's true."

"Besides, as I'm the only one who has experienced a marriage with a long courtship, I can confirm that the amount of time two individuals have known one another hardly matters if their characters don't blend well together."

"And our characters do?"

"I believe so."

Clara exhaled and smiled though it didn't quite reach her eyes. She didn't seem to believe him. She pulled away and looked out over the garden. She was beautiful. In the moonlight, the excessive detailing of her pale blue gown just looked like glints of magic. She reminded him of some sort of fairy.

"You don't want to marry me, Silas," she said softly. "I'm not suited to be a duchess."

"I think you would make a fine duchess."

"You're the only one."

"I'm the only one whose opinion matters on the topic," he said as she turned to face him. "You just said you cared for me."

"I do."

"Is your refusal based on the fact that you don't wish to be associated with a divorced man?"

"Of course not."

"Then what is it?" he asked earnestly. "Why not accept my proposal?"

"Firstly, you didn't propose," she said, adding quickly. "And I cannot compare…"

"Compare to what?"

"Not to what, but to whom."

"To whom then?"

"To you know who," she said, her gaze dropping. While it was dark, Silas could see a blush cover her cheeks. "I should hate to be compared every day to another woman."

Silas was speechless for a moment. He could not deny that had compared them against one another, but not vindictively. It was just that the differences between Clara and Cynthia were so vast that he couldn't help it. Cynthia was classically attractive, cold and ultimately his downfall, while Clara was strangely beautiful, warm and honest. A woman he was more comfortable with than any he had ever known.

He took a step towards her and took her hands into his. She was watching him, seemingly surprised as they had been overtly aware of keeping their distance, physically. He was fighting a losing battle as all he wanted to do was gather her into his arms and kiss her senseless.

"She pales in comparison to you."

"Oh yes, o-of course," she said sarcastically, stumbling over her answer as she glanced at him, but when he didn't join in on her self-deprecating humor, she frowned. "You cannot be serious?"

"I am."

"She is my opposite in every way."

"And we divorced."

"But you loved her."

"I don't see why that would affect your decision to marry me."

Clara let out a sullen laugh, one almost more pained than amused. His brow furrowed, confused.

"No, you wouldn't I suppose," she said. Silas opened his mouth to ask what she meant but in the next instant she continued. "I don't see how a marriage between us would benefit you."

"Well, for one, I'd be more palatable to the general public again," he said. "I may be a duke, but the black mark of my divorce holds me in a contemptible light."

"You are not the only man to get a divorce."

"No, but I'm part of a rare group whose wives forced the issue and publicly humiliated them. It did not help my reputation. You can imagine what has been said of me." By the avoidance of her eyes, Silas wondered what she had heard. "Or rather, what you might have learned on your own."

She tilted her head up.

"I don't believe any of it," she said and Silas felt a small sliver of his heart creak open, like a lockbox being opened only slightly.

"But surely there's a better way for you to get back in the good graces of society, if that is what you wish."

Silas's contempt for society had ebbed and flowed over the years and while it certainly would be more comfortable not to be gawked at by people whenever he went somewhere, the reality of it was, any small perk that came with being married to Clara seemed somehow doubly as important now. If him being accepted in society would make things easier for her, then that was what he wanted.

"Not one I can think of. Besides… I've grown rather fond of you," he said, his tone dipping. "I don't like to think of you as being a monetary prize for some bumbling idiot when this ploy of ours ends. Not when I can offer you something more."

Clara's head dropped and he felt a strange buzzing in his ears.

"You've grown fond of me?"

Her words were soft and the uncertainty in her tone nearly undid him. He took a step towards her.

"Yes, as I believe you've grown fond of me. Haven't you?" She nodded. "Besides, it'll be equally beneficial to you."

"Because I'll be a duchess, you mean?"

"Yes," Silas said, knowing the title of duchess was one of the only things he could offer her. "You would command the respect of every person in the ton."

"I suppose that would be nice," she said, the inflection of her voice sounding wholly unconvinced. "But what about what would transpire between us?"

"How do you mean?"

"I mean, how would we conduct ourselves? With one another?"

"As any husband and wife, I suppose," he said. "It would be a marriage of mutual respect. One of friendship and comfortability."

"Friendship," she repeated. "And nothing more?"

"Well, yes," he said, his brow puckering in contemplation. "What better thing could be between the two of us than friendship?"

There seemed to be a drop in Clara's shoulders. He couldn't understand it. Friendship had been the one thing he and Cynthia never had. Theirs had been a passionate affair, but mutual respect had always eluded them. If what Silas had experienced with Clara in the last several weeks was any indication, he suspected they'd have a perfectly pleasant marriage. A peaceful relationship, the kind he had hoped for so many times before.

"I know certain members of your social standing tend to search outside their marriages for…physical comforts of sorts," she said, not quite making eye contact. "I should like to know now if you have any plans to do so, as to prepare myself. I don't wish to have any delusions going into this, you understand."

Silas didn't answer right away as that familiar feeling rolled within him. His body became stiff as the memories of jealousy, anger, and pain flooded his mind. Images of bodies intertwined, himself both furious and gutted at the sight. He had been able to bury such feelings beneath his own sorrows for over a year, however it all came bubbling up again at her words.

Clara waited patiently for an answer, but when he didn't speak, she looked up.

"No," he said gruffly. "I will not go outside our marriage for comfort." Clara nodded. "Nor I will permit it from you either."

Clara visibly swallowed, seemingly unnerved by the change in his demeanor. Even in the darkness, Silas could see the color change in her cheeks.

"Will we, um… That is, will you require me to," she dipped her head, unwilling to face him. "That game, you spoke of. Will we…"

Silas shook his head.

"No," he said, his tone softening. "I've put that part of my life behind me."

Her eyes lifted and she appeared confused.

"Have you?"

"Yes."

Her cheek twitched as a thoughtful look passed over her face.

"The philosopher David Hume believed that passion rather than rationale drove human kind," she said. "And I'm inclined to agree. I don't think a person can change an essential part of themselves."

Silas felt challenged.

"I'm more than capable of governing myself."

"I don't mean to say that you can't, only that you shouldn't have to." Her eyes bore into his. "I wouldn't try to stop you, I mean, if you so wished."

He stood perfectly still for a moment, taking in what she had said. He wanted to, God did he want to, but he wouldn't. His hand came up to stroke her cheek as a torrent of emotions swept over him. He knew what she was trying to say and while he appreciated her willingness, he wouldn't explore that part of himself with her. Regardless of how much he wanted to, he didn't want to pull her into his depravity.

"I wouldn't make you."

A flash of disappointment shone in her eyes and for a moment he wondered why, when she spoke.

"Very well then," she said softly, her eyes unwavering from his. "I suppose, you may ask me."

A serious sort of feeling fell between them beneath the moonlight and while they were the only ones on the balcony, Silas felt as though a third, otherworldly presence was with them.

"Clara," he breathed as his arms involuntarily flexed around her. "Will you marry me?"

"Yes, Silas," she said softly as his eyes dropped to her mouth. "I will."

Joy burst within his chest at her words and without thinking, he bent down and kissed her, sealing their agreement.

The sweetness with which she kissed him a month earlier had been replaced with what seemed like a yearning desire. She kissed him with a fierceness that surprised him and made his body respond in reaction. His hands came up to her face as she pulled at his lapels. Her kisses felt earnest and desperate, as if she were trying to hold on to something that might slip out of her grasp.

The need to pull her away from this balcony and find a bed was growing, but he couldn't very well do such a thing in someone else's home. Besides, he was going to do this marriage the right way. And so, with a great amount of self-restraint, he held her shoulders and pulled away.

They were both breathing heavily in the dark. When her soft hands reached again for him, he gripped them in his large grasp.

"We should return to the others," he said, his voice was rough and breathless. She only nodded as she stared at him with wonder-filled eyes. "I'll have to discuss it with your father."

"Oh yes," she whispered, her lips slightly puffed by his kisses.

"Perhaps you should go first," he said, trying hard to think of anything that would lessen his reaction to her. "I'll follow soon."

Clara only nodded, but she didn't move. When he tilted his head, she seemed to snap out of whatever daydream she was having. She turned and walked away, leaving Silas with a curious feeling of hope. She seemed both physically eager, yet mindful. A part of him worried that she might come to regret saying yes to him but then he didn't care. She may indeed come to regret it, but he wouldn't let her go now.

Chapter Ten

THOUGH MARRIAGES WERE often the thing of gossip throughout London, resulting in the targeted couple being scrutinized or waxed on about in poetic stanza, no one quite knew how to approach the nuptials of Clara Woodvine and the Duke of Combe. On one hand, it seemed rather sudden that Clara Woodvine would be so quickly attached to someone other than Lord Dilworth, who himself had just recently suffered another disappointment as he and Bettina seemed no longer in each other's good company.

Clara had been warned by Silas that they might be eviscerated by the newspapers due to his past, but the *Times* barely mentioned the previous Duchess of Combe, nor did any of the other publications. Silas had seemed so sure that the gossip rags would bring up his divorce, but as soon as their nuptials were announced, it seemed as if the entire city had forgotten about Silas's first marriage.

While she had consented to marry him, Clara had been flooded with a whirlwind of emotions ever since she had said yes. Silas had been specific about wanting their marriage to be one of friendship but while she was very glad to be his friend, she couldn't ignore other feelings that had begun to simmer between them. Nor could she ignore all he had told her, about the games he used to play with his previous wife.

Clara had decided to see if she could find any philosophies on subjects of control. She had read the Greek philosophers' opinion of eros, passionate love and philia, friendship love, but neither spoke to the sort of relationship Silas had talked about.

There were some other writers, poets and such, who Clara heard about who might explain the nature of what she was searching for, but such works were rarely spoken of. Everyone knew the poet John Wilmot and the Marquis de Sade were libertines, whose works depicted vulgarities that no young lady should ever read. But still, she searched the library in her home for their books, unsurprisingly finding none by either.

Instead, she decided to read *A Treatise of Human Nature* by David Hume, the very philosopher she had quoted to Silas. It seemed there was something to be discovered in his writings and she was eager to learn as much as she could before the wedding. She made sure it was the first thing she packed in her valise when the house began to pack for the wedding, which they had decided would take place at Silas's ancestorial home in Bedfordshire. Clara and her family had often stayed in Bedfordshire while journeying to London from their home in Lincolnshire, though they had never had the privilege of seeing the duke's home. The wedding was taking place at Greystone Manor, as to avoid any fanfare that might lead to more articles being written about them and they would stay for some time afterwards, so that they could recoup from their public romance in private. Time alone, to explore what their relationship would be.

Clara knew that Silas wasn't particularly interested in having the type of relationship with her that he had shared with his first wife, and as much as she told herself that it was fine, she knew she was lying. She wanted very much to explore all Silas's wants and wishes, as well as her own, but he was adamant that they would conduct themselves as friends. He had repeated several times in the weeks leading up to their wedding that their marriage would be based solely on their friendship and nothing more. He said as much the night before they were set to travel north to Nottinghamshire.

Silas had come for dinner and though there was a certain amount of excitement in the atmosphere as they dined, Clara couldn't help but feel a tension in the room as she spooned her potato and leek soup.

"The journey shouldn't take more than two days," Silas said to her father as he picked up his glass of wine. "The midway point is Northampton. We'll be staying at the Rose and Thorn Inn."

Clara's father nodded while her mother beamed.

"We are so happy to celebrate your wedding to our daughter, your grace. Exceedingly so." Her eyes turned towards Clara as she sighed happily. "Imagine. My daughter. A duchess."

"Mother, please," Clara said, the tips of her ears burning with embarrassment.

"Do not dampen your mother's spirits, my dear," her father said, his eyes crinkling in delight at his wife's joy. "She's merely excited."

"Yes, Father," Clara said, her gaze locked on the food she could barely finish.

She wasn't sure why she was feeling so apprehensive. Perhaps the two-day long voyage was worrying her.

"Will there be many guests?" Clara heard her mother ask. "We had hoped to have the wedding in London, your grace, but Clara suggested that it might be in poor taste since… Well…"

Her mother cleared her throat as an uncomfortable silence settled over the room. The heat from Clara's ears spread down to her cheeks. She had made the comment that Silas wouldn't wish to have an opulent wedding, considering it was his second marriage. She stole a glance as she took a sip from her water glass, expecting to see an annoyed looking Silas, but his face was unreadable.

"A very selfless consideration on your daughter's part," Silas said, his eyes on Clara. "Her thoughtfulness is a great attribute. It's why I'm so certain our marriage will be a successful one."

"A marriage based on friendship is a happy marriage indeed," her father said, raising his glass. "My Mary is my closest confidant. It is why our marriage has been a joy these past twenty-three years."

"Heavens, Joseph," her mother said, dipping her head as a blush stained her cheeks.

Clara smiled at her mother's embarrassment before looking at Silas. Her smile faded upon seeing the intensity in his eyes, but then he had just reiterated that theirs was to be a marriage of friendship. While that made her far luckier than most ladies who married into the ton to husbands who didn't seem to care for them at all, she couldn't help but feel like she was missing something.

Later that night, after the duke had left, Clara and her mother sat up in her room, picking out the final touches for their ensembles to wear at the wedding.

Mary was gleeful as she held up a dazzling pair of ruby and pearl earbobs to her ears while she twirled around Clara's bedroom. "I cannot believe it."

Clara smiled at her mother's childlike joy; her eyes crinkled with happiness.

"Have you chosen which jewels to wear then?" Clara asked, noting another pair of emerald and diamond earrings in her mother's hands.

"Well, I've narrowed it down, but I'll simply bring them all and decide the day of the wedding," she said. She sighed and looked at her daughter. "I cannot believe that you will be married by weeks' end."

"Yes, it's all very exciting I suppose," Clara said, trying to sound cheerful.

But her mother stilled at her tone.

"Is there something wrong, my dear? Are you not happy about marrying the duke?"

"Oh no, it's not that," Clara said, shaking her head. "It's just a little overwhelming."

Mary tilted her head.

"Are you concerned about...the wedding night?" her mother asked, sounding rather hesitant.

Clara's cheeks warmed.

"No," she said quickly. Country living had demonstrated to her the finer points of consummation and she was sure Silas would do everything to make the experience pleasant. "I simply meant becoming a duchess."

"Oh," her mother replied, visibly relieved as she exhaled. "Well, I know it must be difficult managing a duke's house, but you will fare well enough if you let the dowager duchess teach you. Besides, the duke chose you and if he thinks you'll make a fine duchess, who are we to disagree?"

Clara gave her mother a half smile, not completely sure that she agreed with her sentiment. It was as if she was constantly trying to convince herself that her feelings for Silas weren't genuine. Yes, she enjoyed their friendship, but she was finding it increasingly difficult to ignore her most private imaginations about their relationship. Clara flatly ignored her growing attraction for him. It didn't matter whether she thought how dashing he appeared when his black hair fell over his forehead, or how considerate he was, like the time he helped her avoid a series of puddles one rainy afternoon, even though her shoes were already soaked. Silas was simply a kinder man than most. Their marriage would be one of pleasant conversation and mutual consideration and Clara had to accept that.

Over the next two days, Clara rode with her parents, hardly seeing Silas until they reached Greystone. Clara had been surprised to discover that they were part of a sort of large convoy travelling to Nottinghamshire. They were being followed by the entire Trembley family, the Duke and Duchess of Egmont—family friends of Silas's mother, the dowager duchess—as well as Holly Smyth and her younger siblings, who had been sent for by Silas at Clara's request.

Silas had told Clara that he had written his sister and mother ahead of time to make preparations for their arrival as well as the wedding, though he had also said that he doubted his sister, Violet, would be much help. Supposedly, Violet had been very fond of Cynthia and hadn't forgiven Silas for the dissolution of their marriage. That information had worried Clara, but only for a moment. Surely, she just needed some time to befriend her new sister-in-law.

But a singular worry in the back of Clara's mind seemed unwilling to release her. What if she wasn't good enough to be a duchess? What if everyone who had known Silas's former wife would realize that she wasn't elegant enough, or calm enough, or good enough to be the Duchess of Combe?

It was a rotten feeling, but she couldn't shake it. Perhaps her worries would prove to be unfounded. As long as Silas was pleased with her, she shouldn't care what others were thinking…and yet she couldn't shake the terrible worry that she would end up embarrassing him in some way.

Clara groaned silently to herself as they rode silently in the carriage north. She did not like being so concerned with how others perceived her. Silas's opinion had become increasingly important to her. Heaven forbid she change the way she behaved only to please him.

She bit the inside of her lip and tried to shake off her worries. Silas liked her just as she was, she reminded herself. And he wasn't going to fall in love with her, so there would be no point in falling in love with him. He only wanted friendship and a peaceful union. Well, she could live with that. After all, friendship was far more than most received.

But Clara wondered if she would be able to curb her growing desires. She had begun fantasizing about what it would be like to touch him. What it would be like if Silas remained perfectly still, perhaps sleeping, while she moved her fingers over his face. There was something very enticing about the strong, straight line of his jaw, the plane of his nose and the fullness of his lips. She wanted to press her fingertips to his mouth and trail her thumb along the ridge of his bottom lip.

Shivering, Clara forced those thoughts from her mind just as the carriage turned. They had arrived.

Greystone Manor was rectangular in shape, with a long center block at the ground floor level, topped by bedrooms and attics above. There were two lower flanking wings joined to the main block by colonnades. To the south of the house was a detached quadrangular stable.

The exterior was both grand and restrained, constructed of fine-grained, silver stone, the genesis of the name Greystone Manor. In line with the Palladian style, it had domes punctuating each corner of the manor.

Standing outside to greet the train of carriages were nearly fifty uniformed servants, headed by a housekeeper, a butler and a cook. In front of all of them however, stood a very tall, very slim woman with wavy grey hair, pinned back into an elegant coiffeur. She wore a plum and black gown that went all the way up to her chin, giving her the appearance of some regal queen. Standing next to her was a slightly shorter girl, perhaps only just seventeen, dressed in a gown of the palest green. She had dark, wavy hair that was held back in a similar fashion as the older woman and Clara knew that these two must be Silas's mother and sister.

Trying to regulate her breathing, Clara exited the carriage following her parents. Their vehicle had been second in line, behind Silas's, who had already exited his carriage and was now standing before his mother. They exchanged a few words before he turned and stepped aside to make the introductions. Clara ignored the thunderous pounding of her nervous heart and tried her hardest not to trip or lose her balance as she approached the dowager duchess.

"Miss Clara Woodvine," the older woman said stoically with a nod as Clara made sure to curtsy extra low. "A pleasure to meet the woman who was so swift to steal my son's heart."

Her tone was tight and didn't quite match her words. She certainly didn't *seem* pleased. Clara was conscious not to fidget in front of this woman. She glanced at Silas who seemed to be trying not to roll his eyes.

"Your Grace," Clara said slowly. "It's an honor to make your acquaintance. His Grace spoke very highly of you and I'm very happy to be able to meet you."

The dowager duchess was silent. Clara's eyes lifted to see one of her brows arched, before letting her gaze drop as she waited for her new mother-in-law to speak.

"She's sweet, Silas. A bit eager, but sweet," she said after a moment. She turned to her son. "Try not to break this one."

Clara felt her cheeks heat up at those words as the dowager climbed the stairs. She studied Silas's profile as a cold veneer shrouded his face.

"Ignore her," a feminine voice said to Silas, catching Clara off guard. She turned and saw his sister approach him, careful not to give Clara any attention. "She's just sour that she wasn't consulted about this rather unexpected affair."

"And you're not?" he asked her plainly, glancing back at Clara.

The girl wouldn't turn around to follow her brother's gaze, but she shook her head.

"Why should I be?" she asked sweetly, Clara was wary of her tone.

Seemingly convinced, Silas nodded and turned to the house-keeper.

"Mrs. Bridges," he said and Clara could hear the genuine happiness in his voice. "It's wonderful to see you."

"You as well, your grace," the elderly woman said, with a curtsy.

"Will you help Boggs show Miss Woodvine and her parents to their rooms?"

"Of course, your grace," she said nodding. She too seemed to be evading Clara's gaze.

Clara tried to make her face impassive as she followed the housekeeper into the cavernous home. It seemed everyone at Greystone was going to ignore her completely. *What had she done agreeing to marry this man?*

Upon entering the grand building, Clara noted that everything inside the manor was opulent, lavish and terrifying. As she followed Mrs. Bridges, she noted the large paintings depicting ancient wars, Persian rugs and gold leaf ceiling murals that seemed to be everywhere Clara's eyes landed. A large, marble staircase to the right of the entrance hall led to the second floor, where another massive hallway opened up into three smaller hallways. An east wing led to family accommodations while the west wing led to guest rooms.

Once Clara's parents had settled in the Lilac room in the family wing, Mrs. Bridges turned to lead Clara out of the east wing.

"Oh," she said, cautiously. "Am I staying in the west wing?"

The housekeeper slowed her steps.

"No, my lady. Of course not. You're to stay in your own room, adjacent to his grace's apartments."

"Oh," Clara said, nervously. "Yes, of course."

Mrs. Bridges nodded assuredly at her.

"Very well. Follow me."

Clara followed Mrs. Bridges up a smaller, but no less elegant marble staircase up a north wing. Grand landscape paintings hung from the walls down the corridor, each more serene looking than the last. At the end of the hallway, there was a large window that went from the floor to the ceiling and had a view of the property. The housekeeper had gone to the last door on the left, but Clara had continued forward until she was looking out the window.

A massive, walled garden, centered by a maze stood beneath her in a sort of courtyard that was outlined with fruit trees. Clara sighed at the beautiful sight beneath her and wished very much to go exploring in the garden, only to be brought back to reality by the housekeeper's throat clearing.

Turning, Clara tried to appear apologetic. She gave the housekeeper a strained smile and followed her into the room.

"Do you like gardens, my lady?" Mrs. Bridges asked.

"Very much so," Clara said, peering over her shoulder before entering her bed chambers.

The minute she walked into the room, her breath caught in her throat.

Red damask wallpaper covered the towering walls and gold framed mirrors seemed to be everywhere. Goodness, how vain had the former duchess been? Surely one person did not need such an excessive number of mirrors but, everything about this house seemed excessive to Clara. She really needed to remember that she was no longer a mere country girl. Still, it was difficult to remember that this amount of opulence was expected of great houses.

Even with that in mind, the lavishness of these apartments made her slightly uncomfortable. Turning about the room, Clara's eyes landed on the bed. This was the most shocking to see. The canopy was draped in black silk and the intricate carvings on the pillars and headboard appeared to be scenes of satyrs and nymphs.

Clara's hand came up to her mouth absentmindedly, her thumb and forefinger plucking at her bottom lip as she stared at one pillar in particular where a satyr's arms were reaching out above him to grab the backside of a nymph.

Clara's head tilted slightly as her eyes traveled up the post. Goodness, was this depicting—

"My lady?"

Clara jumped and whipped around.

"Yes?" she said quickly, as if she had just been caught reading some wicked book.

"I asked if you were also fond of the country?"

"Oh yes," Clara said, trying to smile. "I am very fond of the country."

"Do you and his grace plan to stay in Nottinghamshire?" she asked as Clara's gaze fell around the room.

Plush velvet furnishings and heavy wood pieces adorned the room. She had never seen a room like this one and a singular word came to her mind when she thought to describe it.

Decadence.

"I hope so," Clara said as her fingers trailed against the back of a gilded chair.

Though she didn't say anything, the small pull of the old woman's mouth into a quick smile made Clara feel as if she had just cracked into a safe. She knew now that it was inevitable that she would be compared to the former mistress of the house, but as Silas said, they were nothing alike. Hopefully she would be able to meet their expectations of what a duchess should be like.

Soon a small army of maids swarmed the room, making up a hot bath, laying out several choices of gowns that Clara had brought with her. When none seemed to please Mrs. Bridges, she sent for a few gowns belonging to Violet. Apparently, Mrs. Bridges had once been a lady's maid to the Duchess of Lancaster, a dear friend of Silas's mother. When the duchess passed away however, it was revealed that the Lancaster duchy was bankrupt and Mrs. Bridges was offered the housekeeper position at Greystone. Her taste for fashion was well known as she had a talent for matching her mistresses to dresses that would complement them.

"Oh no," Clara tried to dissuade the maids as one left to collect several gowns from Violet. "I don't want to bother Lady Violet. I'm sure she doesn't wish for a stranger to wear her things."

"It's no trouble," Mrs. Bridges insisted, holding up a string of pearls and an emerald necklace to either side of Clara's neck. "Lady Violet has a vast collection of dresses. Besides, she is more than willing to help her future sister-in-law dress appropriately for her wedding day."

"Are my gowns truly that bad?" she asked.

"No, my lady. But they are a bit…Well…" She hesitated.

"Shiny?" another maid said helpfully.

"Yes. Shiny. Too shiny for the chapel, I think. The dowager wouldn't approve, I'm afraid."

"Oh," Clara said, feeling rather ill-equipped. "Perhaps I should undo some of the beaded stitching in the coming days."

Two maids that stood closest to Clara paused in their preparations as they exchanged glances with one another. Turning to face the housekeeper, Clara wondered if she had said something wrong. Mrs. Bridges had also stopped moving, appearing both surprised and appalled.

"My lady, you'll be a duchess tomorrow. You needn't fix your own dresses."

"Oh no, I just meant—"

"We have a very talented laundress; Miss Kelly is a miracle worker. She'll tend to your gowns straight away."

"All right," Clara said as she was pushed gently towards the bath.

She had tried to protest, insisting that she could bathe herself, but Mrs. Bridges seemed determined to show Clara how the future duchess should be pampered. Lilac oil was added to the bath water and rose scented soaps were used to wash her hair.

Once she was finished, she was dressed in a silk robe and sat before a vanity. Her hair was brushed out and then twisted and pinned in a way it never had been before. When Clara's questioning face met Mrs. Bridges in the mirror, the housekeeper smiled.

"Your hair doesn't need manufactured curls, my lady. A cousin of mine has a similar texture and the heat only aggravates her attempts at curling. She discovered that simply twisting the hair while it's wet will give a more pleasant effect."

"How interesting," Clara said, excited to see how her hair would turn out.

After she was dressed in a pale blue gown that had been brought in from her sister-in-law, she was lightly spritzed with a sweet citrus perfume. The faintest of vegetable rouge was applied to her cheeks and her dried hair was released from its twists.

Clara's eye widened with uncertainty as she saw the results, but after Mrs. Bridges began braiding and pining it, pulling certain strands here and there in a way Clara had never witnessed, she began to see it come together.

Half-moon shaped combs adorned with pearls were used to set a sort of crown-like pattern in her hair, while also holding the mass intact. Once the style was complete, a maid came forward with a wooden box and opened it, revealing an astonishing number of shining baubles.

"Oh, my goodness," Clara said breathlessly as she looked at the magnificent pieces. She felt as though a pirate's chest of treasure had just been revealed to her. She looked up at Mrs. Bridges. "What is all this?"

"These are yours, my lady."

"Mine?"

"Yes. His grace requested that the family jewels be presented to you, so that you may pick out your favorites."

Clara was astonished. Though her family had been able to afford anything she wanted, she had never been very interested in jewelry. That was, until such a bounty had been presented to her.

Her hand rose to the box as her fingers gently touched gold bracelets, ruby set necklaces and sapphire earrings. There was even a diamond tiara. It seemed as though every color of the rainbow had been placed in these shining stones and while each piece seemed more lavish than the last, a small, rose cut diamond, surrounded by seed pearls set on a gold band, caught her eye. She picked the ring up and brought it close.

It was a charming little piece, one that seemed to be lost in the sea of other gems, but Clara quite liked it. Smiling, she placed it on her ring finger and flexed her hand as she stared at it. Yes. This was just right.

Looking up, she saw Mrs. Bridges nod towards the box.

"And what else?"

"Oh, I think this will be enough."

A brief, uncertain expression passed over the maid's face as she looked up at the housekeeper, but Mrs. Bridges didn't show any reaction other than to nod.

"As you wish, my lady."

The maid closed the box and turned to put it away, while a pair of footmen came to remove the tub and bring in her valise. Clara eyed the bag, eager to continue her reading when the housekeeper spoke.

"Dinner will be served at eight o'clock. If there is anything else we can do, please just ring."

"Thank you very much, Mrs. Bridges. I think I will read until then," Clara said as the housekeeper and the rest of the maids left.

She got up and reached for her valise, pulling her book out and began reading. But just as she settled into one of the large chairs positioned in front of her fireplace, a knock sounded from the door. Turning, she saw the door open and Silas walked in.

She stood, her heart leaping as he came to a sudden stop at the sight of her. His eyes roamed over her body and Clara reminded herself that it was silly to always react this way to seeing him. There wasn't anything amorous between them and if she needed to repeat it to herself a thousand times to realize it, she would.

Still, it wasn't completely her fault, when Silas stared at her as though he were a man starved and she was a meal. Clearing her throat, she broke his concentration and he blinked.

"Clara. You look…" He started, but didn't finish.

Clara swallowed, worried that her appearance wasn't pleasing enough when he suddenly cleared his throat. His eyes focused on hers.

"You're breathtaking."

Clara let out a disbelieving breath, that almost sounded like a laugh. A single dark brow lifted in question and she shook her head.

"Thank you," she said quickly, hoping not to invite any more praise as it made her uncomfortable.

"I trust you find your rooms acceptable?" His voice came our rough as he took a step towards her.

"Yes, very much. Thank you."

He nodded as his gaze dropped to her hands.

"What are you reading?" he asked, coming towards her.

"Nothing," she said quickly, tossing the book behind her on the chair. "Philosophy. Again."

"Yes, you're quite fond of it," he said, stopping before her.

Mere inches separated them, but to Clara's surprise, he leaned forward, crowding her until the tips of her breasts pressed against his solid chest. She inhaled sharply as he bent and reached around her. Pulling back, she saw that he held the book she had just tried to hide.

"*A Treatise of Human Nature* by David Hume," he said, reading the cover. "You mentioned him before."

"Yes," Clara said, hating how faint her voice sounded.

"He said passion is what drives people, not practicality."

"Essentially," she said, smelling the faintest hint of scotch. Goodness, he was rather intoxicating.

He frowned.

"I told you, Clara, that you didn't have anything to worry about regarding that. I've decided to never again partake in such experiences."

Clara's hand came up to the center of his chest as she found her courage. Silas fell silent under her touch.

"Don't say that," she said, her tone still soft.

"But—"

"Please," she insisted, her gaze locked on his face.

She wasn't completely sure what she was asking of him but after a long moment he gave her a single nod and Clara felt as though she made another crack in the wall that guarded his heart. If she was diligent, she might be able to reach it fully one day.

His hand came up over hers, touching the ring she had chosen. Looking down, he picked up her hand.

"Is this the only piece you liked?"

"Oh no, they were all lovely. But this one," she looked down. "I felt an affinity for this one."

"It suits you," he said. "I came to escort you to dinner. Shall we?" He held out his arm.

"Yes," she replied, taking it.

Chapter Eleven

DINNER HAD BEEN a happy affair, thanks in part to Holly Smyth's younger siblings. The teenage twins were enthusiastic about the chance to travel, and their energy was infectious. Clara's parents were also cheerful and talkative, seeming oblivious to the tension that had surrounded the other guests. Clara had noted the glares she received from Violet although she wasn't the only one. Fredrick Trembley seemed to annoy Violet a great deal and they exchanged several veiled barbs with one another during the evening.

On the other hand, Clara was flatly ignored by Derek throughout the entire meal. She wondered if the earl was still offended by her speech in his private library. That night seemed like a lifetime ago now and she made a mental note to try and make amends with the earl before he left Greystone. Still, Lady Trembley made it a point to speak with her, as well as the Duke and Duchess of Egmont, who evidently were Silas's godparents.

Once dinner had finished, the gentlemen went to the billiards room for brandy, while the ladies retired upstairs instead of the parlor. The dowager duchess had explained with a wedding tomorrow, there was no need to partake in the usual after dinner activities.

Clara was glad to retire however and was quick to dress in her nightgown. She went to the bed and tried to ignore the growing discomfort at the fact that Silas's previous wife had slept in this very room.

Closing her eyes, she fell into a restless sleep. Though she couldn't recall any faces she encountered in her dreams, she seemed to be running down a corridor full of people, calling her name. But every time she tried to get their attention; they looked past her. Eventually, the image melted away and she saw Silas, standing behind a woman. One arm was pressed against her midsection, while his other hand was wrapped around her throat.

Horrified, Clara came closer. She tried to call out, but no noise came and when she finally reached the couple, she saw that the woman was her.

And she was smiling.

Clara's eyes popped open. She felt confused and slightly apprehensive. The early morning light told her that she had slept for hours, though it had only felt like minutes.

What a strange dream.

Rolling over, she saw a maid adding wood to the fireplace. She turned and when she saw Clara, she curtsied.

"I'm sorry, my lady. I didn't mean to wake you."

"You didn't. I just can't sleep, I think."

"That's to be expected, my lady."

"Is it?"

"Well, yes," the maid said, with a bashful smile. "It is your wedding day."

"Oh, yes. It is, isn't it?" Clara said as the maid curtsied again and left the room.

Clara's mind wandered in the early morning. What had her dream meant? The sight of Silas's hands wrapped around her own throat had made her feel both frightened and, to her shame, tempted. What in the world was wrong with her? Surely, he would never do something like that. He had told her as much, and she believed him. But then a small, wicked part of her wondered if perhaps he might and maybe she wanted him to?

After a few more hours of restless sleep, Clara was awakened by Mrs. Bridges, who came in with her army of maids to ready Clara for her wedding.

She was bathed, dressed, spritzed, brushed and painted over the next few hours. The entire affair was executed with meticulous detail that Clara felt as though she barely had to do anything. Her mother had been with her for the entire time, but had been surprisingly quiet. Clara wondered how strange it must all be for her mother, who was once herself a maid, to now be a guest in a home such as Greystone, watching her daughter prepare to become lady of the house.

When they were finished, she put her ring on the opposite hand and nodded to Mrs. Bridges, who opened the door and led the way. The house seemed empty on her walk down from the duke's rooms to the chapel that stood at a detached end of the manor in the northwest corner. Clara felt as if she were in some type of dream.

She really hadn't expected to be married so quickly and to be instantly made to get ready wasn't the only surprise. She wore a pale lilac-colored gown that was perhaps slightly too snug as she did not have as slender a figure as her sister-in-law, but that was tailored in such a refined way that it would have made even a mule look elegant.

She met her father at the door of the chapel where he handed her a bouquet of ivy leaf, myrtle and lily of the valley. Clara knew the meaning of flowers and was glad to have a bouquet that represented friendship, luck and kindness.

Two servants standing on either side of them opened the chapel doors and Clara and her father began the processional walk. Clara was in awe of the beauty of the chapel, with the setting sun shining through the stained glass windows. There were only eleven people in attendance. The dowager duchess and Violet sat next to the Duke and Duchess of Egmont, as well as Derek Trembley, his two brothers and their mother, while Clara's parents sat with Holly and her siblings.

As her father handed her off before the altar, she took Silas's hand and smiled at him, glad to once again be in his presence, but her smile faltered. He was staring at her with an intensity that she had never witnessed on him before and she was sure he must be feeling a whole mess of emotions. As for herself, she wasn't sure why she felt so warm beneath his gaze.

The vicar spoke about the importance of vows and Clara felt Silas's fingers tighten at the vicar's words. She was curious as to what everyone in attendance must be thinking. Did they think she was too tightly dressed? Was this the same vicar who had married Silas and his pervious bride? Had any of the guests here borne witness to that wedding, as well?

Clara wanted to see the guests, but she couldn't take her eyes away from where her hands were joined with Silas's. His grip was tight, almost uncomfortable, but Clara wondered if he was perhaps somewhat nervous. It seemed a sobering affair and for a moment she wondered if perhaps Silas felt a little sad at having to marry someone again.

He appeared calm and collected, but held her fingers like she was a rock and he was in a raging river. It unnerved her that he should seem outwardly so relaxed, when she assumed his nerves were probably frayed.

She was aware that Silas held no feelings for Cynthia anymore, but a small, nagging something in the back of her mind wondered how he must feel to be marrying again. She lifted her eyes and saw the burning heat in his gaze had been replaced by a somewhat subdued wonder, as if he wasn't sure who she was. Clara felt a powerful urge to tell him things she had never planned on telling him.

Things like she found him attractive, very much so and it made her feel strange and giddy to stare at him for long moments when he wasn't aware. She wanted to tell him that she thought he was humorous and clever and that he was far kinder a man than she had ever expected him to be.

She wanted to tell him that she would never, ever do to him what Cynthia had done. While she wasn't fully aware of all that had transpired between them, she wanted him to know for certain that he could trust her, implicitly.

The ceremony ended and with a very chaste kiss on her cheek, a kiss of friendship and nothing more. And with that, their vows were sealed. The small group cheered and they left the chapel, followed by their friends and family, and made their way to the dining room.

Among their guests were Clara's dear friend, Holly Smyth and her twin siblings, Jasper and Katrina, who were sixteen. All three Smyth siblings shared the same honey brown hair, though Katrina looked most like her sister.

Mr. and Mrs. Geoffrey, friends of Clara's parents, had also attended as had Lord and Lady Bryant, old acquaintances of the dowager duchess, as well as Derek Trembley.

Silas escorted Clara through the house to the dining room where a feast had been prepared. There was a serving of roasted pheasants, venison, duck was served with soups, vinaigrettes, roasted vegetables and creams puddings and pies all lined a long oak table. Wine was poured and general merriment and conversation was had by all. Clara was slightly dizzy when she leaned back from her plate and realized how completely different her life was going to be from this moment forward. Had she made the right decision in marrying Silas?

"What a splendid day," Holly said, distracting Clara, who smiled at her friend. "Thank you so much for including us."

"Of course," Clara said. "I would never get married without you present."

"And I must say," Holly said, her tone dipping as she leaned in. "I'm surprised by the duke. Are you sure this is the same man you wrote to me about?"

"Of course. Why do you ask?"

"Well, he seems so… Intense. You made him out to be some sort of gentle, sweet man. The man I saw didn't come off as gentle. Or sweet."

"That's just because you haven't spoken with him very much.

He's as sweet and gentle as any man I've ever met."

Turning to see Silas, she noted that he appeared as he always did. Her heart thumped faster as her eyes swept over his dark hair and sharp jaw.

"Does he?" she asked faintly, quite enjoying the view of her husband.

She saw his head bent toward Derek as they exchanged words. Outwardly, he appeared unaffected by the day's events, but Clara noticed his left hand, resting on the table's surface. His thumbnail was digging into the knuckle of his index finger.

Frowning slightly, she decided to get closer to him once dinner had finished. He always seemed more relaxed when she was nearby. She turned back to her plate and tried to make conversation with Mrs. Geoffrey for the remainder of dinner.

After the dessert course had finished, champagne was served to everyone as a small string quartet began to play in the drawing room. Since the wedding party was so small, it would have been ridiculous to host a party in the ballroom, but Clara was quite content with the number of people in attendance. It felt intimate and sweet and far more real than she would assume a big, lavish affair in London would have been.

By the stroke of midnight, the guests were ready to retire and Clara said her good evenings beside Silas. Everyone wished them well, particularly Clara's mother who looked as though she might cry.

"Oh, my sweet dear," she said as she placed her hands on Clara's shoulders. "My dear, sweet girl."

"Do not cry, Mother," Clara said, her own voice cracking with emotion. She glanced around at the other guests. "All is well."

"I know, I know," she said, unconvincingly, as she kissed Clara on the cheek.

"Come along dear," her father said, pulling her gently away before glancing at Clara. "All is well."

Clara's throat suddenly tightened at her father's reassurance and she nodded in response, worried that she wouldn't be able to speak without crying.

The couple walked down the line of guests, thanking them all for coming. When they reached Derek, he seemed less than happy. To Clara's surprise, Silas took her hand and moved slightly in front of her, not blocking but seemingly shielding Clara from her husband's oldest confidant.

"Good night, your grace," Derek said to Clara with the barest of nods before his eyes flickered to her husband. "Combe."

"Trembley," Silas said stiffly, before turning Clara away as they climbed the stairs.

Clara frowned, confused as to why there seemed to be tension between the two men. Curious, she squeezed Silas's fingers and he tilted his head in question.

"It was kind of Lord Trembley and his family to travel all this way to show their support." Silas remained quiet as they reached the landing. Inquisitive to a fault, Clara continued. "I suppose I should be grateful that he doesn't hold my harsh criticisms of him from the night of the ball against me." When Silas still said nothing, Clara frowned. "Or does he?"

"I wouldn't worry too much about him," Silas said. "He bears no ill will against you personally. He's just not terribly pleased with this arrangement."

Clara's brows shot up.

"He's not? Why?"

"Because he thinks I've made a mistake," Silas said as they reached the second staircase.

Clara felt the color drain from her face.

"Oh dear."

"I told you, don't give him too much thought. He simply thinks he knows what's best, for everyone, and becomes mulish when his advice isn't heeded." He paused. "He'll come around. He always does."

"Is it because he finds me lacking?"

Silas stopped midway up the stairs, forcing Clara to stop as well since he held her hand. He was a step above her, which only made her feel minuscule as he stared at her.

"Trembley's concerns are not mine and I won't have you bothered by his opinions. Do you understand?"

The authority in Silas's voice sent a shiver down Clara's back. Though he held her hand tightly in the same firm grip as he had in the chapel, Clara couldn't see any anxiety in his eyes. In fact, he appeared almost solemn.

Unable to think of a clever response, Clara nodded. They continued up the stairs and were soon making the long and nerve-racking walk down the northern corridor to their private bedchambers.

Clara kept her eyes on the ground in front of her. To say she was nervous was an understatement. She knew what was about to happen and while she had never experienced anything like it, she had heard that it could be an unpleasant experience if one's partner was unkind or inconsiderate. She knew that Silas *was* kind and considerate, but all the same, she couldn't quite manage to will her nerves away as they approached the third floor.

Chapter Twelve

U PON ENTERING THE bedchambers, Clara felt herself begin to shake. Her nerves were wrought with tension and as she stood in the center of the room, waiting as Silas closed the door, she heard the door click. Then, she heard a deep sigh.

Clara frowned. He sighed? Confused as to why, she turned to see him leaning against the door, his eyes closed as his head pressed back against the wood. He was fully dressed, not changed in any particular from how he had been moments before, but there was a shift in his posture, making him appear almost relived. She studied his face as he breathed, noting the stubble that had begun to grow around his cheeks, chin and neck. His black brows and dark, curling hair that had been held by pomade had dropped slightly, and his dark skin seemed to glow in the light of the candles the maids had lit. He seemed tired, if not content.

His eyes opened and focused directly on her and she felt her heart begin to beat furiously. He really was attractive, far more so than she usually allowed herself to realize, for it was dangerous to admit that she had married a man far superior to her in every way.

Feeling slightly insecure, she held her spot until he pushed himself off the door and came towards her, tugging at his cravat as he did.

"A successful night, I suppose," he said as he walked past her, leaving her feeling slightly empty. There was no heat behind his words, no emotion. He seemed really rather composed. Frowning slightly, she turned to watch him as he walked about the room. "We are married."

"Yes, we are," she said, ignoring the crack in her voice.

He sat on one of the chairs that faced each other at the foot of his bed as he removed his boots. She jumped at the touch of his hand on her shoulders. Turning around, she saw him hold his palms up, his face confused.

"Are you all right?" he asked.

"Yes," she said unconvincingly. She swallowed and nodded at the large mirror that hung on the far wall. This room was nearly identical to hers. "You have a very unique style."

Silas glanced around the room, seemingly unimpressed before he undid the buttons of his vest.

"I did not decorate it."

It dawned on Clara that Cynthia had most likely chosen all the décor.

"Oh. Well, it is, um, quite unique, indeed."

"Yes," was all he said.

Clara wondered what she had said that had agitated him. Perhaps he was offended by her wording?

"I didn't mean to say that I don't like it," she tried. "I only meant that I've never been in a room that was so, well…opulent I guess would be the word. I've certainly never seen black silk drapes," she said, walking to the bed. "Do you have an affinity for mirrors?"

"No."

"Oh," she said, frowning. "Then why are there so many in this room?"

"I'll show you later," he said.

Clara shrugged to herself, curious as to why he was being so short with her. Her hand came up to the bed posts as her fingers gently traced over the suggestive wood carving. "And I've never seen a bed like that before."

He did not respond and after a long moment she turned to face him. Silas was watching her intently and she wondered why his body seemed tense. Swallowing, her eyes shifted back to the bed and then back at him. He followed her stare.

"You wouldn't happen to be nervous? About…" he nodded towards the bed. "…that, would you?"

"Nervous?" she repeated. "No, of course not. What a silly thing to be nervous about."

His brows lifted.

"Some ladies would disagree."

"Yes well, I'm sure those ladies never had the privilege of growing up in the country. I know perfectly well what's expected of me."

Slowly, an unfiltered grin pulled at the corners of his mouth. Clara gulped.

"Do you now?"

"Yes."

"Then please, enlighten me."

Clara's eyes went wide at his suggestion. He wanted her to say it out loud? Good heavens, she might be poorly bred but she wasn't completely without scruples. The humor in his eyes eased her worry.

"Well, I suppose I shall l-lay right over there," she pointed at the bed. "And then you will, um…" She couldn't find the words and nodded her head. "Well, you… will attend to it."

"Attend to it?" he repeated and she nodded again, ignoring the hint of amusement in his tone. "Well, if you say so." His voice was slightly huskier than before and Clara had the vague sense that he was teasing her. "And will you be clothed?"

She blanched.

"Pardon?"

"I ask if you will be clothed."

Clara felt herself begin to panic. Surely people did not stay clothed during the act, but then she had never been privy to such information. Did the upper class stay covered for propriety? Oh, why was he asking her such a ridiculous question?

"No," she said slowly. "I don't suppose so. Is that correct?"

He nodded.

"Quite correct," he said. After a short pause he took a step towards her. "Well then, shall we?"

She took a step back.

"Shall we what?"

"Unclothe you," he said.

Clara swallowed hard, apprehensive, though she nodded to show her consent. But Silas didn't move. He only stood there before her, watching her for long moments before she grew bold enough to look him in the eye.

As she titled her head back, she saw the same heated eyes she had seen in the chapel and her mouth fell open slightly. His eyes dropped to her lips and she was sure he would kiss her, only he didn't. His gaze slowly lifted to meet hers again and the longer he went without touching her or reaching for her, the more disconcerted she became.

"What should I do?" she whispered.

Her question seemed to please him.

"Turn around," he said and she did as she was told.

She saw his bent head in the reflection of the mirror as he worked to undo the buttons at the back of her gown. It was rather fascinating to be able to watch him as he undressed her. She wondered if the mirrors had been hung, not out of vanity but for some other reason. She felt herself flush.

He made quick work of her dress's fastenings and soon she felt the garment sag against her skin. Hesitantly, she lifted her arms and slipped out of the sleeves, letting the dress fall to the floor, leaving her covered in nothing but her chemise. She felt his hands go to her hair next, and to her surprise he began to take out her ribbons and pins until her hair fell loose over her shoulders. The intake of breath she heard from him caused her to turn around and face him. When she did, she saw a mixture of desire and hesitation in his expression. It was a strange thing to see, and she guessed it was probably difficult for him to see her in such an intimate way. They were friends, after all, and she had never had a friend with whom she wished to do these sorts of things. Surely, he was finding it problematic to reconcile himself to being with her this way.

Suddenly insecure, she took a deep breath. Exhaling shakily, she put her hand to the collar of her chemise, but his large hand stayed her.

"I'd like to," he said softly, gently moving her hand back down to her side.

She nodded silently as his larger fingers hooked beneath the strap of her chemise and pulled it down slowly. *What agony*, Clara thought as a mosh of emotions came over her. Arousal slammed into her as well as shivering need and humiliation. She felt as if she were at his disposal. She might have felt rather insignificant in a way, if not for the desire in his eyes.

He was watching her as if she were the only being in the world. And to her surprise, she felt like the only being in the world too.

The strap of her chemise slid down her arms, as the fabric slowly exposed her breasts, then her stomach and finally her legs, leaving her only wearing a pair of silk stockings. Except something caught his eye, just above her knee.

A thin, blue ribbon was tied around her leg.

Silas was motionless for a moment. His dark gaze moved slowly up and she felt her body begin to tremble with trepidation.

"I… I don't know why I…"

She shook her head, unable to finish her train of thought. Lord knows why she had tied the silly ribbon around her knee every day since that night in Vauxhall Gardens, but she had. There had been a draw to do it, a nameless power that had called for her to obey and she secretly relished it.

Her awareness of it at random moments throughout her day had sent a shiver up her spine. She hadn't even meant for him to see it, but she had become tied to the idea, for lack of a better term. The daily secret, a low stakes reminder of him had made her feel daring and slightly wicked.

The heat in his stare made her apprehensive however. Had it been a foolish thing to do? She assumed she would have died of embarrassment at this moment, to be so fully naked before a man, but somehow she was still alive. More than just alive, she was *happy*. Because she felt revered beneath the admiring warmth of his gaze.

"Clara," he whispered, his tone one of genuine surprise as his eyes roamed over her naked body. "You're beautiful."

A paralyzed part of her wanted to laugh at his words, as she had rarely ever been described as such. Strangely lovely, or bizarrely attractive, maybe. She had never simply been described as singularly beautiful, but she wanted to believe him.

"Kiss me," he said.

Clara knew he wasn't particularly interested in anything but friendship with her, but she could almost swear she heard a desperate note in his voice. Consummation of a marriage was the final task for their union needed in order to be legitimized. While it was more a duty than anything, Clara was finding it hard to separate her feelings from the practicality of it all. It didn't *feel* like this was just another duty to him. She decided to kiss him wholly and with every feeling she felt in that moment, even aware that he might chastise her for being too eager.

Her hands went to his shoulders and pulled him towards her as she pressed her mouth to his. An arm wrapped tightly around her back, pressing her against him and she felt like he was consuming her. Clara sought out the heat of his body as she pressed herself closer. The soft, fine fabric of his clothes against her bare skin was a tantalizing experience. She had never once imagined what the sensation of a wool suit would feel like against her nude body and she was almost scandalized at how much she liked it. She leaned closer to him still, eager to be held by his powerful grip.

In an instant he turned his back to the bed as he gently but firmly pressed her down atop the cool silk sheets. She let out a surprised sound as he stood over her and finished undressing. Clara should have averted her eyes, but her curiosity was too much for her and she stared at him as he removed his unbuttoned vest and untucked his shirtsleeves, pulling it over his head and tossing it on the ground.

Clara's eyes travelled down the hard planes and contours of his large, muscular chest, visually tracing the fine dark spattering of hair that trailed down his stomach. Her mouth went dry as her eyes drifted lower, watching as his hand unbuttoned the front panel of his trousers. Hooking his thumbs into the waistband, he pushed them down, his eyes never leaving hers.

Clara's cheeks must have turned red as he kicked away the last of his clothing. She could feel how hot her face had grown— and yet she couldn't bring herself to look away. The hard length of him sprung up from dark curls as he stood back up, seemingly unfazed by his naked state. He reminded Clara of a stature she had once seen in a museum, only he was darker, larger and his member was not at all like it had been depicted in the artwork.

Her breath hitched as he slowly leaned forward and pressed his mouth against her abdomen. Her legs flinched involuntarily, but Silas only moved his hands up her thighs, as if to soothe her body's nervous energy. He kissed her stomach gently and Clara felt her brow pucker, unsure about the purpose of such an act. He moved upwards, pressing a trail of kisses up to her sternum. Clara was practically shaking from excitement and trepidation as he licked between the valley of her breasts. She was sure she might cry out when he moved to her left breast and began nipping and sucking on her nipple.

Clara's entire body shook from pleasure as something over-powering swept over her body. She started to convulse as sheer ecstasy enveloped her.

Silas pulled back and watched her writhe with wonder.

"My god," he said, his words hot against her skin. "You're

sensitive."

Clara couldn't speak, couldn't think as his mouth dropped back to her skin. He moved lower, back down over her abdomen and lower still, until he was positioned between her legs. She was barely aware of his intentions as the hazy afterglow of pleasure fogged her mind. It wasn't until she felt his warm tongue lap at the center of her that she let out a choked cry.

Clara tried to sit up.

"Silas."

"Hush," he murmured inside of her as his hands snaked up her torso and gently pressed her back. "Don't move."

She shivered at his words, vibrating within her like some sort of magic spell. He kissed and licked at her in a way she was sure would send them both to hell, but she couldn't bring herself to protest. Not when another devastating crush of pleasure claimed her. It rose within her, slowly at first, until it was bubbling at the surface and then spilled over like a kettle too filled of water over a fire.

Silas's hand came up to hold her inner thigh in an iron grip. Clara moaned as it slowly slid upward and this thumb pressed into her, just below where his tongue had been. Her eyes closed tightly as it entered her, moving in a gentle rhythm as she felt the pleasure crest, breaking over her like a lightning strike. Soon, Silas's body was over hers, kissing her mouth and cheek as she shook. He leaned forward and spoke in her ear.

"Hold onto me," he said roughly as she felt him position his length at her entrance.

She reached up and held onto his wide shoulders as he moved forward in a single, swift movement.

"Aug!"

A pained cry ripped from Clara's mouth as he paused within her. She felt herself stretch and ache as she settled around his invasion, accommodating him as best as she could. He was motionless for a long moment, and she could feel the tension of his body vibrate beneath her touch. His hand came up and moved against her face, holding her head as she stared at him.

"Easy," he said as he began to move.

In and out, in and out. Clara's bottom lip fell open and trembled as a wave of emotion rushed over her. It was the oddest feeling, to stare into his eyes while he moved within her. It felt as though he were claiming every inch of her. She had never felt so exposed and simultaneously so wanted in her entire life.

Soon, his movements became short and fast and her breath sped up to match. When he fell deep into her on a final stroke Clara tried to lift her knees, almost wishing to wrap her legs around him. Thinking that to be too wanton, she forced her body to relax as the weight of his body dropped on her, making her feel oddly comforted trapped beneath his form.

Some moments later, she heard his breathing even out. He slowly pulled himself from her and got up. She watched with curiosity as he made his way to the water basin that stood beneath a north window that overlooked the garden. When he returned to bed, he had a length of dampened towel, which he used to clean her. Not merely between her legs, but her entire body, prompting her to sit up. She winced when he reached her thighs, but his hand was gentle.

When he was done, he moved the covers down and she crawled beneath them, watching him as he turned out the lamps and blew out the candles. Soon, he rejoined her in bed, his long lean body pressed against her soft one.

Clara wasn't sure if she should speak, and even if she should, what would she say? He hadn't said anything since he finished, but when he laid beside her, she felt his arm unexpectedly come around her waist and pull her tightly against his chest.

"Good night," she whispered, her eyes wide in the dark.

But Silas did not speak. He only left out a gentle snore, leaving Clara alone with her thoughts.

Chapter Thirteen

Silas was up early and out of the house to ride before the sun was even up. Shaken from the night before, he hadn't been able to sleep all night. The moment he heard the steady, deep breaths of Clara's slumber, he pulled away from her and got out of bed. He had sat in a chair facing the bed and stared at her sleeping form for most of the night.

Their coupling had rattled him in ways he hadn't anticipated. Silas had expected to find pleasure of course, but where he hadn't been surprised by their physical compatibility, he had been unexpectedly by the emotional connection he'd experienced. To lay with someone who he not only desired but held in such high regard—someone whose pleasure felt so precious and special to him—well, it felt wonderful and terrifying at the same time. It was all rather confusing.

They had moved in unison during the entire episode and a strange, deep feeling had bubbled up inside of him as he moved deeply within her. Silas had believed it was simply that he was reacting to the fact that Clara now belonged to him as any wife belonged to her husband, but this was different. A possessiveness he had so often beat down while he was with Cynthia had roared up in his chest the moment she said "I do" in the chapel. But while it was similar, it wasn't exactly the same.

With Cynthia, he always felt like he was straining to keep her, like she was always pulling against his hold, right on the verge of breaking free. But Clara wasn't like any sort of caged bird yearning to fly away. Not in his bed, nor in his home, nor in his life. She had seemed a little uneasy at first, and he could understand that. Greystone was likely the largest home she had ever been to and to suddenly be its mistress had to be a daunting prospect. Still, at the same time she seemed relaxed in his company, a detail that he found charming. She had pushed back against his body when his arm went around her waist and the tone of her voice when she said goodnight seemed pleased, as if she were happy to be just where she was.

It unnerved him to no end.

While Silas had longed for a comfortable marriage, void of emotion and desire, he couldn't shake a growing feeling for Clara. He tried to focus on the practical reasons why he had decided to marry her as he rode his horse across the fog covered fields that morning.

She was not a tittering miss or a lady keen on gaining a title. She was attractive, more so now than he had originally thought, though that was not necessarily a good thing—it could be a problem if he ever let himself grow infatuated with her. She had other qualities that he had never found attractive in the opposite sex and those were the reasons he needed to focus on.

But when she had said so softly goodnight, he felt a chip in his amour, like someone had cracked a hammer against a frozen pond.

Silas had been so careful to enter this union without any misconceptions or preconceived notions of love. He and Clara were to have a friendship first and foremost and he would willingly ignore all other feelings, but this creeping urge to go to her, to spend every minute he could with her, sent up a warning within him. If he wasn't careful, he might actually fall in love with her and that was something he absolutely could not do. He had promised himself that he would never allow himself to be at someone's disposal again.

As he rode well into the late morning, Silas couldn't shake the feeling that he was being sucked in. The edges of him seemed already gripped by her.

After his ride, Silas returned to the house. He climbed the stairs in hopes to find Clara in their bedchambers, only to discover them empty. Confused, he turned to search the house when out the window he saw the top of her head as well as that of a red head woman, moving about the maze. Frowning, he decided to catch his new bride and her friend by surprising them at the middle.

Silas was down the stairs, out the back terrace and in the gardens in a matter of minutes. He moved through the old hedge that he had memorized as a boy. It was a yew hedge, put in by his grandmother during the French revival period. He was able to reach the secret garden that laid just north of the center. Pausing, he strained to hear the feminine voices of Clara and her friend. It seemed that they had reached the fountain that sat in the center of the maze, unaware that a pergola, covered in wisteria and climbing rose, was the true prize.

He had barely reached the fountain when Clara's voice caught his ear.

"—I just don't think a marriage should start out like that," she said, causing him to stop in his tracks. "It's dreadful."

Cold dread settled in the pit of his stomach. It felt like every moment of anxiety he had ever experienced had been suddenly validated and his body tensed against the sinking feeling. What had caused her to be so against their match and so soon? Was it because of their wedding night? Surely not, and yet Silas couldn't help but worry he might have hurt her or caused her some sort of embarrassment or discomfort.

"It may not be what I hoped for as a girl, but I don't have many prospects," her companion spoke. "My parents left us little and I've supported Jasper and Katrina as long as I have only because I was able to sell off most of our livestock."

Silas's thoughts were slow to process that Clara hadn't been talking about him. A sickening wave of relief fell over him as he closed his eyes and swallowed back his anxiety.

Taking a deep breath, he opened his eyes and spied through the yew and saw Clara, sitting on a stone bench while her redheaded friend walked around, wringing her hands together. What were they talking about?

"There has to be another way," Clara continued. "You cannot marry that old man. He could be your grandfather. And besides, the terms of his proposal are strange. It's not how a marriage should start out."

"But it wouldn't be a proper marriage. Don't you understand?" her friend asked. "John—Lord Bairnsdale—is a gentle, old soul and he has always been kind to me and my family. I believe he is truly worried about our impending doom."

Bairnsdale? Silas's brow furrowed. How did he know that name? For some reason, it put him in mind of Gavin, but what was the connection? Silas tried to think. Didn't Gavin have an uncle who held some sort of title? A baron perhaps?

"Doom? Oh dear, Holly," Clara said sadly. "I didn't know it was that bad. Why didn't you tell me?"

"A fine friend I would be to complain about my misfortunes while you already had so much to worry about in London. I wouldn't have dreamed of burdening you with my problems."

"Is that not what friends are for?" Clara asked, obviously upset. "To tell one another each other's problems?"

"Clara, our lives have changed drastically these past few years. There's little reason for you to continue bothering with me, especially now that you're a duchess. If you wish to cut ties between us, I would not hold it against you."

"Holly Dora Smyth, how could you say such a thing?" Clara said. "I would never abandon you or our friendship, especially in your hour of need. Do you think so little of me?"

"Of course not—"

"Then I insist you stop talking nonsense and let me help."

"Help? How in the world could you help?"

"I'm not sure, but if there's one thing I know, it's that you absolutely can't marry Lord Bairnsdale."

"Can't I? I have no other prospects, no money and two siblings to take care of, Clara. If a marriage would secure us a future, even if only for a few more years, then I'm inclined to take it."

Clara frowned, displeased with her friend's conclusion.

"And so, this ball you've invited us to, in a few months. It is to announce your engagement?" she asked sadly.

"It will be, if I accept his proposal."

"And there's nothing I can do or say for you to change your mind?"

"No."

Clara's next words sounded discontent. "I wish you would reconsider my help. Silas has agreed to allow me full control of my dowry. I could lend you some money—"

"I couldn't let you do that. Besides, John is not some lecherous old man. He is gentle and sweet and had repeatedly assured me that there would be no sort of bedroom dalliances between us."

"He could change his mind when the ink is dry."

"I'm not exactly his type, dear," she said, but Clara didn't seem to catch her meaning. "But tell me of your duke. Is he truly pleasant beneath that cold façade? How are you feeling now that you are a duchess?"

Silas's brow quirked up, very interested in this turn the conversation had taken.

"He is quite different from the sort of man I always thought I would marry," she said as he strained to hear. "I always assumed I would be madly in love with my husband when I married."

"Peers can rarely claim to be in love with their spouses, my dear. You are aware of that."

"Yes, of course," Clara said. "It's just a silly notion I had. I'm sure all young ladies do. But that's not to say I'm displeased to be his wife. Not at all. In fact, the duke and I have found an amiable friendship." She paused, giving Silas a moment to conclude that he didn't completely enjoy having their relationship referred to as amiable. Even though he had always wanted just that. "I just fear that I won't be enough. I can't quite believe that I'm a duchess. Me. Clara Woodvine."

"Lady Clara Winters now, and yes, it is strange. You used to run around the village barefoot. And that was only last summer."

They laughed and Silas smiled to himself at the vision of Clara, running through a field barefoot. Surely, she wouldn't do so now, but it was an enticing image to imagine.

"I'm sure the duke's taste can be trusted," her friend continued. "He picked you, didn't he?"

"He did," Clara said, her tone suggesting otherwise. "But perhaps that's it. Perhaps he picked me because I'm so very the opposite of what I should be. Of what a duchess should be."

"Why would he do that?"

"Because he doesn't want to repeat the tribulations of his previous marriage," Clara said.

It irked Silas that she would speak about him and his past to someone but it wasn't like the difficulties of his previous marriage were a secret. And anyway, he was the one eavesdropping. If he didn't wish to hear people's opinions, he could simply walk away.

Instead, he took a step closer.

"You said that he spoke of friendship, Clara. That's more than most people have. Especially in these grand marriages that involve peers."

"Yes, I know. And I knew that there wasn't any sort of romantic love between us when I accepted his proposal, but…" Clara paused and Silas was eager to know what she was about to say.

"But what?"

"I don't know." Her voice was soft and somewhat hopeless. It made Silas feel uncertain, but then in the next moment she seemed to recover. "This is a dizzying maze. Perhaps we should ring the bell and have one of the maids come to rescue us."

Silas felt insecure at Clara's answer, but he wouldn't retreat.

Instead, he coughed loudly and took several loud steps as he came into the clearing, revealing himself to the two ladies.

Clara's friend Holly went wide eyed at his approach and he wondered if she was rather scared of him, given the way her eyes shifted downward. Clara turned around and he saw genuine surprise, in her curious grey-green eyes.

"I saw you lost your way from the house," he said, nodding toward the windows high above them. "I thought the chivalrous thing to do would be to rescue you."

"Thank you, Your Grace," the redhead said. "We have been lost for some time."

"We were finding our way through," Clara said. "I believe there is a secret to this maze."

"A secret?" he repeated, looking down at her. "That wouldn't be very sporting, now, would it?"

"No, I suppose not," she said, though she sounded unconvinced. "Very well, lead the way."

He nodded and turned.

"Follow me," he said.

He knew the maze had a fairly simple exit from that point, but he made a point to make a wrong turn here and there, feigning confusion. Clara's companion seemed worried, but the inquisitive stare Clara gave him proved that he wasn't fooling her and he wondered what it would take to trick his clever little wife.

His wife. The words gave his heart pause as he continued out of the maze and up to the house. He wanted very much to ignore the feeling of possessiveness that enveloped him, knowing that it had been the exact reason Cynthia had abandoned him. His need to be in control, to possess had been his undoing and while Clara was her exact opposite in every way, he doubted very much that she would allow his boorish, jealous behavior to manifest.

Taking a deep breath, he pushed the feelings away and turned back to wait.

"Do you have plans to go to London this season, Miss Smyth?" he asked, trying to be conversational.

"Oh, no, your grace, I couldn't possibly attend this year's season." She paused and gave Clara a pointed glance. "Next year perhaps. My sister will eventually make her debut, though not for another year or so."

"Well, if you ever require any assistance, don't hesitate to ask," he said. "I am aware what you mean to my wife." He paused, having not wished to say *wife* in conversation and certainly not out loud, fearing his own reaction. "We should be very happy to perhaps sponsor your siblings, if they are so inclined to accept it."

"Oh! That is very kind of you, your grace," Holly spoke, her eyes lighting up. "I can't imagine a more generous offer."

"It would be no trouble," he said, noting the expression in Clara's eyes. She stared at him with a calculating glare. "If you'll excuse me."

"Yes of course," Holly said.

"Actually, I had something rather important to discuss with you," Clara said loudly, taking a step towards him. "I'll be right along, Holly."

The redhead nodded and disappeared up the stone steps that led up into the house. Silas did not move, only watched as Clara turned around to face him. He wondered if she would be pleased with his offer.

"That truly was a generous proposal," she said, her tone emotionless.

"Was it?" he asked, feigning a casual air.

"Yes, especially considering Holly is planning to marry this year." Clara squinted her eyes. "A sponsorship from someone like you could give her a reason to reconsider."

Silas suspected that she believed he had overheard the conversation. He had, but he wasn't going to let her know it.

"Well, I wouldn't want to come between her and a marriage prospect, especially if she is fond of the young man."

Clara took a step towards him.

"You know very well he isn't a young man," she said softly.

"You were listening."

"Are you accusing me of eavesdropping?"

"I am."

"In my own garden?" he countered. "It's hardly the place for a secret conversation. Anyone could have happened upon you."

Clara smirked at his haughty answer.

"So, you *were* listening?"

"To admit to such a thing would call into question my character."

She took another step and suddenly there was very little room between them. He wasn't the type of man to be cowed by a female, but Silas couldn't deny that his body responded to her closeness. Clara seemed completely unaware of her effect on him—or the proper amount of distance to maintain when speaking with someone. She was wholly unfazed by societal norms.

"I would never question your character, sir," she said, her eyes full of gentle teasing. "A man who won a wife."

"I did win," he said huskily. Her eyes seemed to sparkle with mischief. It both intrigued and worried him, though he knew not why. Without thinking, he raised his hands to her arms to gently stroke her. "How do you feel? After last night, I mean."

A blush touched her cheeks but she smiled.

"Very well," she said, her tone soft. "And you?"

"There's no need to worry about me. It was new for you."

"It was new for you too, Silas. We had never slept together before."

He cocked his head.

"You're right. In any case, I feel very well too."

Her smile brightened.

"Good," she said, seeming happy with his response. "I'm glad."

Silas felt pleased that she should be so satisfied and in an instant of sheer joy, he leaned down and kissed her. For years, Silas had kissed women with the single thought of seduction, but this was something else. This was simply a desire to show her that he was pleased. The beat of his heart seemed suddenly more pronounced as Clara leaned into him, kissing him back with unconcealed enthusiasm.

He pulled back for a moment, mindful not to lose himself to his desires out in the open, particularly when they were hosting so many guests. But all the same, he noted the heightened color of her cheeks, her swollen lips with decided satisfaction.

"Perhaps we should go inside," he suggested prudently.

"We could," she said coyly. "Or we could take a stroll in the maze?"

Her innocent prodding gave him pause. While he was more than willing to continue their rendezvous, the strength of his reaction to her was concerning. His previous relationship had been based off of physical feelings and he had intended to avoid that in his second marriage.

He hadn't considered that he would find himself so constantly excited by her. Hopefully it would wane over the next several weeks as the novelty wore off…but a nagging feeling told him that his reaction to Clara might be permanent. If that was the case, he would most likely have to put some distance between them, if only to preserve his control of the situation. It wouldn't do to fall in love with Clara, not when she deserved so much more than the shattered pieces of a broken heart that were all he had to offer.

He moved her back a fraction.

"Perhaps tonight…" he said. He needed to control himself. "…we should tend to our guests."

"Oh. Of course," she agreed, sounding disappointed.

He nodded and moved around her, convinced that it was the right choice. This would surely prove to be a different sort of marriage than before. He would simply have to lead by example.

However difficult that might be.

Chapter Fourteen

AFTER AN ENTIRE month of living with Silas, his sister and his mother, Clara had concluded that while they all seemed to care for one another, they each had very firm—and very different—ideas of how things should be done. Clara unfortunately, was outnumbered every time.

It wasn't that she didn't appreciate the help her new family provided. She had never even imagined that she would find herself running a household so extensive and she was grateful that her mother-in-law was more than willing to coach her in the finer points of running a household. She was a bit less grateful that the lessons included etiquette coaching, as well. In fact, she had been asked to join her sister-in-law in etiquette lessons. Clara had been curious at first, but she found the sheer number of rules and regulations they were supposed to follow was rather daunting. She didn't wish to insult anyone by not attending, even if she found many of the rules arbitrary and rather silly. Not to mention, many of them didn't truly apply to her, since she already had a husband and wouldn't have to worry about how a lady was meant to behave while courting. Still, she was determined to become every inch the duchess Silas deserved.

Married. It had been a month and she had quickly learned what everyone meant about having a peerage marriage. While Silas was obviously attracted to her, as he proved nearly every night, Clara found that their daytime interactions were limited, if not completely nonexistent. He was respectful, courteous and distant when they did happen to cross paths during the day. Clara was often left feeling unsure of herself, until the evenings of course.

At night Silas was like a different man. He seemed to relax tenfold the moment their door closed. *Their* door, since they had forgone the tradition of sleeping in separate rooms. She returned to her rooms to dress, but she slept in his bed every night so that he could worship her and ravish her. They'd spend hours making love, talking (although never about anything too important) or simply holding one another. They connected in a way Clara had never experienced before. But by the time the sun rose, Silas was back to being his stoic, polite self—a stranger to her until night came again.

Worse than a stranger, really. A stranger would feel obliged to keep his opinions to himself. Silas was frequently openly critical, particularly of her choices as the new duchess.

It's not his fault, Clara told herself one morning as she reflected on one particular instance the previous week, when she had requested the cook to make clangers.

Clangers were a long, suet crusted pastry that covered two different fillings. On one side was a savory stuffing while the other end contained a sweet center. Clara's favorite had been a pork and caramelized onion partnered with an apple cinnamon finish. She had loved them as a child and perhaps had been feeling homesick when she'd asked for them for dinner.

The look on her mother-in-law's face when they were revealed had made Clara's heart sink.

"What in the world is this?" the dowager duchess had asked.

"They're clangers," Clara said, shrinking a bit into her seat.

"Rather a plebian dish, isn't it?"

Clara saw Violet wedge her fork underneath the edge of the pastry and lift it to examine the interior. Her lip curled up in disgust.

"They're really quite good," Clara tried, her gaze going to Silas, hoping for some support. "I thought it would be nice to try."

Silas had appeared unsure, his own gaze shifting between her and his family. After a moment, he gave her a reserved smile, and took a bite. To his credit, he ate the whole thing, but later commented that it was beneath their cook to prepare working class dishes for the family's table.

Clara had thought that was a rather snobbish thing to say, but she didn't want to cause a problem, nor did she wish to offend the kitchens.

That wasn't the only time that she had noticed the striking difference in Silas while it was daytime. He seemed to behave like a proper peer, all stuffy and tight laced. He even spoke to her as she was a servant who was still learning her position.

It grated her nerves severely.

Still, she hadn't mentioned it to him, unsure if what she was experiencing genuine slights or if he was wanted to help and was simply inept at explaining himself to her. To be honest, she felt as if she were in some kind of fairytale. Her husband would transform every night into a different person. It left her confused. She wasn't sure how to broach the topic to Silas and so continued with their arrangement as it unfolded.

She told herself that she should be happy to have this sort of arrangement with him. If he was half as attentive to her during the day as he was at night, she wouldn't be able to get anything done. All the same, she wished she could see him during the day, if only to spend some time together that didn't involve sleeping together, the way they had back in London when they were courting. But given how powerful the attraction was between them, she reluctantly admitted that if they did meet during the day, they would probably end up naked somewhere. And that certainly wouldn't do.

They hadn't laid together last night, or the previous six nights as Clara had just finished her monthly courses. She had noted the tension in Silas's shoulders that morning when he left their room and she hoped that her courses would finally finish today.

Sighing, Clara tied the strings to her bonnet as she prepared herself for her second trip to visit the tenants. The first trip had happened during the first week of marriage and she had gone with the dowager duchess. This time, however, she was to ride with Violet.

Silas's sister had been her oddest acquaintance since arriving to Greystone. Violet never went out of her way to see or speak to Clara, and remained completely indifferent when she did see her, without showing any emotion, like or dislike. It had unnerved Clara at first. She felt rather like she was speaking to a plant most of the time. Whenever Clara had tried to ask her questions or show curiosity in her interests, Violet remained largely apathetic.

Undeterred however, Clara was hoping their outing today would prove beneficial to finally building a friendship.

They left the house at half past nine with twenty baskets all made up with strawberry jams, fabric, bottles of port and the various other odds and ends that each household was in need of. For example, The Farleys' young daughter had suffered a sprained ankle a few days earlier and Cook had made up a tea blend specially made to help with swelling.

It was a little frightening to be attending to this work without the dowager to supervise, but Clara was determined to rise to the occasion. Violet's presence was decidedly useful, since she had a sharp memory for names. And by the fifteenth house, her sister-in-law was even showing signs of conversation. Well, perhaps a cough wasn't exactly a plea for conversation, but Clara saw it as an opportunity.

"Are you well, Violet?" she asked as her sister-in-law covered her mouth. "I hope you are not coming down with a cold."

Violet let out a noncommittal hum.

"It has been unseasonably cool this time of year," Clara tried again.

"I'm fine, thank you."

"Are you sure you don't have a chill?"

"No."

Clara tried not to frown. Instead, she pulled her shoulders back and tried again.

"I do hope the weather holds out," she said, looking up towards the grey skies. "It would be a shame if it rained." Violet didn't speak at all in response to this, so Clara tried again, hoping this time to shock her. "I'd hate to return home without my slippers."

That seemed to catch Violet's attention. Her sister-in-law stared at her for a long moment before her curiosity got the better of her.

"Why would the rain have anything to do with your slippers returning home?"

"It's an old Lincolnshire custom. Or perhaps not Lincolnshire so much as the village of Kimberton. And really, to assume everyone in the village of Kimberton participates would be a gross overestimate. In truth, it was mostly just one person, Miss Hilda Franklin—and those who chose to follow her example. But there was good reason to follow in her footsteps, as it were, given that she never caught a cold."

"What are you talking about?" Violet asked, obviously confused by Clara's train of thought.

Clara smiled. *Got her.*

"Mm? Oh yes. Well, Miss Hilda Franklin was the oldest woman to ever live in Kimberton. That's where I grew up. She was a very sweet old woman and she was one hundred and two the day she died, not five years ago."

"One hundred and two?" Violet asked, disbelieving. "I don't believe it."

"I might not have either, except that there was a record of her baptism in the Kimberton Chapel. Everyone could confirm that Miss Franklin had lived in her family cottage for over a hundred years. She lived with her great grandnephew by then, but she was still spry the day before she died."

"And what does she have to do with slippers and the rain?"

"Well, Miss Franklin was a very proper sort. A good, God-fearing sort of woman who never let her skirt come over her ankle, or wore a neckline below her collar bone. She was completely prim in every way. Except that whenever it rained, if she was caught outside in a storm, she would remove her slippers and walk barefoot right through the center of town."

Violet stared at her. "What?"

"It's true. Whenever Miss Franklin was caught in a storm or a summer shower, she would remove her shoes and carry them in the crook of her arm as she would march through the middle of town back to her cottage."

"Why?"

"No one understood exactly. Even her own family tried to dissuade her from doing something so bizarre, but it never failed that on a wet day, she would be seen barefoot." Clara tried not to smile at the confusion on Violet's face. "Of course, there were rumors as to why she did so."

"What rumors?"

"Oh, there were a few stories. One suggested that she had been cursed in her youth by a witch. Another said that a gypsy woman told her that she would live to be a hundred if she never wore shoes in the rain. Others believed she was simply mad, though you wouldn't have assumed as much from talking to her."

"But no one knew the truth? Did no one ask her?"

"Oh, everyone asked her—but she would never give an answer." Clara shook her head. "And it would have been a strange story on its own, except for the day that she died."

"What happened?"

"Well, it was a day, not unlike today," Clara said, glancing up at the sky once more. "And Miss Franklin was out attending morning mass. Supposedly, it hadn't started to rain when she left church, but then she never made it home and it rained and rained all that day. The family went out to search for her, and it wasn't long before they found her. She had passed away, seated beneath an old oak tree. They said she appeared as peaceful as any person ever did."

"Was she wearing her shoes?" Violet asked.

"She was, but that's just it. Usually, Miss Franklin wore slippers, which were easy for her to take off. That day when they found her, she was wearing a pair of new leather ankle boots, tied tightly all the way up."

Violet's eyes went slightly wide.

"Did she wear them on purpose?"

Clara shrugged.

"No one knows. But then, no one ever did when it came to Miss Franklin."

Violet seemed contemplative as she rested back against her seat and Clara hoped that her little story had cracked her hard exterior. It was a silly tale, but one that always seemed to intrigue people. Of course, when Violet didn't speak for the next five tenant visits, Clara assumed she'd failed miserably.

After the last visit, Clara and Violet returned to the carriage. About halfway home, a loud roll of thunder boomed in the distance. Violet's eyes snapped to Clara's. Bending toward Clara, she spoke at last.

"Was that a true story?" Violet asked. "Or did you make it up?"

"It was true," Clara said. She dropped her hand to her ankle and took off her slipper, first one and then the other. Violet watched her with a perplexed expression. "And while I can't very well practice the custom in town, I do so in the countryside, whenever I yearn to take a stroll."

"You're a duchess. You can't walk around the countryside barefoot. It's beyond improper."

Clara smiled.

"I can and I will," she said and held up her slippers.

Then it happened. Violet laughed. "Silas will have a fit," she managed to say through her giggles.

"Will he? Whatever for?"

"He's very rigid about propriety. He won't like it."

Clara shrugged.

"Well, I don't wish to offend him. But it's hardly a scandal."

The word scandal seemed to make Violet's smile shrink and she looked away swiftly.

"No. My poor brother has suffered enough scandal for one lifetime."

Clara wanted to ask Violet about Silas's past, but she wasn't sure how to do so without offending the girl. It seemed Violet too had suffered. Silas had told her that the girl had formed a close bond with her former sister-in-law.

"I've heard the two of you were quite close," Clara said, broaching the subject carefully. "You and the former duchess, I mean."

Violet nodded, her eyes not quite meeting Clara's.

"For a time, yes," she said, somewhat sadly. "She was like a sister to me. I was so angry at Silas when she told me she couldn't stay. I thought him a brute for hurting her and making her leave him."

Clara wasn't sure how to respond. From what Silas had told her, she knew that pain had been part of his marriage with Cynthia—but it had been a part that Cynthia had wanted. Indeed, it had been something she demanded. Still, Clara didn't know how to explain that to a girl as young as Violet. In truth, it wasn't really something that she fully understood herself.

"It can be difficult, even for family, to understand what happens between a husband and wife," Clara said carefully. "There are parts of that relationship that are only for them. But still, I would never consider your brother to be a brute. Would you?"

"I wouldn't have thought so," Violet said. "But that was what she told me. And of course, I was aware of the fights they had. You could hear the shouting all over the house," Violet said, shaking her head. Violet glanced up at Clara. "I should apologize for being so cold to you. I was angry that Silas chased Cynthia away. His getting remarried feels like a betrayal of sorts. Only, the more I think about it, the more I realize that I was also worried about you."

"Worried about me?" Clara repeated, surprised. "Whatever for?"

"If he was cruel to Cynthia, then he might be cruel to you and chase you away as well." Another crack of thunder sounded over them as their carriage pulled onto the long drive that led to the house. "It's why I've kept my distance, not wanting to get attached."

"Oh, Violet, I'm not going anywhere," Clara said reassuringly. "Your brother does not have the same feelings for me as his former wife. Ours is a marriage built on mutual respect," she said, but the term seemed lacking. "And friendship."

"Friendship?" Violet repeated, seemingly unimpressed. "I always heard marriage was supposed to be a practical endeavor. Feelings towards one's spouse, whether friendly or otherwise, should not be considered as a deciding factor."

Clara's mouth fell open slightly and she stared at her sister-in-law with a mixture of pity and horror.

"Goodness gracious. What about love?"

Violet blinked, as if she had no idea why Clara would bring up something so irrelevant. "What about it?"

"Haven't you ever heard that one should marry someone they love?"

Violet's brow creased.

"Amongst commoners, I suppose," she said. "At our level of society, it is quite rare indeed. And since Silas's divorce, I have come to believe that that might be for the best. I would have said that they were a love match, but after witnessing how it hurt them, I would not recommend it."

No, Clara mused, she probably wouldn't. Clara swung the slippers that she held in her hands back and forth and shrugged.

"A friendship is a far more stable thing than romantic love," she heard herself say. "And there is love in friendship, but it is a hardier, sturdier sort of love."

"Do you love Silas?"

Although they had been speaking about it, the question had caught Clara off guard. *Did* she love Silas? She found herself uncertain as to how to answer. Yes, they were married and had slept together, but that wasn't the same as love. Clara had felt a deep pull towards him since the moment she first saw him, but that wasn't love, either. Not truly. It was the *potential* for love, maybe, but she knew better than to allow it to develop further. Not when Silas had made it clear that romantic love was not something he would offer her. But there was more than one kind of love, as she had just explained.

"Y-yes," she stuttered quietly, unsure why. It was a dangerous thing to admit, but she hardly assumed Violet would suffer from it. "Yes, of course. As I love all my friends."

Violet gave her a half smile as the skies opened up. Sidetracked by the torrential downpour, Violet quickly bent down and took off her shoes as well.

As the carriage pulled up to the front of the house, both women were helped down by a rather shocked footman as they ran through the rain. They reached the house at the same time, laughing as they stepped inside through the door that was held open for them. It seemed they were about to fall into a proper fit of giggles when a stern male voice echoed throughout the foyer.

"What on earth are you doing?" Silas asked, coming down the stairs.

Clara smiled at him, expecting him to return it, but there was only seriousness in his eyes. She swallowed and tried to smother her grin.

"We were caught in the rain," she said.

"I see that," he said, glancing down. "Where are your shoes?"

"Oh, well, that's a funny story," Clara said, when Violet took a step forward.

"Don't be angry, Silas," she said, her tone anxious. "It was just a bit of fun."

"Fun?" he repeated, coming up to Clara. "Walking around in

a rainstorm barefoot is fun?"

Clara smiled and tilted her head.

"Yes, it is. You should try it."

"I think not. And you shouldn't be behaving so carelessly," he said coldly.

Clara bristled at his words as a heavy silence fell around them—especially when she looked over to see Violet watching them with tangible dismay. It was obvious that Violet was worried this would escalate into a fight like the ones Silas and Cynthia used to have. While Clara didn't appreciate Silas's words, she wouldn't make the poor girl suffer through an argument, having been so aware of them in the past.

She peered over her husband's shoulders and forced a bright smile to her face.

"Would you excuse us, Violet? I wish to tell your brother a story," she said, winking at the girl.

The gentle sendoff seemed to pacify Violet and she gave Clara a half smile before heading towards the stairs. When she was at the top, Clara turned her focus back on Silas, who appeared vastly annoyed.

Well, so was she.

Lifting her chin, she walked past him without a word.

"Where are you going?" he asked, though it sounded more like an order than a question.

She didn't answer. Clara headed towards the back hall, reaching the door that led to the terrace. She opened it and walked out directly into the rain, only to have her arm held back by Silas's grip. He spun her around, a rising fury in his eyes.

"Do not walk away from me," he growled.

"I do not wish to speak to you," she said as the rain fell on them.

"Why not?"

"Because I do not wish to argue with you."

"Argue? What would we argue about?"

"About your behavior."

"*My* behavior?" He sounded outraged. "You're the one walking around without shoes. Devil take it, will you come inside?"

"You have no right to speak to me that way," she said hotly, not moving. "I am not a child for you to scold."

"No right?" he repeated, his countenance hostile. "I have every right as your husband to take your wellbeing into consideration. When you showed up with no shoes during a bloody storm—with my sister, I might add—my right is to inform you that such disregard for your health is not acceptable. It's hardly becoming of a duchess."

Now that, Clara would not allow. If Silas thought to cow her with nasty words, she would show him just how un-duchess-like she could be. She squared her shoulders. Taking a step forward, she lifted her finger and poked him directly in the chest.

"Do you mean to shame me? For something as silly as footwear?"

His large hand closed around her finger and tugged her closer, setting her off balance.

"I was merely pointing out what's expected of you," he said, unfazed.

"So, my lack of shoes undermines my position?" she asked.

"No, your lack of propriety does."

"You said I would be free to be me if I married you. Are you rescinding that promise?"

"If you plan on walking all over England barefoot, I might," he said loudly as his hand moved up to her wrist. He yanked her as he turned, trying to pull her inside, but she wrenched her arm away. He paused, appearing both puzzled and furious. "Come indoors at once."

"I don't want to."

"You're going to catch your death out here."

Clara wasn't sure what she was doing or what she wanted from him, but she knew she couldn't let this stand. She couldn't deal with him behaving like a caring husband every night but then shifting into a scold as soon as the sun rose. She needed to know that he respected her outside of the bedroom—that he believed that she was a suitable duchess. And she needed to be absolutely certain that he was not comparing her to his former duchess.

It was a bothersome feeling, one that had grown over the past few weeks. Her curiosity about Cynthia had only grown more and more since her arrival to Greystone. She had wanted nothing more than to forget her, but every turn, every glance from the servants or her in-laws, made her question everything about herself and whether she measured up. She had never been so uncertain of herself and though she had tried very hard to behave like the perfect duchess, she felt the pressure of it buckling on her shoulders. She wanted a little reprieve from it, and the rain had seemingly unlocked the part of herself that was willing to rebel.

She stared at Silas, his eyes dark with anger. The rain had wet his hair and was running down his face, turning his white shirt translucent. If only she could make him forget too…

Clara slowly lifted her fingers to beneath her chin and tugged at the satin ribbon of her bonnet. Pulling it away, she felt instant cooling relief as the raindrops fell onto her hair and face. She took a step away from him and dropped the bonnet on the ground as she turned, heading towards the maze.

"What are you doing?" Silas called out, but she didn't answer.

She wasn't sure what she was doing. When she reached the entrance of the maze, she unlatched her cloak and let it fall to the ground as well. Giving him a final look, she paused before disappearing behind the yew.

Since coming to Greystone, Clara had walked the maze every day and had studied it from the window of their bedchamber. She had found it easy to reach the center now, she still hadn't found a way to the wisteria pergola at the back. Convinced that there had to be a secret door somewhere that she hadn't found, she let her hand trail along the hedge as she went deeper into the maze.

She hesitated before taking the first turn, wondering if Silas would follow her, but after several moments, he didn't appear and Clara felt a little hope go out of her. Perhaps they didn't suit as well as she thought. If a barefoot duchess was really too much for Silas to handle, she supposed she could give in and wear her slippers, but Clara so desperately wanted Silas to relax, like he did at night in their bedroom. She wanted him to smile—which was something he rarely did, even at night.

There was something guarded about Silas that she had recognized since the beginning of their acquaintance. But while most everyone in England believed the rumors about him being a cold and cruel man, Clara saw something else. She recognized the way that his anxiety forced him to keep people at a distance. Even with his sister and mother he kept his guard up, and while Clara had perhaps the best chance to get close, he made sure never to speak to her too openly about anything.

Clara let the frustration of her relationship wash away as the rain intensified. She wanted to forget everything about Silas's past and her feelings of insufficiency. The harder the rain fell, the more her feelings bubbled up within her. She walked faster, wishing she was in some open field rather than a suffocating maze. Turn after turn she felt as if she were falling deeper and deeper into a tangled web of emotion that relented only slightly when she reached the fountain in the middle.

Breathing heavily, she felt panicked when she saw movement to her left. Stumbling backwards, she was shocked to see Silas standing there, completely soaked. A part of her felt guilty that he was drenched in rainwater, but the rest of her felt so relieved that he was *willing* to get drenched in rainwater…for her.

"Care to explain what you're doing? Running through this maze in the pouring rain?" he asked, his tone loud and biting.

What could she say? That she wanted him to open up to her? That she needed to understand the evident pain he carried within him? That she wanted to help?

Good lord, it all sounded too dramatic to put into words. And yet, she needed to tell him everything or she would explode.

"I don't think I'm a very good duchess," she said, embarrassed that her voice cracked at her confession. The rain sounded loudly in her ears, forcing her to raise her voice in order to be heard. He stared at her as she spoke. "Or at least, I have the impression that you don't think I'm a very good duchess."

"When have I said that?"

"I never believed that it would matter much, my lack of social etiquette, but I was wrong. I am inadequate."

"Clara—"

"No, please let me finish." She held her hand up as he came towards her. "I know you wanted this to be a marriage of friendship, Silas and I've tried, but what sort of friendship only lives in the dark? We barely talk. I never see you."

"I see you every night."

"Yes, at night when we…" She paused, her cheeks flaring at the mention of their coupling. "When we sleep together, but I need more, Silas."

Silas stared at her, his whole body unmoving as if he were carved from stone, his gaze was alit with heat.

"I told you friendship was all I could give. I explained that to you."

Her heart ached at his words and she debated continuing to hold in all the terrifying emotions she had been feeling for weeks. It would be easier to simply smile and apologize, to go about their lives quietly and courteously—and separately in far too many ways.

But Clara wouldn't be doing herself any justice in lying to him. No, she needed to be honest.

"Yes, you did," she nodded. "But I'm afraid… I mean, I realize now that I need more. More of you. More of *us*. I want you to trust me, Silas. I want you to have faith in the fact that I would never do anything to hurt or embarrass you." Silas stared at her, his expression set in a way she couldn't decipher. Was he anxious? Angry? She couldn't tell, and so she continued. "I want more from this relationship. I want you to stop avoiding me during the day and to talk to me when you have an issue as opposed to just dictating to me how you'd rather I behave."

Thunder crashed somewhere in the distance, but Clara barely registered it against his silence. For a moment she feared he might never answer. His body shifted as he looked away and she was sure he was about to leave. But then suddenly, he turned back to face her.

"I'm sorry if I've been neglectful," he said, practically yelling over the storm. "I *have* been avoiding you."

"But why?"

He glanced upwards, almost hesitant, before looking back down.

"It's…easier for me, to go about my day when you aren't near." Clara's mouth fell open a little with surprise and Silas rushed to explain. "That's not to say I don't like being near you. It's just that I find myself, well, unable to focus when you're near. I thought it was best to keep my distance."

"Oh."

"And I do trust you." He sounded torn. "But I told you before, Clara. I can't give you anything more than friendship. There isn't anything else."

Clara felt her heart break a little at his words, but she stepped towards him. He was staring at her like she was some sort of specter. Placing her hand to his chest, she felt the shudder of his body beneath her fingers.

"There is," she said softly. She knew he wouldn't be able to hear her, but she wanted to say these words out loud. "But I'm afraid you've locked it up so tightly, you'll never let it go." Following an instinct, she let her fingers curl against the wet fabric of his shirt and pulled him towards her. "I wish you would, Silas."

Before she realized it, he was kissing her, deeply and purposely, and she met him with her own need. She kissed him as if to tell him that he was safe with her. That no matter what had happened to him, she would understand.

Her hands came up to the sides of his face, cradling his cheeks in her palms as she kissed him deeper. She needed him to feel the depth of her feelings for him, but she was left lacking when he pulled back. Eyes opened, she watched the mix of emotions battle their way across his face. Abruptly, he grabbed her hand, his strong fingers wrapping tightly around her cold ones and pulling her to follow him.

"Not here," he said as he walked.

"Where are we going?" she asked as he led her away from the center of the maze, but he didn't answer.

She wiped the rain from her face as it continued to fall. Within minutes, they were beneath a vine covered pergola that sat against a rock wall. The pergola was so covered in thicket that it blocked nearly all of the rain from falling on them. They could also hear each other more clearly.

"Silas?" Clara said with question, gazing up into his grey eyes.

"I can't offer you what you want, Clara," he said, his tone somewhat shaken. His eyes shifted down at their joined hands and Clara wondered if he was nervous. "I can't…"

Sensing that it was too much for him and ignoring the pain she felt pinch her heart at his refusal to try, she took a step towards him. She was desperate for him to feel the way she felt, but she couldn't force it. All she could do was support him.

"You don't have to," she whispered. "It's all right—"

"You don't understand," he said, his grip tightening on her fingers. "It's not a choice. I am truly unable to give you more."

The painful pinch in Clara's heart grew. He really believed that there was nothing left to give her. The hurt he had endured from his previous marriage had been a deeper cut than she had realized and she felt momentarily shamed for not crediting him with feeling that deeply.

But she wouldn't give up. She would simply have to love him more than he had ever been loved before, to show him just how much he was worth it.

"Silas?" she asked, leaning towards him. "Will you kiss me?"

"Did you hear me?" he asked, his brow furrowing in confusion. "I can't love you."

Clara ignored the frigid ache in her heart at his words.

"I'm not asking you to love me, Silas. I'm asking you to kiss me."

Silas's brow was creased as he glared at her.

"Damn it," he muttered as he crushed his mouth to hers.

Chapter Fifteen

W*HAT IS WRONG with this woman?* Silas wondered angrily as he kissed her. She wasn't listening to him. Why did she refuse to accept that he was unable to provide her anything more than friendship? He had no heart to offer anymore. Not after the way it had been crushed to dust, pulverized by a woman who had never genuinely cared for him. And yet, in this moment, as Clara pressed her body against his in earnest, he couldn't for the life of him remember the shape of Cynthia's mouth, or even the exact color of her eyes.

Features that had once held such power over him had become fuzzy. It was increasingly difficult to recall every aspect of her face, especially since his wedding to Clara had taken place. It had been his own fault, he supposed. He hadn't had the time to wallow in his own misery anymore the way he had before he'd begun to share a bed with Clara.

His hands dropped her hips, wide and full beneath his strong grip. God save him from her curves. At night, after she'd fallen asleep curled onto her side, Silas's eye would roam over her sleeping form, a landscape of rolling hills and valleys bared for his touch. She would make the strangest sound when he touched her as she slept—a content, purring noise that always made him equal parts hard and envious. That she should be so responsive to his touch, even in sleep, undid him. That she could find such peace and pleasure bothered him.

An unfounded anger surged through him as he kissed her, pressing her body fully against the rough rock wall that encircled the garden. His hands found her wrists and pulled them up over her head as his tongue moved against hers, savoring the taste of her mouth. This was all he could give her—but he intended to give her so much that it overwhelmed her.

He crushed his body against hers, enjoying the gasp that dropped from her lips as she felt his length press against her. He could give her all the physical enjoyment her body could handle.

"This," he spoke, tearing his mouth from hers and leaning against her ear. "This has to be enough, Clara."

To his annoyance, she defiantly shook her head.

"No, Silas," she whispered back. "I want more."

"There is no more."

"There is," she said as she pressed her lips against his neck, making him shake with desire. "I want it all. I want all of you."

He silenced her again with his mouth, both furious and unrepentantly aroused by her persistence. She would have all of him, he thought savagely as he gathered her wrists against his palm. His other hand moved down her body, gripping her soft breasts beneath the see-through fabric of her chemise. Never in his life had he held such perfection. It made him want to worship her...but this wasn't meant to be a gentle coupling. Not when he had something to prove.

His hand moved down to the front of his breeches and with a quickness that seemed to surprise Clara, he released himself while he gathered her skirts up. Her eyes were on him, he could feel it as he bent his knees. Bringing both hands down to the bottom of her thighs he lifted her and in a swift, singular motion, pushed up into her.

Clara gasped, her eyes fluttering closed as her arms fell to his shoulders, holding onto his neck. Silas had to fight off the very real wave of emotions he felt in the moment. Awe at the beauty of her flushed cheeks, strands of wet hair plastered against her skin, her face the epitome of pleasure. Fear over the way she caused the broken parts inside of him to vibrate. Triumph at the knowledge that she was his completely.

No. He moved against her, roughly. He had believed Cynthia was wholly his once and she had destroyed him. Never again would he allow himself to trust a woman.

But damned if Clara didn't make him want to try.

She began to make the same soft, purr-like noise she made in her sleep, and the sound of it enraptured Silas. The wet warmth of her wrapped around him contracted and while he was moving with a definitive rhythm, he felt his control slip.

"Silas."

Her voice was filled with pleasure, her eyes remained closed as he moved. He pumped into her with increasingly harder strokes as he kissed the breath out of her mouth.

Her desire was his to master and yet at the same time, he felt entirely under her power. He would do anything, give anything to bring her to ecstasy. He was both her reverent servant and her dominant protector. The conflicting feelings flooded him, muddling his mind. If he thought too hard about what she actually meant to him he wouldn't be able to live with her anymore. He pushed those ideas from his mind. He had no intention of losing her.

"Silas, please," she begged softly as he pumped into her. "Deeper."

Silas nearly spent himself then and there at her request. His hands moved further back around her buttocks. Holding her in what he was sure was a painful grip, he pulled her fast and hard against him. Clara let out a broken sort of cry as she writhed against him. Silas couldn't stand it any longer and he slammed into her one last time before he exploded within her.

Operating on nothing more than base instinct, Silas bent his head to her shoulder, his teeth biting down on her smooth skin as he shook in the aftermath. Only after several moments did he notice the damage he had done—not just to her shoulder, but to her back where it had scraped against the rough-cut stones of the garden wall. With a bitter curse, he pulled himself from her and her legs dropped to the ground as his hands came up her back.

"I didn't hurt you, did I?" he asked, worried.

"No," she said breathlessly. "Although I suspect you were trying to."

He scowled at her accusation.

"I shouldn't have taken you against the wall like that."

"I wasn't talking about the wall," Clara said, her gaze intent.

It was true that he had hoped to scare her off with his words, to pulverize whatever silly hope she had at breaking down his walls, but it seemed that plan had been doomed to failure. This stubborn, impossibly gentle, gorgeous woman seemed undeterred. Of course, that only frustrated Silas even more.

He steadied her shoulders before he took a step back.

"I wasn't lying, Clara. I can't love you."

The words felt hollow as they dropped from his mouth, but he knew they were true.

Didn't he?

"You don't have to," she said after a long moment, her unwavering eyes on him. "But could you let me love you?"

A strange lump seemed to grow in his throat as he stared at her. Why did she want to do something so dangerous? To love someone who didn't return the love was a misery he would never wish on anyone, not even his worst enemy. Especially Clara.

"No," he said decisively as he bent down to gather her dress.

To his surprise, Clara came forward, her short index finger poking him in the shoulder again. What was her obsession with poking him?

"Why not?" she asked, her tone no longer gentle and serene. He helped her dress in her wet gown. "Why are you so hellbent on being miserable forever?"

"I'm not hellbent—"

"Aren't you?" she asked as he buttoned her dress. "For God's sake, Silas, all I want to do is care for you, in the way a wife should care for her husband—"

"And I don't want you to get hurt," he said as he stalked away from her, back through the maze.

"Are you planning on hurting me?" she countered, causing him to spin around.

"No, never," he said, the sincerity of his declaration apparently lost on the incensed Clara.

"Well, the only way I could be hurt is by you. All I'm asking is that you let me love you. I don't see why I'm not permitted to try."

Silas shoved a hand through his wet hair as confusion and aggravation coursed through him. Was she being purposefully obtuse?

"Fine, do as you please," he said after several seconds of an internal struggle, continuing his walk.

He was glad he was walking ahead of her and couldn't see her reaction to his words. No matter what she did, he intended to hold firm to his resolve to keep her at arm's length. Otherwise he actually might hurt her. For god's sake, his love for Cynthia had nearly destroyed him. Love was a treacherous, soul crushing sort of thing and he wouldn't let Clara suffer it. He didn't have the working equipment to do so. He was a broken man and she needed to accept that.

"I will," she said once they reached the stone steps of the manse. "I love you, Silas Winters, and I shan't ever stop."

Silas froze in the doorway. The words sent a shock through him, as if he were standing next to a box of fireworks that had abruptly gone off without warning.

He turned and stared at her incredulously. She was determined, with her chin in the air, her mouth in a flat line and her eyes glowing, as if ready to argue her point.

"Why?" he asked after a deafening long time. "Why would you want to love someone like me?"

The heat in her glare diminished. She took a step towards him and her small hand reached out for his. His instincts told him to pull back, to refuse her intimacy, but he was frozen beneath her touch.

"Oh Silas," she said softly. "Why wouldn't I?"

He stared at her as if she spoke a different language. He couldn't comprehend why she was so set on having feelings for a broken man, but something within him rallied against his self-destructive behavior. Silas found that he wished he could be someone worthy of her troubles.

"I'm sorry, Silas. I've been trying so hard to be patient, to understand things that don't quite make sense to me—"

"What do you want to know?" he asked, his throat tight. He had no doubt that she wished to know more about the games he used to play with Cynthia.

He had sworn never to broach the topic to anyone. His relations with Cynthia had been too miserable, too embarrassing to speak of. But it was terribly hard to deny Clara anything, especially when she was so bull-headed and determined. She was ridiculous. Ridiculous and unnervingly persistent not to mention brave. To admit that she loved him, when she knew he would never, could never love her back…well, he found himself in awe of her bravery.

She deserved to at least know why he felt the way he did.

"Can we change first?" Clara asked, looking down at herself. "I'm worried we might catch a cold."

She folded her arms across her chest as she shivered and Silas frowned with worry. Damn him for having her outside, like some sort of animal.

"Hawkins!" he bellowed behind him.

Instantly the butler appeared.

"Yes, your grace?"

"Have the bath drawn and send several trays of food up to my room," he said. "Along with tea and a bottle of brandy."

"Very good, your grace," Hawkins said with a bow before disappearing.

"Come," Silas said, holding out a hand to Clara.

The shadow of a smile passed over her face as she took his hand. He didn't know what he'd done to deserve it, but he felt oddly pleased that he had caused it.

A half hour later, the storm continued to rage outside, but neither Clara nor Silas seemed aware. Tucked away in the warmth of their rooms, Clara sat in a thick, burgundy colored velvet nightrobe that belonged to Silas, with a black satin quilted pattern on the lapels. She had dressed in one of her nightgowns but had still been rather cold and asked him for something that she could wrap herself up in. He helped her tie it at her waist. It dragged beneath her feet as she crawled up into their bed while Silas, dressed in nothing more than a length of towel he had wrapped around himself once he got out of the bath, brought her a cup of tea with a liberal dose of brandy added.

"Are you warm?" he asked after she took a long, slow sip.

"I will be," she said cheerfully before her stare turned serious. *This is it*, he mused. She was going to ask him.

"Yes?" he asked, his tone slightly brittle.

"What happened between you two, Silas?" she asked. "What did she do to you?"

Silas chuckled, unsure what he found so amusing about her question. It all seemed rather ridiculous, he guessed as he sat on the bed, one leg bent on the edge while the other stayed on the floor. He wasn't sure how much he should tell her or even where to begin, but then he took a deep breath and decided to be as honest as possible.

"Cynthia and I were similar in many ways. When we were first introduced, we learned that our backgrounds were nearly identical. Cut from the same cloth, you could say," he started, tracing his finger along the end of the label of the bottle of brandy he held in his hands. "We both appreciated the arts, as well as languages, although I believe our shared interests ended there. We were both the offspring of dukes who had little care for their children, resulting in our being rich, bored, and lacking morals. That's not to say my father was a cruel or immoral man. He was simply preoccupied as any man of his position would be." His brow creased. "Cynthia's father was eager to marry her off, as she'd proven too spirited for his liking. I hadn't planned on marrying so early in my youth, but then I hadn't met her."

Silas's gaze lifted to Clara to see her reaction, but her face remained impassive so he continued.

"When we did meet, it was a surprising attraction. I was infatuated with her instantly, and she appeared to feel the same, but it wasn't an easy sort of courtship. Cynthia liked to play games," he said, his tone soft. "I did too."

"What sort of games?" Clara asked, her tone curious.

"Vile ones," he continued. "Ones that hurt people and played with their emotions. She would try and make me jealous so that I would react." Silas felt his throat tighten slightly, disliking his need to share these parts of himself with her. His eyes locked on hers. "And I would."

"What would you do?"

He shook his head, an unsteady breath escaping as he debated internally how much he should reveal to her. As he stared at her, unwavering and understanding, he felt another crack in his heart open.

"Punish her."

"Like you told me before. Where you would control her, restrain her."

"That too," Silas agreed. "But sometimes, I gave her what she really wanted—which was pain. Pain was her addiction and control was mine. It was always part of our little play. I allowed it for a time, to appease her, but she always wanted more. None of it was supposed to be real, or at least I didn't think it was real because I was so sure she and I were the same person." He frowned, not quite believing it anymore. "We were supposed to be two sides of the same coin."

"I'm not sure I understand," Clara said after a moment.

Silas exhaled, hesitant to proceed.

"I have…had…particular tastes in my youth," he said lowly,

knowing full well that Clara would not understand. "There are times when pleasure and pain can be shared, to heighten certain feelings and reactions. I wasn't particularly fond of the pain aspect, but the control was intoxicating."

"Oh," she said, color rising to her cheeks. "Like when you, um… That is, I mean, when you…"

"When I held you down?" He finished her sentence. She blushed wildly and Silas felt both depraved and drawn to her. Lord how he loathed himself. "Yes, like that. But it wasn't enough. The pain I could manage to give wasn't enough. She wanted more."

"More?"

"Much more," he continued. "And she didn't care that I wasn't interested in it. She wanted me to hurt too." He glanced across the room, feeling odd. He was reluctant to tell her everything they had done, but the more he spoke the more he felt relieved. "I was foolish. I asked her to marry me in a desperate attempt to try and keep her. She accepted and we were wed."

"But not for long?"

"No," he said, standing up. He placed the brandy bottle on a side table. "Not a week after we returned from our honeymoon, we began to fight. At first, I tried to appease her, but she didn't like that. She didn't want me to make her happy. She wanted to argue. To continue the games that tormented us. She thrived on it."

Clara's brows knit together.

"She didn't want to be happy? But why?"

"As I said, the pain was her goal all along. It was why she enjoyed the arguments, the jealousy. That was what caused the disconnect between us. Once our game was played, I wanted peace, but she wanted torture. Constantly. And when I did not comply, she decided to do it on her own."

Clara was quiet and he could see on her face that she was confused. Lord, he hated himself for telling her these things.

"She found comfort outside our marital bed, at first to get a rise out of me. I was constantly enraged, furious and threatened to murder any men who had touched her. She enjoyed how rough I could be when I was staking my claim, but it was more than that. She reveled in my agony. My pain was for her consumption and even then, I was happy to provide it to her."

"Oh dear."

"And it didn't matter how many times she made a fool out of me. I was hopelessly in love with her. I would do anything for her. Except…"

Here it was.

"Except what?" Clara asked, her voice nearly a whisper.

Silas didn't want to look at Clara, but something forced him to turn. She was watching him with the gentlest and most understanding eyes he had ever witnessed. They unnerved him. Taking a deep breath, he continued.

"She wanted me to share her," he said lowly. "With one of her paramours." Silas's eyes shifted down, focusing on the edge of the bed, unwilling to see Clara's pity. He huffed, humorlessly. "To show you how far gone I was, I actually considered it, even though it went against my entire being. Maybe I even could have gone through with it if it had been a simple fantasy—achieved once and then forgotten. I was willing to do anything for her, as I told you. But what she wanted was something that exceeded even my limits."

"What did she want?"

"She wanted… She needed a full relationship with someone else. There was some sort of pit, I believe that she was trying to fill. I'm not sure what it was, but she insisted that she needed another man, another relationship as well as ours and I could not abide it." He took a deep breath before continuing. "When she told me this, I felt a break from her, from myself."

"Our fights got uglier. I tried to make accommodations, truly, but it seemed every inch I gave her, she would demand a mile and then throw it back in my face," he said lowly. "It was as if she were purposely trying to push me to the point where I'd shatter completely."

Silas flexed his hands as his eyes landed on a small, dark walnut vanity table tucked in the corner of the room. The memory of that last conversation filtered through his mind.

"This isn't working, Silas. You can't make me happy," Cynthia had said, sitting at the vanity in this very room. "This marriage was a mistake."

Silas had felt a bizarre mix of rage and misery course through him at her words.

"I've done everything to make you happy," he had hissed back at her. "I've been made a fool of, mocked openly, all to appease you and your insatiable need to hurt me and ruin my name."

"You're being dramatic," she had said, standing up in a dismissive manner. "Why should I have to curb my tastes to appease you?"

"I don't ask that you curb them, only that you consider me before you act like a trollop."

"Consider you? Why must you always be at the forefront of my mind? Every action, every pleasure is sullied by the need of your approval." She sneered, her expression full of bitterness. "Every single fiber of my being is supposed to seek your approval and I hate it!"

"When have you ever sought out my approval?"

She shook her head, unwilling to answer as she caught sight of herself in the mirror.

"This is not what I wanted. I never should have married you."

"I had hoped that we would settle—"

"Settle all you want, Silas. I won't be here for it. I want a divorce."

He had sensed a break coming for some time, the blood in his veins had turned to ice. He had never actually expected to divorce anyone. It was practically unheard of, even for the wealthy. But she had been determined to push him into it. And what Cynthia wanted, she always got—sooner or later.

He shook his head as if to brush off the memories. Turning back to Clara, he saw her patient face watching him.

"I should have known better. I take full responsibility for the collapse of that marriage."

"Oh, but how could you?" Clara asked, standing up. "It wasn't your fault that it didn't work out."

"It didn't succeed because of me either," he said shaking his head. "Cynthia was not someone who would ever be content with the sort of conventional relationship I wanted to give her. I was a fool to think we could be happy together—but I paid for my arrogance with years of lies and betrayals. Shame has been my only companion for the past year. How could I have let her get away with such things? It was why I had planned on remaining alone after our divorce." He glanced at her. "I didn't want to share my miserable self with anyone, to plague another human being with my desolation."

"Then why did you propose to me?"

Guilt washed over him as his gaze dropped.

"I suppose, in a moment of selfishness, I wanted to keep you."

"Because I help with your anxiety? Or was it something else?"

Silas swallowed as he looked at her, unsure how much to reveal. Clara came towards him tentatively. Her hands raised and she touched his chest. He felt his heart begin to beat faster beneath her fingertips.

"You shouldn't feel any shame, Silas," she said, allowing her last question to go unanswered. "You're only guilty of trying to appease your wife. A wife who didn't have any idea how to react to the sort of support you gave her," Clara said. "She was the luckiest woman in the world and she squandered her good fortune. And you—"

"And me?"

"And you," she repeated, coming closer, her hand moving over his cheek. "You should forgive yourself. Your only crime was loving her."

Silas looked down at his wife, rather captivated by her words. No one had ever told him to forgive himself. The few friends he had left had disparaged Cynthia as a wicked harlot. His mother and sister had blamed him for his inability to keep his marriage together. All of London thought he was a scoundrel.

Everyone except Clara.

"I don't want to hurt you, Clara." His hands moved over hers. "It's why my friendship is all I can give you. It's why I can't accept…"

To her credit, Clara didn't weep or argue. Instead, she only squeezed her fingers around his.

"Shhh, Silas. It's all right," she said softly, her expression hopeful. Her hand pulled his to her chest and placed his fingers over her heart. "It will be all right."

Silas felt a snap within him, as if a steel band had broken from around his heart. She was wrong. It wasn't all right. Clara didn't deserve his excuses and if he were a better man, he would feel guilty for stealing her chances of a loving marriage away from her, but he couldn't bring himself to do so. Nothing would be enough to heal him, but he wouldn't bring himself to squash her optimism. Without realizing it, his arms went round her.

"Very well," he heard himself say. "Do as you please."

The smile she gave him made his stomach do an odd sort of flip. She was so happy in that moment. His shoulders, that were so tense the entire time he told her his history with Cynthia, relaxed and he felt as if a weight had been permanently lifted. Like a ghost had gone out of him.

Leaning forward, he kissed her. Almost instantly, her arms were wrapped around his shoulders. He tugged her towards him. Leaning on the leg that hung off the bed, he maneuvered her off the mattress and into a standing position, his mouth on hers the entire time.

She pulled away for a moment, confused.

"What are you doing?"

"Showing you what the mirrors are for," he whispered

against her mouth as he turned her around to face the largest one that hung on the opposite wall.

"Oh."

His hand moved over her shoulders, pushing down the robe to reveal her breasts. His eyes locked on her reflection as her mouth opened. The shock in her gaze sent a jolt of yearning through him and as his hands came up around her, he waited for her to protest.

But Clara wouldn't stop him and the same, terrible urge to control bubbled up within him. *Why is she so perfect?* he wondered as he kissed down her neck. His teeth grazed over the soft skin of her shoulder and he bit down again, not as hard as he had in the garden, but enough to elicit a response. And yet she still remained unfazed. Her grey-green eyes filled with challenge and he knew she was daring him.

Lord above, he thought miserably. *This woman will be the death of me.*

Chapter Sixteen

Clara peered out over the fields and rolling hills of the surrounding countryside, contemplative and quiet as she, Silas and Violet rode to Lord Bairnsdale's home in Bedfordshire. It was half a day's journey from her childhood home, just outside the town of Kimberton and she was eager to see her parents while this far south.

She and Silas had been half expecting an invitation from the baron as Holly Smyth had decided to accept the elder man's wedding proposal, much to Clara's dismay. She wanted so much more for her friend—but now that the decision had been made, she would not pass judgement on it. Holly needed support, not condemnation. At least they would be able to spend the week-long hunt together, which would hopefully reassure Clara that the baron truly was as kind as Holly claimed.

Silas hadn't been particularly interested in attending, but he'd relented when Violet had insisted and Clara had encouraged it. He'd told Clara that he'd rarely seen his sister ask passionately for anything. He didn't know why she was so eager to attend, but he was curious enough to want to find out.

As the carriage gently tottered down the country lane, Clara felt the duke's eyes on her. She wasn't sure how or why she was always aware of when he was staring at her, but it had become second nature at this point. She kept her unfocused gaze out the window and wondered if her husband might soon relinquish his claim that he was incapable of loving her.

Clara had had her work cut out for her in that respect. Since Silas had confessed his inability to love nearly a month ago, she had been patiently working to demonstrate that her love was enough for the both of them. Silas and she were married, joined together forever and she took her vows quite seriously. More so than Cynthia.

Don't do that, she scolded herself silently. She had tried very hard not to think of Cynthia as the enemy—it wouldn't help anything, and it seemed unfair to judge the woman without hearing her side of the story—but it was hard to let go of the anger over how much she had hurt Silas.

She sighed quietly. Since that night, they had settled into a strange, comforting sort of dynamic. Silas hadn't kept his visits to strictly evening appearances anymore, having realized that trying to distance himself from her was futile. Clara and Silas had since returned to being more open with one another, as they had before their marriage. She often saw him during the day and they had even started to take rather long walks through the south fields, since Clara wasn't very proficient at riding yet. He had offered to teach her and even if she was rather nervous, she had agreed, secretly happy to be in his company for any reason.

During their walks, they had conversations about nearly everything. Clara explained in detail about her childhood—how she and her parents had lived very modestly up until her father became a success. It had been a strange transition from living frugally to extravagance, and to suddenly be thrusted into a different social circle, one that barely tolerated them because of their low birth rank. Above all, it had been lonely. It was why she was so protective of her friendship with Holly.

The two had been friends as children, long before either one of them knew about society and ranking. They had simply liked one another and had spent their youth running through fields and playing in streams together. When Holly's mother died, some time after losing her father, she was barely sixteen and had taken on the responsibilities of the entire household, as well as her two younger siblings. Without any prospects outside of her limited circle, having never been introduced to London society, Holly had focused her attention on maintaining her family home. It was a task that had proved increasingly difficult over the years. While Holly's life had become increasingly difficult, Clara's life had shifted as well, in a far opposite direction. And yet despite it all, they had maintained their friendship and loyalty to one another throughout the years.

Silas had listened intently to Clara every time she spoke about her youth. She had explained to him that she had always had a very good sense of who she was as a person, but the past few years had left her confused.

Silas in turn had divulged into his own upbringing. It had been, to his way of thinking, a fairly normal childhood. His parents were stern, but not cruel. Affection was rarely physical, even between his parents. His mother was more diplomatic than kind, often keeping a distance between herself and her children, maintaining the formality with which she had been raised. His father had been elderly when he was born, an important man with far too little time on his hands who had died at the age of seventy-five, just as Silas turned seventeen.

He had been close with the Trembley family having met Derek at Eton as boys. He had regularly visited Derek and had even come to appreciate Lord Trembley as a sort of surrogate father. Clara had felt sorry for the young man he had been, but Silas assured her that he had come through adolescence with only the usual bumps and scratches. And yet, he'd been lonely too. Not to the same extent perhaps…but lonely enough to throw himself into his relationship with Cynthia—to relish, at first, the way their lovemaking had been so intense, so all-consuming.

His lovemaking with Clara had certainly felt more intense since that day in the rain, but the most Silas seemed capable of was pinning her wrists above her head and even then, he was always exceedingly careful. When she tried to ask him about it, he only ever told her that he didn't wish to sully her mind with such depravities, but every once in a while, it seemed he couldn't help himself. Sometimes his fingers would dig into her hips, holding her exactly where he wanted her, or he would tell her to change positions, quickly, or else. Of course, there was never any repercussion if she was too slow or didn't obey. But it always made her pulse jump and she found herself curious what he might do if only he allowed himself. She was eager to learn more, even if Silas refused to teach her.

Besides their standstill, they found a content and peaceful sense in each other's company. Every day they grew closer, and every night, well, every night Clara could almost swear that he did love her, even if he refused to say it.

She let herself float back to the previous night. She and Silas had made love slowly, purposefully. Clara had been sure that she would become tired with the constant lovemaking, but it proved to be her favorite activity of the day and she often had to distract herself to focus on other tasks.

However, last night had been different. Silas had always made sure that she reached the pinnacle of pleasure before him, this time he had seemed especially intent. He'd penetrated her slow and fully, with his eyes on hers. She had felt exposed for some reason, more vulnerable and more naked than she ever had been before.

Neither spoke and when they reached orgasm—together no less—Clara had to turn away to hide the tears that unexpectedly stung her eyes. Even Silas, who was usually rather flirtatious afterwards, was quiet and contemplative.

When they woke that morning, all seemed to be in order again and they moved and spoke without distraction. But she hadn't been able to stop thinking about it.

"Nervous?" he asked as the carriage moved across a particularly bumpy section of road.

"No," she lied.

In truth, she was rather worried. This would be their first official coming out as husband and wife and she felt anxious. Violet's earnest request had distracted Clara from her fears however and when she inquired why her sister-in-law was so adamant on going, Clara had been sworn to secrecy before Violet had revealed the reason.

In the month since their run in the rain, Violet had gradually opened up to Clara. It was during that time that she had admitted to Clara that she had been madly in love with a man named David Lutz since last year. From what Violet had told Clara, the baron was a devoted patron of the arts, in particular writing, and had been sponsoring the young writer for some time.

Violet had met Mr. Lutz the previous summer when he was visiting a family friend in Bedfordshire. Mr. Lutz had asked to write her and they had been in correspondence ever since. According to Violet, he was terribly romantic, but was petrified of Silas. Violet knew Silas would never approve of a courtship since David was a novelist. He'd had some success in a serial series in the *Times*, but in all honesty, he was the penniless fifth son of a barrister with no option but to make his own way in the world. Nothing about him fit with what Silas expected from anyone seeking his sister's hand. But Violet was determined to have him and she hoped Clara would help her convince Silas.

"Clara will be splendid, I'm sure of it," Violet said with conviction, smiling at her. "Is this truly the first time you've been invited to a country house?"

Clara felt her cheeks flush.

"I'm afraid so, at least, to a baron's home. I hope you do not have any expectations of me, Violet. I've never been accused of having pristine social capability."

"You'll be brilliant," Silas said, leaning towards her.

The smile he gave her made her want to squirm. Instead, she pursed her lips and tried very hard not to appear pleased. She needed to talk about something else.

"Will all the Trembleys be in attendance?"

"I believe Fredrick and Alfred will be accompanying their mother. Derek has a previous engagement," Silas said. "Supposedly the baron was close with their uncle. I believe he may even be a cousin of Lady Trembley."

"Oh, is he?"

"I think so," Silas said, his brow furrowing for an instant. "I can't remember how I know that exactly."

The rest of the carriage ride was filled with happy chatter until they reached their final destination. The baron's home was set far back behind two very flat fields of wheat that appeared as if they were just about ready to be harvested. The golden sea of wheat, swaying gently against a blue sky made Clara smile. She had missed this part of England.

The house was a large Tudor-style brick manor. It was nearly three hundred years old and the dark, nearly black planks of lumber stood out against the red brick, making it a very visually interesting and beautiful building. Clara tried not to gawk at it as she was helped out of the carriage by Silas.

"Welcome to Kingston House, your graces," an elderly gentleman said, coming forward with a slight head nod.

The man was quite tall and rather frail looking. Clara wondered if she had ever seen a man so thin, noting that his clothes seemed to hang off his body. His kind blue eyes gazed at her with a sense of warmth. She smiled at him, but a part of her was still resistant to the idea that this man would be a good match for Holly.

"Thank you," Clara said with a curtsy.

"Miss Smyth has told me so much about you, your grace. She arrived little more than an hour ago. I'm so pleased that you could attend our humble hunt," he said with a nod, before turning to Silas. "And I heard you are an acquaintance of my nephew, your grace. Gavin is my brother's only son and the heir to this barony."

"Gavin rarely mentions that he's set to inherit a title," Silas said.

A shadow passed over the elder man's face. Clara was curious what seemed to bother the baron, but she kept her face blank.

"Yes, well, Gavin is rather preoccupied with his own gallivanting, isn't he?" He smiled, but Clara felt like he was speaking as if he were guessing at his nephew's activities. But the baron extended his arm behind him and changed the subject. "I'm sure your journey was long and you wish to settle in. Shall we?"

Clara pushed her speculations out of her mind as she took Silas's hand and was escorted into the house. After a brief tour of their rooms, the baron left Clara and Violet with Silas so that they might recover from their journey. Once they were put to rights, Clara sought out her sister-in-law and they headed down to the parlor where several guests were conversing.

Clara noticed the Trembley brothers right away and they each gave her a welcoming smile. Surprisingly, Fredrick was wearing a sling around his arm. Clara took a moment to wonder what had happened, but she was distracted when a familiar face peered into her view.

"Holly!" she exclaimed. She was wearing a peach colored gown, her curled hair adorned in pearl pins. "I'm so happy to see you."

"And I you," she said, turning to face Clara's sister-in-law. She curtsied. "How do you do, Lady Violet?"

"Very well, thank you," Violet said, her gaze falling back to Fredrick. "Miss Smyth, do you know what happened to Mr. Trembley's arm?"

"Well, yes, actually," Holly said, peering over her shoulder before returning her attention to Clara and Violet. "Supposedly, Mr. Trembley was racing his horse with several friends in London last week and fell from his horse when a carriage had turned a corner, spooking his steed. Thankfully he only dislocated his shoulder, but his mother has been incensed. He escorted her here to the baron's home for the hunting party as a way to make amends."

"Oh my," Clara said. "Thank goodness he is all right."

"I hear it's quite painful."

There were several other couples, fine ladies and seemingly unimpressed gentlemen who leaned in to whisper to one another as Clara and Violet came into the room. Clara tried to give the impression that she was equally as bored as everyone else, but her heart was pounding viciously. She was quite uncomfortable.

"Oh," Violet said softly, reaching for Clara's wrist as she turned towards her. "He is here."

"Who?"

"David Lutz," she whispered. "Oh heavens, I didn't expect to see him until dinner."

Clara glanced around Violet and saw a young man, possibly only twenty-five or twenty-six, with flaxen hair and an easy smile on his face as he stood in the doorway. He was handsome, Clara supposed, in the way all youthful girls thought a singular sort of man was handsome. He had a charming sort of face and dark, playful eyes that seemed hellbent on seeking out mischief. She could certainly see why Violet was so attracted to him.

Leaning towards Violet, she whispered, "I think he's searching for you."

Violet blanched.

"Oh no, I couldn't possibly speak to him. Not after everything I've written to him."

"Chin up, it will be all right," Clara said hurriedly as the man approached. She gave him a bright smile and gently turned Violet around to face him.

"Clara, this is Mr. David Lutz. Mr. Lutz, this is my sister-in-law, Clara Winters, the Duchess of Combe."

"Your grace," he said with a deep bow. "It is a pleasure to make your acquaintance," he added, coming back up, his eyes set on Violet. "Lady Violet. It is wonderful to see you again."

"Y-yes," Violet stuttered.

He turned back to Clara.

"I'm so grateful to have been invited to the baron's hunt. I am anxious to meet Lady Violet's brother."

"Mr. Lutz…" Violet said with a slight shake of her head.

"Then it is fortunate that you would be invited to a party that my husband is attending," Clara said, her brow knit with confusion over Violet's uncharacteristic shyness. "Tell me, how are you acquainted with the baron?"

The young man's eyes flashed with excitement.

"The baron has sponsored my writing career for two years now. He's even been kind enough to mentor my work. He's a talented writer himself and knows nearly everyone in publishing." His cheer seemed to dissipate for a moment. "I hope I will be able to repay him for his kindness one day."

"I'm sure you will," Clara said, peering around the room. "I don't see the baron at the moment."

"No, I believe he and a few of the men have gone to see his latest acquisition."

"What is that?"

"A brewery building," Mr. Lutz said. "The baron finds himself enraptured by a new venture from time to time. Last year, he was fascinated by glass blowing. I'm not sure why, but he tends to obsess and buy a business outright—but then he bores of it just as quickly."

"He must be a well-versed man to have so many interests."

"He is, but just as fast as he falls in love, he falls out of it," he said smiling. "Still, his resale skills are unparalleled. He's always quite successful at relieving himself of those same businesses."

"Then may he find many more indeed," Clara said, matching the young man's smile, while something seemed to tickle at the back of her neck.

Mr. Lutz began speaking with Violet, but Clara barely heard their conversation as her smile dipped away and her gaze drifted down past the young man to the floor just behind him. It was the strangest feeling. Almost as if she could tell she was being watched.

She turned slightly, her eyes snapped back up to the parlor entryway when she saw him. Silas was watching her intently as

Lord Bairnsdale explained something to him.

Clara felt her heart thud against her chest, a strange, fluttery feeling seemed to climb up into her throat as she glanced at her husband. His face was blank, but she couldn't help but feel pinned to the spot where she stood.

In the next minute, Silas approached her, leaving a slightly confused Lord Bairnsdale behind. Why should he appear so striking, Clara wondered as she pulled her shoulder back. He was so handsome and she was aware some might melt beneath his hard gaze, but she felt rather pleased to be the entire focus of his attention.

When he finally reached her, she nearly spoke when he did.

"Violet," Silas said, his tone unreadable.

Clara closed her mouth, suddenly aware of her sister-in-law at her side. Turning, she saw the pair leaning rather closely to one another. To Clara's surprise, Mr. Lutz was holding Violet's hand, palm up, and pointing at the creases with his forefinger. It was close to being improper.

Mr. Lutz dropped Violet's hand, and Clara felt momentarily unbalanced.

"Your grace," Mr. Lutz said with a bow. "I was just showing Lady Violet a palm reading trick I learned from a Romany woman in Austria when I was there this past spring. A most fascinating practice."

"I'm sure it is," Silas said, sounding as if he thought the exact opposite.

Neither man spoke and it was obvious Silas was dismissing the young man, but the worry on Violet's face prompted Clara to try and smooth things over between the two.

"Mr. Lutz was telling us about the baron's brewery. Apparently, it's right here, on the property," she said facing Silas. "Has he shown it to you?"

One of his black brows lifted.

"He has."

"I find it fascinating," Clara lied, turning to Violet. "Violet and

I were wondering if we might be able to take a tour."

Silas tilted his head and looked back and forth between his wife and his sister.

"Is that so?"

"Oh yes." Violet nodded dramatically.

"I would be more than happy to show you the brewery," Mr. Lutz said, his smile dropping at the glare Silas gave him. "With your permission of course, your grace."

"I think the baron would be happy to give us a tour," Silas said as Violet's hopeful face turned sour. "Tomorrow."

"Of course," Mr. Lutz said, seemingly eager to be out of their company. "Ah, if you'll excuse me, I've something of importance to discuss with Mr. Trembley."

With that, the young man left. Violet turned to her brother, a picture of serene feminine composure.

"Why must you ruin everything?" she asked through smiling teeth.

"Curb your dramatics," Silas replied. "I didn't ruin anything."

"Didn't you? He probably thinks I'm a fool," she hissed back. She leaned toward Clara. "Come, Clara, lest we be berated for having a conversation."

Clara wasn't exactly sure why Violet seemed so put out by her brother, but she certainly couldn't choose between the two. To pick Violet would be a mark against Silas, and to choose Silas would lose her a trusted confidant in Violet.

With both of them staring at her, Clara was struck with a brilliant idea.

"You know," she said, hoping to distract the two from their disagreement. "I've always heard that plays are put on at these sorts of gatherings."

Both Silas and Violet gawked at Clara. She swallowed as Silas's brow creased. He shook his head, confused.

"Excuse me?" Silas asked.

"A play?" Violet repeated.

"That's what happens at big house parties like this, isn't it? I should very much like to, well, you know. Do all the things I've suspected these parties to pertain to," she said before turning to Violet. "And I'm sure a young author would take particular interest in the works of playwrights, no?"

Clara felt Silas's glare on her check, but she refused to acknowledge him. Neither sibling spoke for a moment, and Clara was sure they were debating on whether she sounded ridiculous, when Violet nodded slowly.

"A play. That is an idea. A romantic play," she added, challenging her brother. "And you and I will put it on, Clara."

"Of course," Clara replied, not terribly thrilled with the idea of speaking in front of everyone, but happy to distract her sister-in-law. "I'm sure the baron has a book or two of plays, considering Mr. Lutz's praise for the baron's taste."

"Yes, I shall go ask him," she said before departing.

Clara smiled as she watched Violet leave, happy to have avoided whatever it was that had been building.

"You're managing us," Silas said quietly at her side.

Clara turned to face him.

"You don't mind my handling, do you?" she asked, alluding to something else.

Silas grinned down at her.

"No, not at all," he said softly.

Clara felt a thrill go through her, feeling particularly excited about the coming days. Surely this would be a week to remember.

Chapter Seventeen

SILAS'S EYES OPENED while it was still dark.

He hadn't been pleased to see Clara smiling so warmly at Mr. Lutz. He'd had to beat down the aggravating jealousy that all but consumed him in those moments when he entered the parlor yesterday afternoon. Upon discovering Violet's connection to the young author, Silas had hoped to push his sister away from Mr. Lutz, but it was Clara's close proximity to the smiling young man that had affected him most. He knew Clara wasn't they type to try and make him jealous, but memories from his past had gripped him and refused to let go. Soon, he was feeling the familiar tinges of anxiety bubbling beneath the surface.

It bothered him to recognize his jealousy and anxiety seemed to be muddled together. Surely he wouldn't start having attacks every time his wife smiled at someone.

Would he?

Silas had been up with the dawn that morning to join the others for the hunt. He had been able to garner that the baron was a patron to Mr. Lutz, which was even more of a reason to stop Violet's infatuation with him. The poor man could barely afford to support himself, let alone a wife and children. Even though they would be able to live comfortably on Violet's dowry, Silas wasn't interested in his sister becoming some sort of benefactress to her own husband. He had no wish to see her settle for someone who couldn't even provide for her. No, it would be best to shift the young man's focus a bit.

Mr. Lutz had gone off the main path that cut through the forest and seemed to be struggling to get his horse back to the others. Coming up alongside him, Silas noted how uncomfortable the young man was on horseback. Finally, Mr. Lutz noticed him.

"Ah, your grace," Mr. Lutz said. "A fine day for a hunt, wouldn't you say?"

"Yes," Silas said. "Are you fond of hunting, Mr. Lutz?"

"Well, I've not had the pleasure to do so often," he said as he tried to duck beneath a branch. "But it seems to be a pleasant form of exercise." Another branch caught his cheek and he batted it away. "To be honest, I've rarely ridden on horseback."

"You don't say."

"Well, I suppose I'm not terribly clever at hiding my lack of riding skills. But there's so rarely a need to ride in London. Not when I could walk or go by hackney."

Silas wondered if the expense of keeping a horse stabled would also be an issue. Clearing his throat, he turned his horse to the left, avoiding a downed tree.

"I've heard you've written a series, for the *Times*. Is that so?"

"Yes, I have. Although it hasn't quite garnered the amount of attention I hoped it would. It is my own fault. I thought the people of London would be quite interested in the American wilds."

Silas reined his horse to a stop.

"I didn't know you had traveled to the Americas."

"Oh, well... I haven't. But I have read about it. That's why I believe my next piece will do quite well."

"What is your next piece about?"

Mr. Lutz smiled.

"It takes place in New Orleans. Fascinating city, or so I'm told. My antagonist, a Mr. Dubois, is a merchant. Well, not quite a merchant. He has hopes of becoming one."

"Is that so?" Silas said, completely uninterested. He had

planned to steer the young man to taking a holiday and focus more on novel writing than serials, but another opportunity had presented itself. "You are aware that the baron speaks very highly of your writing."

Mr. Lutz flushed.

"Has he spoken about it with you?"

"He has. For my part, I find that what's lacking in serials is authenticity."

"Authenticity?"

"Yes. I find that I can always tell a writer who has experienced life's tribulations compared to one who hasn't." He flicked his horse, as they continued through the woods. "For instance, have you read *The Solider*, by E. S. Helms? About Colonel Lennox and the events leading up to the Battle of Quatre Bras?"

"I have, yes."

"And how did you find it?"

"Well, honestly, I found it rather derivative."

"I agree, and that's because E. S. Helms didn't serve in the war."

"Yes, but he did interview Colonel Lennox extensively, as well as many of the generals from that engagement."

Silas waved his hand.

"But imagine what it would have been like had Lennox written the book himself," he said, watching the young man's face. "I imagine a book written in the colonel's own hand would have been vastly more interesting and far from derivative."

"I suppose so," Mr. Lutz said, his tone unsure. "But Helms did have success with his book."

"Because it was a successful topic. Now, had he been there firsthand and written about it, I think it would have been far more successful."

"I suppose that is true. I myself find words written from firsthand experiences to be infinitely more interesting."

"And a talent like yours, Mr. Lutz, shouldn't be squandered on secondhand knowledge."

He turned to Silas.

"Do you mean I should go visit New Orleans if I'm set on writing about it?"

Silas shrugged, hoping to appear disinterested.

"I cannot say, but for your craft, I think it would be worth it."

Mr. Lutz frowned.

"But I've never been away from England. I don't even have the means to travel," he said, before realization dawned on his face. Tipping his chin up, he continued. "Besides, I have too many people I care for who I could not abandon."

Silas fought the urge to roll his eyes.

"I'm sure you do," he said stiffly. "Well, good luck to you then, Mr. Lutz. I look forward to reading your next piece based on the experiences of others."

Tucking his heel into the side of his horse, Silas galloped ahead of the young man, confident that his words had affected him.

Silas and the rest of the men spent the remainder of the morning moving across the baron's forests and fields. By noon, they had decided to return to the house. Silas had observed Mr. Lutz speaking with the baron and two other gentlemen on their way back to the stables and wondered if his plan was working.

Upon his return to the manse, Silas had learned that his wife and sister were in the library, researching the play they hoped to put on. Reaching the library, he saw that the Trembley brothers had been recruited as well as Holly. Two other young ladies, who were giggling while reading their respective parts, were tucked away in the corner, eyeing the Trembley men with interest.

Clara was directing the entire thing, seemingly happy to be out of the spotlight. When she saw Silas approach she went to stand, but he shook his head to dissuade her from making a fuss on his account. He wanted to watch her and so she continued reading at his unspoken command.

"This is a bit flowery, is it not?" the youngest Trembley, Alfred, said. "People don't talk like this at all."

"How would you know?" the other Trembley, Fredrick spoke, wincing slightly. His arm was drawn up in a sling around his neck. "You never could woo a lady."

The two cloistered ladies laughed gently behind their hands, but Violet seemed determined.

"Great men throughout history have always commanded the English language to their advantage," she said, her shoulders pulled back as if to demonstrate said command. "Besides, I'll have you know that their greatest treasure is a fair lady's attention."

"God forbid I ever receive the attention of a lady who thinks this piece is any good," Fredrick mumbled, causing his brother Alfred to snicker and earning a piercing glare from Violet.

"Are you refusing to play your part?"

"It's trite. Listen to this." Fredrick held the book up and cleared his throat. When he spoke, he changed his voice dramatically. *"Tell me dearest, what is love? 'Tis a lightning from above, 'Tis an arrow, 'tis a fire, 'Tis a boy they call desire. 'Tis a smile Doth beguile."* Fredrick sneered with disgust. "It's awful."

"It's beautiful," Violet challenged, glaring at him. "Beaumont was a genius."

"No, he wasn't. Everyone only assumes he was because no one wants to think for themselves."

"I quite like Beaumont," Holly chimed in, flipping through her book.

"See?" Violet said, as if Holly's taste confirmed something.

"Well, I don't," Alfred stated.

Fredrick tilted his head towards his brother, though his gaze never left Violet. She let out a half sigh, half growl.

"I don't see why you insist on being here then," she snapped. "If only Mr. Lutz was available…"

Silas was curious as to why Mr. Lutz hadn't joined them, but then he had overheard the baron say something about wanting him to make the acquaintance of a gentleman who had recently returned from New York. For Mr. Lutz, the request of his patron would have to come before everything else. He paid the young man's bills after all.

"Believe me, I'd trade places with Mr. Lutz in a heartbeat, if I hadn't dislocated my shoulder," Fredrick said, painfully lifting his arm that sat in a sling. "Although compared to this play, I think I'd rather have my other arm broken."

"One wonders if your shoulder's dislocation also dislocated your good taste."

"Well, I've always found plays at house parties a bore, especially when Beaumont is involved, so I don't think my tastes have shifted."

Violet glared at him.

"You arrogant—"

"Now, now, let's not fall into an argument," Clara said, motioning with her hands to settle those around her. "Some people enjoy Beaumont, some do not. There is no right or wrong answer."

By the expressions on Fredrick and Violet's faces, it seemed there was very much a right and wrong answer. After a long moment, Violet squared her shoulders and turned away from Fredrick.

"It doesn't matter," she said. "A good actor could make the worst lines poetry. I doubt Mr. Trembley could summon enough emotion to display any ability even to his own mother."

"Now see here," Fredrick started, his tone agitated.

"Please," Clara started again, standing up now. "There's no need to argue."

"Silas never questioned the material when we did plays. Did you, Silas?" Violet said, turning to her brother.

Everyone in the room turned to look at Silas.

Bloody. Hell.

"Keep me out of this, Violet," he said, batting down the abrupt feelings of discomfort that came when he was the center of attention.

"But you were always the epitome of perfection when it came to our plays."

"Plays?" Clara repeated, turning to fully face him. A slow smile crept over her visage. "You wrote plays?"

"Violet wrote plays," Silas corrected, giving his sister a withering glance. "I only performed in them."

"Please, Silas, will you read the part of Jasper? Just to show these other gentlemen how to do it properly," Violet said. "The way it should be done."

Silas was very close to saying no when Clara spoke up.

"Oh, yes, please do," she said, mirth in her eyes. "I'd very much like to hear it."

Silas silently swore to make Violet pay for this. But in the meantime, he wouldn't let Clara push him out on stage alone.

He grinned wickedly at her.

"Of course," he said, coming forward. "If my wife will play Luce."

Clara's eyes went wide.

"Oh no—"

"Oh yes, please do, Clara," Holly said, beaming at her friend. "It will be a pleasure to see."

Clara glared at her friend then at Silas, who was glad to have caught her. She seemed rather uncomfortable with the idea, but then stood up, determination on her face. Silas hadn't fully appreciated the gown she wore that day and was pleasantly surprised to see the seafoam dress. Though they hadn't been to London since their wedding, Silas had recognized that Clara's gowns had changed. He'd learned from his mother that the maids at Greystone had taken it upon themselves to remove the excess beading on her apparel, and the results had been fantastic. The one she wore now, for example, appeared much simpler, allowing Clara's beauty to be highlighted instead of lost in competition. He also appreciated that its cut was generous to her curves, and he liked the way the color of the material seemed to light up her eyes.

She walked towards him, stopping when she reached him. Holly handed them a book and winked at Clara.

"Good luck," she said with a grin.

"You'll read from the same page," Violet said, pointing to the passage.

"Very well," Silas said. "Shall I begin where you left off, Mr. Trembley?"

"By all means," he said, smirking.

Silas took a deep breath and read.

"The poor hearts of men that prove. Tell me more, are women true?"

Clara leaned over the book they shared, held open in Silas's hand. He inhaled the sweet, familiar scent of her hair.

"Some love change, and so do you," she said.

"Are they fair, and never kind?" he asked, feeling oddly connected to these words.

"Yes, when men turn with the wind."

"Are they froward?"

"Ever toward, those that love, to love anew," Clara said, her cheeks turning a sweet shade of pink.

Silas was very aware how close they were standing to one another. While they were married, it felt slightly illicit. These ridiculous words seemed rather familiar, even if they had never spoken them before, and they seemed to be having some sort of effect on them.

"Dissemble it no more, I see the God of heavy sleep, lay on his heavy mace upon your eyelids."

"I am very heavy."

"Sleep, sleep, and quiet rest crown thy sweet thoughts: Keep from her fair blood, distempers, startings, Horrors. and fearful shapes: let all her dreams Be joys, and chaste delights, embraces, wishes, and such new pleasures, as the ravished soul Gives to the senses. So, my charms have taken. Keep her you power divine, whilst I contemplate Upon the wealth and beauty of her mind. She is only fair, and constant: only kind, And only to thee."

When his gaze lifted, the warmth in Clara's eyes set his heart on edge. What a bizarre feeling to have. He had been aware of Clara in every way for months, but he felt in that moment as if another layer of her had been revealed. It was quite like witnessing a rose bloom before his eyes. Caught up in it, he hardly registered the sudden shift in the air that happened around them.

But then a cold snap shot down his spine, and he frowned.

"Well, how sweet," an eerily emotionless, familiar female voice echoed into the room.

Chapter Eighteen

SILAS DIDN'T HAVE to turn around to know who it was. By the expression on Clara's face, he knew she was just as surprised as he. Turning around he saw Violet, Holly, and the others in the room holding a collective breath as they faced the entrance way of the library. Eyes following their direction, he saw Cynthia, the former Duchess of Combe, enter the room, on the arm of a tall, finely dressed blonde man who had an air of arrogance about him.

Tension seemed to crackle in the air, but Silas was hardly concerned about it. He had often imagined what it would be like to meet her again, face to face, but the only thing he could think to do was take a step in front of Clara, in an effort to protect her as well as a stab at self-preservation. Strangely enough, his anxiety didn't rise at all as everyone in the room turned to see him, waiting.

It seemed no one would address her until Silas did so first.

For a moment he considered grabbing Clara and his sister and leaving the room without acknowledging her, but before he could decide, he found Clara's hand on the back of his arm. The small warmth from her curled fingers gave him pause. All the while, Clara kept her eyes fixed on Cynthia.

Turning back to face her, he cleared his throat.

"Cynthia," he said quietly, his eyes hard.

A flash of something, challenge perhaps, shone in her eyes as she and her escort stopped their advance. They were a few yards away from him and Clara. Cynthia's long neck stretched as she peered over Silas's shoulder.

"Is that Violet?" she asked, her voice a soft coo. "My, how you've grown in only a year."

"Nearly two years now," Violet said after a moment of silence.

It was evident that she didn't wish to betray her brother, but the stilted hope of seeing a former confidant was obvious in the sound of her voice. Violet remained immobile, however.

Cynthia cocked her head.

"Come, friend," she said, hands outstretched. "I wish to see you closely."

Violet didn't move and Silas saw displeasure pass over Cynthia's face. Instead, Violet turned to her brother, as if waiting for his signal. As he looked up, he saw that everyone was watching him. He needed to be cautious. Whatever move he made, whatever word he spoke next, would solidify Cynthia's treatment for years to come.

A surge of vengeance coursed through him, urging him to make her pay for the pain she caused him. But it was a dull feeling, not as strong as it had been before. Clara's fingers neither released him nor tightened, but they remained as if she were giving him support in whatever he chose to do. In truth, he would have liked for Cynthia to disappear.

Instead, he glanced back down at Clara once more. She was staring at him with patience and understanding. In that moment, he felt very glad indeed that she was his wife. Turning to his left, he nodded at Violet before facing Cynthia once more.

Cynthia, who had always been very attuned to body language, was visibly displeased at the display. Firstly, that Violet had chosen her brother instead of her and then, Silas's lack of reaction. He could guess what she was searching for. She fed off emotion, good or bad. Had he been pleased to see her, she would've relished it. If he had been furious, even more so. But indifference? That was something she could not stand. He hadn't done so on purpose, though. Silas couldn't muster any sort of feeling, good or bad, towards her now.

Violet took a step towards her, but Cynthia held up her hand to stop her, instead trying a different approach.

"Miss Clara Woodvine," she said, a sneer in her tone. "What a stellar choice, Silas. I have read about you, Miss Woodvine. It truly is a pleasure to meet you. I had hoped Silas would find a suitable replacement one day."

The cut was intentional and obvious, but before Silas could speak, Clara took the smallest of steps around him, seemingly unwilling to be protected. In fact, she came to stand in front of him.

"My name is Clara Winters," Clara started, her sweet, even tone hard as steel. "Duchess of Combe." Her title seemed to echo through the room and challenge snapped between the two women. "Unfortunately, my dear husband has married a prideful woman. Pride is in fact my worst sin, and while I do pray that the good Lord helps relieve me of such a vile attribute, I'm afraid he hasn't thus far. Therefore, you may address me as 'your grace' to appease my wicked sense of self."

Cynthia's mouth set in a hard line; her eyes lit with acrimony. Rarely, if ever, had she been set upon by someone, especially in front of a room full of people. Silas had never heard Clara speak so calmly yet forcefully towards another human being. While he was rather pleased that she had been so straightforward and earnest, a part of him wanted to tell her she needn't bother. Cynthia's presence, while a nuisance, was not worth the aggravation. Nor would it be worth her retaliation.

Just then the expensively dressed man who had been standing next to Cynthia came forward.

"Your graces," he said with a bow of his head. "May I introduce myself? I am Lord Randall Valle, son of the Earl of Pinehill."

"Lord Valle," Clara said, the picture of manners.

"You'll have to forgive my fiancée," he said slowly as his words seeped through the room. "We have been out of England for so long, she may have forgotten etiquette altogether. You see, we've been in Paris for over a year."

So, she was to be remarried. Silas was rather numb in that moment and couldn't quite think of anything to say. He might have reacted before marrying Clara—in fact, he was sure he would have—but as monumental of a revelation as it was that Cynthia was engaged, it seemed to fall a little short of making him care.

How very strange.

"Well, I've heard rumors that Paris will do that to one's manners," Clara replied smoothly, unaffected by the news.

Silas had to admit that he was surprised that Cynthia had decided to marry again, but the surprise did not affect him in the way he thought it would. There was no heat behind his heart, no anger. To be honest, he only felt a sort of mild pity for the young lord.

"There's no need to apologize for me, Randall," Cynthia said, turning to Clara. "Your grace—"

"Thank you very much, Lady Cynthia," Clara said, cutting her off. "While it has been thrilling to finally meet you, I'm afraid we are rather pressed for time. We're rehearsing a play, you see, and I don't want our players to be unprepared for our performance. So, if you'll excuse us."

"I—"

"Thank you for understanding and I look forward to continuing our conversation again during dinner. Good day."

Clara turned her back on Cynthia who, while nearly shaking with fury, turned to leave, if only to stop herself from being ridiculous. Silas knew Cynthia would seek revenge for being so humiliated by Clara and while he would never have assumed Clara was capable of behaving like that, a small, selfish part of him had been thrilled. She had put Cynthia in her place immediately. She hadn't cowered or waited for Cynthia to embarrass her.

Still, it might not have been the best idea to anger Cynthia. She was a reactive, volatile person as Silas could attest, and Clara had certainly incurred her wrath. Clara, on the other hand, had hardly seemed affected. Everyone went back to their respective spots, including Fredrick, quietly taking over his role as Jasper. It seemed everyone involved with the play had decided to behave themselves under Clara's direction, who had taken a seat in a tall, wingback chair.

Silas watched her for a moment, noticing that she appeared the picture of demure serenity, except for her foot. The heel of her right foot was bouncing rather uncontrollably beneath her skirts.

Without thinking, Silas went to her, bent down and kissed the corner of her face, just at the temple, in front of everyone. It was a chaste kiss and one that hardly conveyed anything important, but Clara looked up at him with surprise.

"What are you doing?" she asked breathlessly, her cheeks coloring at such an open display of affection. "There are people here."

"Indeed," he said before glancing up at everyone else. "I'm afraid I have an appointment with the baron. If you'll excuse me."

Silas bowed and left the room, feeling the eyes of everyone on his back. He intended to find the old baron and learn why Cynthia was here.

Surely the old man hadn't done something like this on purpose? If so, it would demand consequences. Silas truly hoped the baron had simply made a mistake, because if he had purposely tried to humiliate his wife, Silas wouldn't be able to hold back his growing fury.

Oddly enough, his anger seemed to eat away any anxiety he might have felt over Cynthia's arrival. Was it because anger was more prominent an emotion? Or could it be that Clara's presence had given him some sort of underlying strength to face Cynthia?

Unwilling to dwell too long on such intrusive thoughts, Silas stalked down the hallway until he reached the baron's private study. Without knocking, Silas stepped into the room, finding the baron sat behind his desk.

The old man's soft blue eyes lifted beneath his white brows as he sat back in his chair.

"Ah, Combe. I was just—"

"What is your game, Bairnsdale?" Silas all but snapped. "Why is Cynthia here?"

The old man frowned.

"Cynthia? Who the devil is Cynthia?" the baron asked before his eyes opened wide as the connection was made. "Good lord, the woman accompanying Lord Valle, Lady Cynthia, is *your* Lady Cynthia?"

"She is not mine," Silas said.

The old baron stood up and came around his desk, shaking his head.

"I was unaware of it, I assure you. Pinehill is an old friend, and I always invite his offspring to this party. I was unaware young Lord Valle had even become engaged until he arrived. Pinehill and his son are on the outs, you understand, and I've been trying to see if I could broker a sort of peace between them, but I had no idea that he would bring a companion here." He frowned unhappily. "I offer my sincerest apologies, Combe."

"It's not your fault," Silas said, the heat of his anger dissipating. "I was just rather surprised. As was my wife."

"Your wife!" the baron repeated, angst in his voice. "Oh dear, how uncomfortable this will be. I'm so sorry this has happened."

"Nonsense," Silas said, shaking his head. It was apparent the baron was mortified. He didn't wish to add on to it. He cleared his throat. "We're all adults, Bairnsdale. It will be fine."

"Are you sure? I would have them leave, truly, except that I had so hoped to be able to bring Lord Valle and his father into reconciliation. I owe the man a debt, and this seemed an excellent way to repay it."

"It's fine," Silas said. He didn't want to cause Bairnsdale any trouble. Even though Cynthia's presence had been an unfortunate surprise, he wouldn't have her thrown out and appear as though he were still affected by her. "Do not trouble yourself."

Bairnsdale looked as if he didn't believe a word of it, but nodded, his forehead puckered with worry.

Silas left the baron's office, unsure of what to do. He supposed there was always the option to leave himself, but the idea had barely formed in his mind before he pushed it out. He had given into his own anxiety for far too long where Cynthia was concerned and he wouldn't continue to do so. He was a duke for God's sake, and though he had once suffered heartbreak at Cynthia's hands, he wouldn't dishonor Clara.

The image of his wife, her pin-straight back when she faced Cynthia, made him feel both proud and hostile. He wanted to protect Clara from all the hardships of the world, especially the hurt that Cynthia could cause but she had stood up to her, fearlessly if not recklessly.

The devil himself would be wary at the prospect of facing Cynthia.

Then, as if the mere thought of her had summoned her like a demon, Silas rounded the corner of the hallway and crashed directly into her.

"Oh!" Cynthia said, her hands held up to brace herself as she caught him by the lapels to steady herself.

When she realized who it was, her surprised eyes flickered with excitement. Her fingers pressed into his chest as she leaned forward. Annoyed that she seemed to think this was a game, he glowered down at her.

"A word. Now," he said as he headed down the hallway. Seeing a door slightly ajar, he walked to it. Peering into the room, he found that it was some sort of private drawing room and that it was currently unoccupied. He held the door open and waited for Cynthia to cross the threshold.

Her brow arched and she deliberately took her time as she crossed the hallway and entered the room. He had to beat down the desire to push her forward as he closed the door, but he was instantly set upon.

Cynthia's arms moved around his neck as she tried to press her body against his, but he recoiled from her in disgust, pushing her backward. She stumbled as her face turned thunderous.

"What is the matter with you?" she asked, smoothing her skirts. "What else do you want to do in private?"

"What are you doing here?"

Her expression changed in that moment from annoyance to intrigue. Smiling a wicked smile, she took a step toward him.

"To see you, of course," she said, her tone sickly sweet. "It's been far too long."

"We're divorced. Or have you forgotten?"

"How could I? When every lady from here to Greece won't seem to let me forget," she said bitterly.

Then Silas saw it. Regret. Cynthia had not been able to live down her divorce. While she had often been able to thumb her nose at society's dictates, protected from notoriety by her wealth and status, it seemed she had finally gone too far. Their divorce had demoted her position. Now, instead of a duke's daughter or wife, she was a divorcee.

"Not for long," he said slowly as he watched her as if she were a snake set to strike. "Your Lord Valle is set to have you."

"And what good will that weakling be to me?" she all but spat. "He's disowned by his father, though Valle believes that our marriage should satisfy the old bastard enough to resume his allowance. I had to be engaged to even think about travelling back to this godforsaken country." Her eyes flashed with mischief. "But I am grateful to be back. I've been in the company of foolish boys for far too long. I've missed what it's like to be with a real man."

"Tired of pulling their strings, are you?"

Her eyes squinted.

"I've never had any complaints, but yes. It's wearisome," she said, taking another step forward. "He isn't half the man that you are, you know." She took another step, as her voice turned soft.

"I've missed you, Silas."

How long had he ached to hear those words from her mouth? For far too long he had hoped for Cynthia to return. She had broken his trust a thousand times, and yet he still would have taken her back in an instant back when he was still under her spell. But she had left him behind, and his eyes had finally opened to who she truly was. He had realized that the woman he had loved had never truly existed.

Ignoring her words, he continued.

"I want you to listen to me, Cynthia. There is no place for you in my life and I won't have you making problems for anyone associated with me. Do I make myself clear?"

Cynthia's eyes flashed with challenge. She sauntered up to him and he wanted to retreat, but he knew better than to show her weakness.

The familiar deep buzzing of Silas's unease began to cumulate beneath his skin. This was the beginning of his anxiety, but for some reason it felt further away than usual, almost as though it was trying to reach him over a vast distance. It had been suffocating before, all-encompassing whenever he'd experienced it only months earlier, but when Silas recognized the panicky feeling, his thoughts instantly turned to Clara's words.

Let it be.

Her ridiculously simple words had aggravated him when she first spoke them, but he now found a strange sort of comfort and strength in the simplicity of her sentence. He took a deep breath and repeated her words in his mind as he turned his attentions back to Cynthia. She would not summon anything from him. Not anger, not worry, not fear.

Instantly, Silas felt as if a chain that had been wrapped around his lungs had snapped. It was an odd, light sort of feeling such as he hadn't known for years.

Let it be. Let it be.

"My, how grave you've become, Silas," she said, her tone sultry. Her hand reached up and touched his face. "Since when have you become the aggressor?"

Silas's hand seized her wrist, and she gasped. The pleasure that surfaced in her eyes would once have set his body on fire. But now he only felt cold.

"Keep away from me and my wife," he said, tossing her arm away from him.

The mention of his wife caused Cynthia's face to cloud with hostility.

"What are you doing with such a crass peasant, Silas?" she asked, her voice annoyed once more. "She's not even of your class."

"Don't speak of her."

Her eyes rounded. "Or is that why you decided on her? Couldn't stand to be the weak one any longer so you sought out someone whose strength was half of yours."

Such words might once have riled him up but Cynthia's game was monotonous at this point.

"Strength is something you know nothing about," he said quietly, ignoring the fury in her eyes. "Although from what I can tell of your upcoming nuptials, that must be your plan with Valle."

"How dare you?" she asked as her hand came up to strike him, but he was too quick. Once again, he caught her wrist in his hand and as his grip tightened, he saw her desire heighten. Her moods flickered like the flame of a candle. "Oh, Silas."

He dropped her hand again.

"Stay away, Cynthia. Or so help me God, I will finish you."

He turned and tore open the door, storming down the hallway without a backward glance. He was nearly around the corner when he heard her yell from behind, her voice tinged with sick amusement.

"I wish you would! I truly wish you would."

Chapter Nineteen

CLARA HEARD THE actors perform their lines, but her head and heart were miles away. So, that was Cynthia, the woman who had robbed Silas of his heart and broken it into a thousand pieces. She hadn't expected her reaction to be so visceral, but she hadn't been able to stop herself.

When the woman had first entered the library, it seemed no one had noticed, except Clara had experienced a chill just before Cynthia had spoken. A flash of pain shone in Silas's eyes before he turned to face her and while he had originally stepped in front of Clara, she had felt the distinct need to protect him from Cynthia, as much as she could.

She had held her head high and tried desperately to sound indifferent and dignified. She knew Silas was helplessly tied to her. It hurt her heart to think that he could love a woman like Cynthia and not her, but she couldn't ponder on that for too long or her heart would truly start to ache. Instead, she did her best to spend another hour dictating the others into positions and reminding them about their enunciation, while also keeping Fredrick and Violet away from one another. Those two seemed hellbent on bickering for argument's sake and while Clara might have enjoyed watching the verbal parley any other time, her mind was indeed elsewhere.

Just then, Holly came to sit next to her.

"Are you all right?" she asked softly as they watched the others perform. Clara nodded, but didn't speak. "I'm so sorry that happened."

"What could be done?" Clara asked honestly, her voice barely above a whisper.

"I wonder if John was aware of who she truly is," Holly said, her brow knitting together. "It does not seem like something he would manage on purpose."

"I doubt the baron was aware of her coming. She seems the kind of woman to show up when she chooses to, doesn't she?"

"I suppose. Perhaps I should speak with John about it. He could ask them to leave—"

"Oh goodness, no, Holly. I will not be cowed by that woman. Not in front of Silas."

The mention of her husband's name caused Holly to appear even more worried.

"He must be furious."

"He isn't pleased."

"I can't imagine what it would be like. To be suddenly face to face with someone who was once your spouse. What he must be thinking."

Although Holly had clearly meant to be sympathetic to Silas, Clara couldn't help but feel as if her friend had pointed out something grievous. What would it be like to be faced with someone who he had been so intimate with? Clara had never intruded on Silas's private yearnings, but she had found herself wondering what had transpired between Cynthia and him.

Silas didn't appear pleased at all at the sight of her, but would there not be memories between them? Clara felt her face grow warm with jealousy as the others finished the scene. She mumbled a few words to them before leaving the library, eagerly beating down the feelings of envy that were overwhelming her. In truth, by the time Clara reached her rooms to get ready for dinner, she was less than excited to happen upon Silas, who was seated at the desk in their room.

"Oh," she said, coming into the room, stalling for a moment at the sight of him. He was without a jacket and his shirtsleeves were rolled up, probably in an effort to keep ink from getting on his cuffs. She ignored the surge of need and swallowed. "I didn't realize you were here."

He stood up and came towards her, and she felt trapped.

"How are you?" he asked, his eyes filled with concern.

"Fine," she said, feeling uneasy.

He stood before her, unmoving for a long moment before he spoke again.

"I think we should talk," he said and for some reason Clara felt a warning shoot through her. "About getting through the next few days."

Was he going to tell her that he was still in love with Cynthia? That he would resume some sort of relationship with her? That their marriage was a mistake?

Clara had rarely ever been so unsure of herself or her life and it shook her to the core.

"There's no need," she said, moving around him in an attempt to avoid the awful conversation he wished to have. "I'm sure there's nothing to say."

She was vaguely aware of him turning as she went towards the wardrobe where her gowns were hanging. The sapphire color gown was probably her most flattering dress, but on the other hand, the soft yellow was darling, she thought to herself, trying desperately to ignore her husband's presence.

"Clara," he said, but she shook her head.

"Silas, I'm quite all right," she said, giving him a false smile.

His eyes seemed to darken at her dismissal, but for the life of her, she couldn't understand why. What really needed to be said, anyway? While Clara supposed she had been rather haughty when talking to Cynthia, she wouldn't feel sorry for it and had no intention of apologizing, even if Silas told her to. She'd felt the need to stake her claim to the title and to her husband. Unlike her predecessor, Clara was happy to be the Duchess of Combe. She was proud to be Silas's wife.

"I'm not," he said lowly, but to Clara it was deafening.

Of course, he wouldn't be. She tried to swallow her foolish feelings. He wouldn't simply be fine seeing the woman who broke his heart. What a fool she was to be standing here, worried about her own silly nonsense.

Dropping her hands from her gowns, she turned to face him.

"I'm sorry, Silas, I didn't even consider how you might feel at seeing her," Clara admitted. "I was so consumed with my own reaction to her that I didn't think of how hurt you must be at confronting her again."

Silas's head cocked slightly, his brow furring above his dark eyes.

"Hurt?" he repeated.

"Well, yes. Aren't you?" she asked, confused.

They stared at one another for a long moment and the shadow that had plagued Silas face vanished. He took a step towards her, his large hands going to her elbows.

"You think seeing her hurt me?"

"Yes," she said. "Didn't it? You said you were not all right."

Silas shook his head.

"My feelings are on your behalf. I hate that there was no warning—that she was sprung upon us so abruptly. I didn't wish for you to ever meet her, let alone be surprised by the encounter."

"Surely you did not think we would never cross paths?" Clara said, confused. "Besides, I was perfectly fine seeing her. I may have been a bit rude, I admit, but it wasn't a traumatic experience."

"I'm glad for that."

A strange, stilted silence followed. Clara was sure there was more to say, she wasn't sure exactly what. She gave him a small smile, which he returned, but when she tried to move out of his grasp, his grip tightened slightly.

Glancing up, she saw a heat in his eyes that hadn't been there before.

"Silas?"

"Is there nothing that phases you?" he asked. "You always seem so wholly unaffected by things that would bother most people."

Clara shrugged.

"Most people care about foolish things," she said softly. "Like their own popularity or importance. I couldn't begin to explain why those things never mattered to me. Perhaps because I spent the first half of my life as a schoolmaster's daughter before my father's inventions gained traction. In that quiet life, I never had hopes of impressing anyone." She inhaled and exhaled slowly, as she averted her eyes, worried about her next words. "But to say I am unaffected would be an understatement. I'm neither happy nor mad that Cynthia is here, nor do I much care what she has done with herself or whom she now intends to marry. I am not interested in her or her escapades in the least. What I do care about... is you." She swallowed, trying to remove the sudden lump in her throat. "I have fears, Silas, and insecurities and worries, just like everyone else. I am half confident, half full of doubt at all times regarding us."

"What do you doubt about us?"

"That no matter how much I might love you, it won't ever be enough to extinguish the pain from your past," she said, ignoring the slight squeeze of his hands at her elbows. She looked up at him, which was a mistake as his face had become thunderous. "I know you said you couldn't love me. And I wouldn't want to force any sort of lie from your lips, but please, Silas, don't... Just don't..."

"Don't what?" he asked.

"Don't be tempted," Clara said as her throat constricted painfully.

For a fragile moment neither of them moved as her words sank in.

Silas's finger dug into her arms as the meaning of her confession seemed to dawn on him.

"You think I would be unfaithful?" he grounded out in a guttural tone.

To Clara's humiliation, tears formed in the corner of her eye. She tried to brush them away, but he held her.

"I don't think you would mean to," she tried. "But she has a power over you."

"She does not."

"She does, Silas," Clara said. "And I am not asking for things you cannot give, but—"

"What word could that woman possibly give that could command me to do anything at all?" he said, his words angry. "She is nothing to me."

If only that were true... but Clara knew it wasn't. He had told her himself that he was incapable of loving her and Clara felt certain that it was because he still held Cynthia in his heart.

Pulling from him slowly, she put her hand to his chest.

"It's all right," she said through tears, cursing them. "I would just like it if you were careful."

That didn't seem to be the correct thing to say, as in the next moment, Silas pulled her fully against his hard body.

"Silas—"

But whatever she was going to say fell away as he kissed her. It was a rough, earnest sort of kiss, one that conveyed anger and need and desire all at once and Clara melted into his hold on her. She was surprised that a kiss could be so punishing and she wondered what she had done to deserve it.

Whatever she did, she found that she didn't really care as she let herself fall in the familiar warmth that always enveloped her when he kissed her. Only a second later, he tore his mouth from hers and found her ear.

"There is no woman, no creature on this earth who could tempt me to be unfaithful to you," he said. His hot, angry breath sent shivers down her shoulders.

Clara was desperate to believe his words, but for the two

months that they had been married, she had seen how utterly consumed he still was by memories of his previous wife. She wanted to believe him and really, he had never shown any sort of signs that he would stoop to unfaithfulness, but having seen Cynthia and the reactions between the two, she just couldn't help worrying. Clara had been accused of a lot of things: poor fashion, ill manners, a lack of respect for her betters, even reaching above her station. But she had never considered herself a fool. Would she be betraying her good sense by believing him?

She didn't speak, unable to alleviate his anger because she wouldn't lie to him. He seemed to read her feelings and his brow cinched together, forming a deeper set of vertical lines between his eyebrows.

"You don't believe me?" he asked, half incredulous, half furious.

Clara opened her mouth to answer him, but Silas silenced her with his mouth. His kiss was filled with anger and determination and she felt herself break as he held her roughly, trying to convey his fury at her lack of faith.

Silas's hands dug into her back as he lifted her body effortlessly and moved her back against the wardrobe door. Clara let out a huff of breath as he kissed her, consuming her with desperation. His mouth was all over her skin and she felt his hand tear at the front of her gown, breaking the fabric with ease.

"Silas!" she said, worried that he'd ruined her gown, but he would not be deterred.

Pulling the bodice of her gown down, Silas's mouth covered her breasts with aggressive kisses, sucking and biting a path down to her nipple. Clara let out a painful cry, but much to her surprise, the hurt she felt wasn't nearly as prominent as the ferocious pleasure that flooded her body.

Clara's body shook and she felt herself become bold. She wanted to meet his desire in every respect. In an instant, her arms fought against the tight bands of steel of his arms and wrapped around his head as she held him tightly to her chest. Letting herself be taken by the basest of feelings, she clawed and tore at the fabric of his jacket as she kissed his forehead.

Encouraged by her reaction, Silas's hands pushed at the fabric of her gown until it slipped past her hips, falling in a heap on the floor. Her chemise was torn, but that didn't seem to register. One of his arms crushed around her waist, clutching her soft form to him while his other hand undid his ties.

Clara breathed in raggedly as his rough touch found the spot between her legs. She groaned as he moved his fingers within her, growling to discover that her body was wet and waiting. Shame might have filled Clara if she had given herself a moment to think, but in the next instant, Silas pushed her up and pulled her down on his hardness, impaling her against the wooden door of the wardrobe.

A curse tore from his mouth as he moved inside of her and Clara's eyes closed as his mouth slid up her neck. She hissed as his tongue moved into her ear, causing a tremor to course through her body. He pushed his hardness deeper into her, far deeper than she believed he ever had and just as she was about to protest, he spoke.

"Take it."

Clara's heart slammed against her chest and her eyes flew open at his words. The biting tone of his command was amplified by his angry gaze and she kept her gaze intently on him, wordlessly accepting every bit of him.

A guttural sound came from him as he pumped into her, causing a ferocious feeling of pleasure to roll within her. Lord above, she wasn't sure why his anger about the whole situation appealed to her so much, but she very much wanted to take in all the anger from his body. She was desperate to please him.

Worried that her words would fail her, she shook her head slightly as she stared into his eyes, acknowledging his statement. Emboldened by her acceptance, Silas's fingertips bit into her buttocks as he held her up, pushing into her repeatedly as her breath caught.

"Tell me you believe me," he said.

"I—I," she tried to speak, but he continued to move inside her.

She nodded, but his grip tightened, unsatisfied.

"Say it," he demanded.

"I believe you," she whispered against his mouth.

"Have you always doubted me?" Clara closed her eyes. She did not want to say. "Answer me."

"Silas, please," she begged, but he wouldn't let her skirt away from his questioning.

"Answer me."

"No!" she said louder than she had intended. "I never doubted you, Silas. I just… I just…"

"You just what?" He sneered.

"I just want you to be happy."

It was a pathetic statement, but Clara couldn't possibly tell him that she wanted him to love her. She had desperately wished that Silas could love her just as ferociously as he had Cynthia but to say it out loud, to beg him to care for her, would be too much. Her pride wouldn't allow it, not when she was so frightened that he would never be able to love her after all.

"Please," she said, tears coming to her eyes. "Silas, please."

"Tell me," he began through clenched teeth, his voice gruff. It seemed her words had affected him greatly. Her fingernails dug into his shoulders as his muscles tightened beneath her hands. "Tell me you…"

Clara felt her heart break for some reason when he couldn't finish. The desperation in his voice, the desire to be in complete control of himself, made her think back to the panic attacks he had suffered in the beginning of their relationship.

"What? Tell you what?" she asked.

But the words would not come. Silas's strong body seemed to barely contain itself. His head dropped to her shoulder as he breathed and for the faintest of moments, Clara heard him speak so gently that he almost sounded desperate.

"Tell me you love me."

Clara's arms clutched to him with all her strength. She did. She really did.

"I love you, Silas," she said softly into his ear.

Silas's mouth found hers and the urgency with which he kissed her tore at her heart. Clara wrapped her arms as tightly as she could around him as he crushed against her. The heavy need she felt break over her just as Silas's body became rigid seemed to hold itself in limbo. He shook and jerked in her arms, and Clara peppered his head with kisses, disappointed that her own release had not come but thankful to be in his arms.

As their breathing calmed, Clara waited for Silas to release her. But even after a long moment, his grip did not slack.

Clara frowned.

"Silas?"

Without warning, Silas turned, Clara high in his arms against his chest as he walked across the room. She gasped slightly as he dropped her on the bed. Clara pushed herself onto her elbows as she watched her husband undress fully, removing his jacket and shirt, before coming over her once more.

Surely, he didn't mean to do that again so soon? But when he crawled over her body, his mouth moving over her chest and stomach, she felt herself relax under his touch. He was far gentler now than he had been moments ago and yet, he was so intent on the task, as if he was completely unaware that he had already reached his peak.

Clara wanted to ask him how he could be so ready to continue, but then his hands were on her and she couldn't think quite right.

Silas moved his hand down her body, the pad of his thumb pressing against the bud of her. Clara arched into his palm as he worked, and she squirmed beneath his mouth as it descended to meet his fingers. She wanted to push him away, to clean herself before he continued, but it was as if Silas was possessed. He didn't have any thought to stop and his sheer determination to bring her to orgasm sent a carnal sense of power and pleasure through her body.

Silas pushed her knees down and when his tongue finally reached her, lapping slowly at her most intimate part, Clara felt a sudden break. Her body convulsed with the rapid jolts of pleasure that enveloped her. She cried out as her hips tilted up and Silas's hands moved around her hips and buttocks as he pulled her up, feasting on her without restraint.

Shockwave after shockwave pulsated through her for what felt like eternity until her body finally sagged. It felt as though her bones had melted as her insides fizzled. Her hips dropped down to the bed as her convulsions ceased and Silas moved up over her body, curling behind her as his arm pressed against her chest, pulling her into a tight embrace.

Clara's mind was foggy, like a night sky after a firework show. She could barely think, let alone decipher what had happened between her and Silas. Worried that trying to put it into words would somehow lessen the fragile state of their relationship in that moment, Clara's hand came over his and squeezed his large fingers beneath her small ones.

Tomorrow, she mused vaguely as her eyes shut. She would speak with him tomorrow.

Chapter Twenty

S ILAS SPENT MUCH of the night demonstrating to Clara just how much she meant to him. But even as she slept—sated and relaxed—by his side, his mind seemed to refuse him any sort of peace and so he woke before the sun rose. He had been so sure about his own heart up until yesterday, but even with his growing relationship with Clara, he couldn't help but think he had been wrong from the beginning.

His friendship with Clara had become the most important thing in his life. While he didn't want to ruin it by falling in love, an act he thought impossible, he couldn't help but have feelings for her. Feelings he had never actually felt before. Feelings of security. Of comfort. Not once could either of those words have described his relationship with Cynthia, which made him wonder if perhaps he had never really loved her to begin with.

His steps slowed as the realization dawned on him. Had he ever really loved *anyone* before?

Surely he had. The sheer amount of passion and excitable fury that had boiled between him and Cynthia had to have been love. It had been intoxicating and painful. Yet even now as he considered it, the memory of those emotions seemed dull and unfocused. Compared to his feelings for Clara… well, the whole experience was completely different. Clara was warm and kind, and it was always a pleasure to be in her presence, even if she baffled him more often than not. She was constantly surprising him with her startling honest and unique perspective.

With Clara, their lovemaking was endearing and poignant. With Cynthia it had been furious and excruciating. While the sexual pleasure he'd shared with Cynthia had been exciting in the moment, he could see looking back on it that passion of that sort was destined to burn itself out. But what he shared with Clara... well, that was something he wanted more than he'd realized.

Clara was the only woman he wanted.

Having woken too late to join the hunt, and finding that he wasn't particularly interested in joining the baron that morning, Silas instead decided to take breakfast on the terrace, where the servants had explained it would be served.

Upon exiting the house, the familiar scent of cheroot smoke wafted on the breeze, causing him to search his surroundings. It had been months since last he smoked, as he had realized Clara didn't particularly care for the smell of smoke on his skin and clothes.

Searching the terrace, his eyes spotted Lord Valle, whose back was turned to Silas as he looked over the western woods, hand on his hip, pushing back his grey tweed coat. In that moment, Silas realized how very similar he and Valle were. They were alike in height and stature and while their coloring was different, they shared similar shaped faces and an arrogance only one in their positions could be born with.

Valle turned then and saw Silas. His face was troubled for a moment before a cool smile came to his lips as he hid his expression.

How odd.

"Ah, your grace," Valle said, coming towards Silas. "I had hoped to see you."

The glint in the young man's eye made Silas both wary and annoyed.

"Whatever for?"

"Come now, let's not be enemies. Cynthia has told me quite a bit about you," he said, grinning. "I think we could be friends of sorts."

Silas was unimpressed. The lad was barely twenty-two, likely brand new to the sort of depravities Cynthia could show him and probably fancied himself something of a devilish rouge. Silas should scare him off, he thought as he rolled the cheroot in between his fingers. He took a step forward, deciding to demonstrate his own dominance.

"Perhaps we could be," Silas said, his voice velvety and low as he came to stand before him. "Perhaps I could make you beg like I made her beg." The young man's sneer faltered as his eyes flashed with both worry and wanting. "Is that what you mean, Lord Valle?"

"I would, um…" He coughed, bringing his fist up to his mouth. "I mean," he said, dropping his voice to a whisper. "Yes. That's exactly what she wants."

Silas gave him a pitying glance.

"Yes, it's always about whatever she wants, isn't it?" he said, shaking his head. "Where did she find you?"

"Excuse me?"

"She must have seemed quite enrapturing. She was to me when we first began our affair. But I assure you, Lord Valle, you will not find your peace with her."

The young lord sneered.

"Much that you know about it. She's the only person in my whole world who accepts me."

Valle was angry, but it didn't hide the pain that crossed his face. Yes, Silas was sure Cynthia accepted him, but it wouldn't be the sort of life he hoped it would be.

"But only because she can get you to do her bidding," Silas challenged. "You shouldn't have to settle for that."

"What do you know about it?" the young man argued. "You couldn't understand what it's like."

Silas couldn't and he did not envy the position the young man was in. Although, as a man who was not restricted by gender when it came to his attractions, he wouldn't tell anyone else how or what to do with their lives. He only meant to warn him away from the devil herself.

"There are people who would accept you, Lord Valle. People who might care for you, as you are. Regardless of what you can do for them."

"I've never met one," he said bitterly.

Silas sighed.

"Perhaps you should keep searching," he said as he left the young man alone, but before he could go, he felt Valle's hand wrap around his wrist.

Having rarely been touched by anyone, Silas gave him a sharp glare, which caused the young man to release him. But when he spoke, Valle's voice was low.

"She wants you back. She means to do what she can to get you."

"She can go to hell."

Valle shook his head.

"You don't understand, Combe. She's obsessed. It's all she's talked about since learning about your marriage. Our engagement was decided on so that we could return to England. My father finds me, shall we say, undesirable, while Cynthia wasn't aware just how ostracized she would be following her divorce. But our coming here? It was at her insistence."

Silas squinted at him and saw the young man's façade drop for a moment. In an instant, he suspected that the young lord was growing tired of his game with Cynthia, a feeling Silas knew all too well himself.

"Why are you telling me this?"

Valle shook his head.

"I… I don't know exactly," he said. "But just know that she won't stop."

Silas looked at the young man for a long time before nodding and walking away. Leave it to Cynthia to engage a man with no support. It was a weak thing to do on her part, but then Silas was realizing that Cynthia was nothing if not cunning.

Regardless, he didn't wish to think about Cynthia's motives. The time had come for Clara and Violet's play, and he was determined to give it his full attention.

Upon entering the parlor, Silas saw that the guests had begun to take their seats. He made his way to an empty settee that stood towards the back and took a seat. Without failure, Cynthia entered the parlor just as his knees bent and she made her way straight towards him, as several heads turned to watch. She seated herself next to him. Silas wanted very much to leave but he remained, strictly to show he wouldn't be chased as the play began.

To his surprise, Violet and Fredrick did an excellent job portraying two people in love. An observer never would have guessed how much they disliked one another. Silas had half a mind to tell his sister that she might have a career on the stage should she ever be desperate enough to need one, but all thoughts of praise fled from his mind when Cynthia leaned ever so slightly towards him.

Her hand wandered to the side of his hip as she tried to get his attention. Annoyed that she would try something so publicly, he shifted away from her, but she only grew more brazen. Her fingers gently found the hem of his pants pocket. Without thinking, he silently grabbed her hand and squeezed her fingers together tightly before glaring at her. Cynthia's eyes fluttered closed, her mouth open slightly, as if she were enjoying his biting grip.

As the scene ended, everyone stood and cheered except for him and Cynthia. Turning his attention to the front of the room, his eyes caught Clara's, whose face dropped at the sight of them sitting together with their hands joined.

Blast. Silas dropped Cynthia's hand and stood, making his way towards Clara. Unfortunately, it seemed she wasn't interested in hearing his explanation.

"Please, Silas, not here," Clara whispered fiercely as she

turned away from him.

"Clara," he said, his tone pleading, which caused her to pause—but only for a moment.

A beat later, she peeled away from him quite easily, and Silas watched her as she disappeared in the crowd.

Chapter Twenty-One

CLARA WAS HARD pressed to keep her temper in check. The sheer jealousy that had torn through her when she peered behind the makeshift curtain to see Silas sitting next to Cynthia had been all consuming. Although she knew it was beneath a duchess to feel anything so strongly, she couldn't help it. Clara was a human being first and foremost, and she was madly in love with her husband, a man who refused to love her back.

Feeling rather sorry for herself, she was surprised when she was approached by Fredrick Trembley to dance. While he was easy with conversation, Clara couldn't help but notice that he was constantly peering over at Violet who was waiting against the far wall. Several yards away, Mr. Lutz stood with the baron and two other gentlemen, seemingly deep in conversation. It was obvious that Violet wished for Mr. Lutz to tear himself away and ask her to dance, but the young man seemed too engrossed to notice her.

"Mr. Trembley," Clara said, nearly halfway through their dance. "Do you think you would be so kind as to ask my sister-in-law to dance?"

Fredrick's eyes snapped to hers.

"Pardon?"

"I know it's uncouth of me to ask and I pray you won't ever tell her, but Violet has been rather gloomy these last few days and I do wish she would smile. I think a dance with you would suit her very well."

His brow furrowed.

"Lady Violet doesn't quite like me, your grace."

"Oh, but she does," Clara lied. "She's said that she's never so challenged as when you are in the room. While it might sound like a complaint, I can assure you, Violet is bored with being so often appeased. To be challenged by anyone is a joy for her to experience."

"Is that so?" he asked, his eyes searching for Violet again.

When the dance ended, Clara curtsied her thanks and went to find the refreshments while Fredrick made his way to Violet. After an exchange of words, a visibly annoyed Violet followed Fredrick onto the dance floor. Holly was being led to the dance floor by some officer who Clara hadn't had the pleasure of meeting, as the baron looked on cheerfully. She watched them as her mind began to wander absently to Silas—and from there to Cynthia.

Clara was aware that Silas was worried that she would be approached by the former duchess, but so far, she hadn't been bothered by her since their initial meeting. She sensed that it would be dangerous to fall into a false sense of security when it came to that woman, but she did not wish to spend all her time worrying about a potential meeting, either. That seemed like it would be giving Cynthia far too much sway over her mind.

Thankfully she had her share of distractions. Holly's presence was reassuring, and since the dance had just ended, Clara started to move around the room, searching for her friend. Unfortunately, she was stalled in her search for several minutes when the baron introduced her to an older woman, the Viscountess of Sunderland. Apparently, she was an old friend of the dowager countess and was eager for Clara to send her mother-in-law her regards.

Once Clara was able to pull herself away from the conversation, she gazed across the ballroom to see if she could find Holly, only she was nowhere to be found. Frowning slightly, she made her way across the ballroom, ready to search the hallway—but she paused when she overheard a barely familiar male voice speaking.

"…and I'm sure I do not know where Miss Violet has disappeared to, though I did see her with that Fredrick Trembley character not too long ago."

Upset by the implications of the man's words, Clara turned around and spotted Lord Valle. In a moment of sheer madness and indignation, she approached the man. Holding out her hand to him, he stopped speaking mid-sentence as his eyes caught on her.

"Your grace?" he asked, sounding confused.

"It is your turn to dance, Lord Valle," she said smoothly. "I have you written down twice on my card and I shan't be disappointed."

Both knew he had never asked her for a dance, and that she certainly wouldn't have permitted him one if he had, but to say no in front of these people would be shocking. He was a gentleman and couldn't actively cut her. He extended his hand.

She hesitated to meet his eyes until they reached the dance floor. When the music started, she began her questioning.

"What do you think you were doing? Are you trying to cause some sort of scandal for Violet and Fredrick?"

His eyes snapped to hers.

"Of course not. I was merely mentioning that I haven't seen either of them for nearly a half hour."

Clara's mouth set in a thin line. She leaned forward.

"I don't know what you've got planned for my sister-in-law, but I promise you, Lord Valle, should anything untoward happen to Violet, you will incur the wrath of my husband. While most men might be able to forgive those who work against their families, I assure you, the duke shall neither forgive or forget."

Lord Valle swallowed visibly, the color draining from his cheeks.

"It wasn't my idea," he whispered back as they danced. "Cynthia put me up to it."

"Whatever for?"

"Why does she do anything?" he hissed, more to himself than to her. "She's a harbinger of chaos. If I was in a better position I might…"

He shook his head and Clara's brow lifted. It was surprising to hear the young lord's critique of his fiancée. He seemed rather put out by Cynthia's meddling.

"Can you tell me what her plan is, so that we might undo it?"

He shifted uncomfortably, but after a moment, Lord Valle nodded.

"Cynthia wanted me to lock Lady Violet away with Mr. Lutz. Apparently, she learned that your sister-in-law has feelings for the man."

That had been true at the time of their arrival, but in the days since, Mr. Lutz had been far too busy conversing about a trip to America or something of the sort to acknowledge Violet. In response, Violet's affection for the writer seemed to have cooled.

Turning to search the room, Clara caught sight of Mr. Lutz, flanked by two elderly gentlemen. He seemed to be deep in conversation with them. Clara frowned.

"Mr. Lutz is over there."

"Yes, I know," Lord Valle said. "But Cynthia wasn't particularly worried about who Violet was locked up with, just that she was locked up."

Clara looked at him.

"Who is she with?" she asked quietly.

"Mr. Trembley," he said. "I didn't want to do it, but she threatened… I mean, she insisted."

Clara was surprised to find herself feeling sorry for Cynthia's fiancé. What threat could she have used against this man?

"You must find them and set things right, Lord Valle. My husband will be incensed if he discovers your fiancée's plot."

"She's with him," he said. "It was her idea to cause a distraction so that she might try to… to revisit her relationship with the duke."

Though Clara felt a sudden stabbing feeling in her heart, she tried to ignore it. If Silas had been speaking the truth—and she hoped he had—he wouldn't fall victim to her feminine wiles.

"Thank you for telling me. And please hurry," she said as the music came to an end. She curtsied as he bowed and nearly went their separate ways when Clara spoke. "And Lord Valle?"

"Yes?"

"I think, for the sake of your health, you should be gone from here within the hour. And perhaps you should consider going alone."

A sad shadow passed over his eyes.

"Always."

"No," she said, taking a step towards him. "I only think to preserve you from my husband's wrath, but when he learns that you helped... well, I daresay you'll always be welcome to Greystone." She nodded. "If Violet's reputation remains intact, that is."

A hopeful smile shone on the young lord's face before he turned to leave the room. Clara was now on a mission to find Silas.

Hurrying from the ballroom, Clara first searched the parlor then the card room, making several excuses as she was cornered and nearly roped into conversation. After searching the library and even the billiards room, Clara had begun to worry that they had gone somewhere out in the gardens when she saw the baron's private office. Deciding just to peer into the room before heading to the back terrace, Clara pushed open the door.

There, on the other side of the room, she saw Silas's back facing her, with long, delicate arms wrapped around him at the waist.

A ringing sound echoed in her ears as her cheeks warmed. Clara had always thought herself a level headed woman, she had never felt so dejected, nor so furious, in her entire life. Even when she was being gambled away by Dilworth, she had never felt lower than she did at that moment. The man she loved, embraced by that wicked woman, a woman he had once loved. It was almost too much.

Thankfully, Silas seemed eager to have Cynthia off of him and pulled at her hands, stepping back as he did.

"Cynthia, stop it."

"Don't you remember it, Silas? How painfully wonderful it was? How terribly gutting it was between us?" Her words caused Clara to feel ill. "It was the most satisfying feeling in both of our lives."

"No—"

"*Ah-hem.*"

Clara was sure that her shoulders were straight and her chin was high when she made the throaty little noise that called both of their attentions away from one another. Silas pulled away from Cynthia's desperate grasp, causing her to stumble slightly. He walked purposefully towards his wife.

"Clara—"

"Please, Silas," Clara struggled to say, her tone shaky. "We don't have time. You have to find Violet."

Silas tilted his head, unsure.

"Excuse me?"

"Have the little love birds been caught yet?" Cynthia's voice sounded from behind him.

Clara ignored her, focusing instead on her husband.

"Lord Valle told me that he locked Violet and Fredrick away. I'm not sure where but he went to undo it. I'm worried that her reputation is at risk." Clara nodded at Cynthia, causing Silas to turn around. "Lord Valle said it was her idea and that she somehow forced his hand to commit it."

"How dare he say that," Cynthia hissed. "I should turn him out for being such a weakling."

"What game are you playing at?" Silas bellowed at Cynthia, who seemed startled by his tone. "Violet has never done anything except support you, even when you left."

"It's just a little fun, Silas," she said, her brow furrowing. "We used to have such fun together."

"Stay the hell away from me and my family," he thundered.

Clara's hand went to his bicep and stilled his rage. The violent jealousy that shone in Cynthia's eyes made Clara curious.

"There's no time for that. Find them, Silas," Clara said earnestly.

With one last disgusted look at Cynthia, he tore from the room. Clara turned to follow him, eager to be away from this woman, but Cynthia's voice stopped her.

"He'll eventually come back, you know," she said, her shrill tone filled with bitterness. "Silas and I are meant for one another. We don't belong with anyone else. We are one and the same, if you will. He may think he can live without the pain, but he's wrong. It's an addiction, and no sweet kisses from you or any other woman can block it out. It's too delicious to stay away from. When he realizes you can't give him what he wants, he'll come back to me."

Clara turned slowly to face the woman she had once believed was her rival. Rival would be the word, if she felt like she compared to her at all, but she didn't. Clara would always be happy because she was pleased with herself. Cynthia would never be content because she couldn't bear to be at peace with anyone, including herself.

It almost made Clara feel sorry for what she was about to do.

Almost.

She watched a smug smile appear on Cynthia's lips as Clara walked towards her.

"What could he possibly see in someone like—" SMACK. "AHH!"

Clara shook out her hand, the sting biting her palm. Never in her life had she ever struck someone and she was surprised by how much it hurt.

"You stupid cow!" Cynthia screamed through the hand she held against her face.

"Stay away from my husband," Clara warned. "I am not as refined as other ladies of my position, but do not mistake my lack of polish for a lack of conviction. I may not know how to play clever games, but I will not tolerate threats to my family." Cynthia seethed at her as Clara rolled her shoulders back. She took a deep breath and continued. "Do not cross me, Cynthia. Silas does not belong to you anymore. Do you understand?"

"You stupid—"

"If you try to hurt anyone I care about again, I will not hesitate to use every bit of my position and power to see that you never step foot in England again. From what I understand, your situation here is already quite precarious. I've no doubt you were hoping to marry Lord Valle to try and repair your reputation. If you were set on that plan, I suggest you leave and chase after him before he gets away." She took a step towards Cynthia, who took a step back. "Do you understand me?" Clara said slowly.

It was evident that she wanted to argue, but Clara's words were not hollow. It was apparent that Cynthia would not be welcomed into the homes of any members of the peerage so long as she held the stigma of her divorce. Even if she did manage to marry Lord Valle, she would be shunned if Clara wished her to be. In all honesty, Clara was in a very powerful position.

Realization seemed to break over Cynthia, and defeat immediately began to seep through her. After a moment of silence, she nodded.

"Yes. Yes, just leave me alone."

"I plan to," Clara said, turning on her heel as she left the room.

Once she was in the hallway, Clara let guilt wash over her. Never in her entire life had she ever sunk so low as to harm another person through physical violence. In fact, she had often thought those who acted out and claimed to be controlled by their baser emotions were foolish. Reprehensible, even.

Lord forgive her.

She would be lying if she didn't admit a small part of her

found a bit of satisfaction in knocking Cynthia off her proverbial high horse. It was an instance she hoped never to repeat or return to, but she also knew that she would not hesitate if she found Cynthia lurking about her family again.

All the sense of rightful justice she felt in putting Cynthia in her place did not take away from the very real pain that Silas seemed unwilling to love her. Perhaps he had been right all along. Perhaps their marriage was one of friendship and nothing more.

When she reached her rooms, she found Silas and a distraught Violet, who was weeping openly.

"Goodness, what's going on here?" Clara asked.

"We're leaving," Silas said, his tone gruff. "Now."

"Tonight? While the ball is taking place?"

"Yes," he spoke. Violet whimpered and Silas gave her a furious expression. "Not a word out of you."

"You're a brute!" Violet yelled.

Clara gave her husband an uneasy glance.

"Silas, you didn't hurt anyone, did you?"

"Yes, he did!" Violet hurriedly exclaimed as maids and manservants moved about them. "He nearly murdered Fredrick Trembley."

"Fredrick?" Clara repeated, her face crumbling into confusion. "Why on earth would you have done that?"

"Care to share?" Silas asked his sister sarcastically as a bright red stained her cheeks. "No? Well, then, it falls to me to tell her that that bastard Fredrick Trembley had his hands up your—"

"Oh, stop it! Stop!" Violet shouted, putting her hands to her ears. "Don't say it!"

"You can't even talk about it! What makes you think you'd even be ready to do… that?" he said, seemingly stumbling over his words. Clara saw an embarrassed flush come to his cheeks. It appeared Silas was less than eager to talk about his sister's situation. "Besides it was a godsend that I got to you before that roving pack of gossip mongers found you," he said, turning back to Clara. "Did you know Valle sent out a damn search party for them?"

"I wish they had found me!" Violet snapped, which caused her brother to stop what he was doing and come up to her. "It wouldn't have been nearly as mortifying."

Clara took several steps forward and placed both hands up between them.

"Violet, I'm sure whatever embarrassment you've endured here tonight shall not live forever, and whatever has been ruined can be mended. Your brother was worried about you, and I know you do not hate him." She took a breath. "Now, please make sure all your things are gathered from your room and meet us downstairs. Promptly."

Violet gave Clara a small nod and ran back to her room. When Clara turned to face Silas, he seemed far too distracted to discuss what had transpired between him and Cynthia, although from the words he spoke next, it was clear she was at the forefront of his mind.

"That vile snake of a woman," he cursed, running his hand through his hair. "To go after Violet that way. I should strangle her."

"Cynthia won't be an issue any longer," Clara said evenly, as she went behind the silk screen to change into her travel dress. "In fact, I think she may leave the country again as Lord Valle will not have her."

"Not an issue?" Silas repeated, coming behind the screen. "How?"

Clara snapped her dress tightly.

"Silas, please."

"What do you mean she won't be an issue?"

Clara's cheeks flared hot.

"We had words," she said, avoiding his eyes. "She threatened you."

"Did she?" he asked, unimpressed. "Empty threats, I assure you. She has no sway over me."

"No, but it seems that was enough for me to do something,"

Clara admitted. "I slapped her."

Silence followed for a long moment before Clara looked up. Silas was staring at her, dumbfounded.

"You what?"

"I slapped her," Clara repeated, shame bubbling within her. "I'm not proud of it."

Clara held her breath, worried about how he might react.

"You slapped her?" he said, the words seemingly too hard for him to comprehend. He reached for her. "In the face?"

"Yes, Silas, in the face," she said, pushing him away so that she could finish dressing.

"Because she threatened me?"

"Yes."

"What did she say?"

"It's hardly worth repeating," Clara said, putting her arms through the sleeves of her travel dress.

"But—"

"Please, Silas, I just wish to be away from this place." She paused, her heart aching for some reason. "Please."

A cloud of worry passed over Silas's face before he nodded.

"Yes. Of course."

Within the hour, Silas, Violet and Clara were packed away in a silent carriage as it pulled away from the baron's home. Uncomfortable and unsure, it seemed that no one wished to speak about the events that had transpired at Bairnsdale's home.

Clara felt at odds the whole ride home. Unable to sleep, she spent the night replaying the entirety of their stay at the baron's and wondering if she could have done something differently. Guilt seemed to be her only companion, for every time she tried to make eye contact with either Violet or Silas, they avoided her eyes. Perhaps Violet was too preoccupied with her own worries, but that Silas should be ignoring her carved at her heart.

Doubt like she had never known crept into her veins as the night wore on. Silas was probably ashamed that she had struck someone. It wasn't something a lady in her position should ever do. There was no reason for her to stoop to such behavior. Surely, he was aghast at her conduct.

Falling in and out of sleep, Clara was tormented with dreams of Silas and Cynthia, locked in one another's arms. Her words filtered through Clara's mind. When they finally reached the halfway point to Greystone late the next morning, stopping to refresh themselves at an inn called the Fox and Horn, Clara could barely move her stiff body.

Silas left the carriage silently, while Clara and Violet waited patiently for him to return. After only moments, he returned and escorted both women inside the inn.

Upon entering the room, Clara saw a hip bath had been prepared and while she desperately wanted to wash herself, she wasn't eager to do so in front of Silas. Thankfully, he left her alone, escorting Violet to her own room.

Tired and miserable, Clara slowly undid the front buttons of her travel gown, which was dusty and dirty from the tavern's yard. She quickly removed the rest of her clothes and dropped herself into the hip bath. Taking a sliver of soap, she lathered a piece of cloth and scrubbed herself clean. When she was done, she quickly dressed in a chemise, lifted the covers, and dropped into the bed.

Clara closed her eyes, hoping to get some sleep before they continued their journey.

Chapter Twenty-Two

S ILAS OPENED THE door to Violet's room, positioned just across the hallway from his and Clara's. She brushed past him in a huff. While he was certain he had been fully justified in ripping Fredrick off of his sister, a pang of guilt shot through him at her distress.

"I was only trying to protect you," he said gruffly, causing her to stop. "I don't know why you think I'm constantly trying to ruin your life, but I promise you, my only intention is to preserve your reputation and possibly save you some heartache."

For a moment she didn't speak and Silas assumed she would continue with the silent treatment he had suffered from both women during their trip from Bairnsdale's home. Turning to leave, he was halfway out the door when Violet spoke.

"I am not so fragile that I cannot suffer a bit of heartache, Silas," she said over her shoulder, her eyes cast down. "If I was ever allowed to meet someone."

"You met Lutz, didn't you?"

"Yes, last year before you went into hiding," she said, turning around to face him. "I've been kept up in Greystone with you for over a year. Don't you think it a bit unfair that I should have to be locked away from the world simply because you refused to participate in living?"

Silas frowned.

"I didn't stop living. I married—"

"Yes, you did," she said pointedly, her eyes becoming expressive. "You went to London at the behest of Lord Trembley after being confined to your wing of the house for nearly a year. Then you returned home several weeks later married to a complete stranger." She shook her head before he had a chance to open his mouth to defend Clara. "And I do not mean to disparage her. I quite like Clara and am glad of your marriage, but you cannot imagine how shocking it was, especially after your yearlong internment. Not to mention how unfair it was."

Guilt hit Silas square in the heart. He hadn't realized how deeply his actions had impacted his sister. She sat on the bed with a gentle plop and Silas drove his fingers through his hair. He had thought he was protecting her.

Coming forward, he shook his head.

"I didn't realize that my actions had caused you suffering."

Violet rolled her eyes.

"It wasn't suffering exactly. I did have my correspondence and I was permitted to stay with our cousins in Bedfordshire," she said. She shrugged gently as she inhaled. "I just wish you weren't so determined to see me unhappy."

"I don't want you to be unhappy."

"Don't you? You scared Mr. Lutz off. He told me last night that he was making arrangements to visit New Orleans of all places. He said he got the idea from you."

Silas's brow pinched.

"He wasn't focused on you, Violet."

"He also lacked a fortune."

"He lacked an entire means of providing for anyone more than himself, but his lack of standing wasn't so great a mark against him. The minute I mentioned traveling, his eyes lit up. He is focused on his career and there's no blaming him for that." Silas frowned. "But he wasn't ready to settle down."

"And Fredrick?"

Silas felt his anger grow remembering the moment he walked

in on his sister being manhandled by the fool. He glowered.

"That bas—ah," he stopped himself from cursing in front of her, her brows hitched up. "Fredrick knew better than to do what he was doing."

Violet smiled weakly at him.

"You're much too judgmental, brother," she said.

He watched her, a mixture of sibling reverence and overall disgust.

"Good lord, Violet, don't tell me you actually like the idiot?"

"He's not an idiot," she said with a slight frown. "And I do."

"Then he can court you the proper way. With a chaperone." Violet frowned peevishly until he added, "Clara will surely be happy to act as one."

His sister smiled up at him, knowing full well that Clara would not be nearly as stringent with the rules of propriety as others might be. She tilted her head.

"You know, I think you made the right choice, marrying Clara almost as soon as you met her."

Silas nodded, glancing at the door. He wanted to return to his room and speak with his wife, but not before he procured them something to eat.

Turning back to Violet, he smirked.

"Perhaps I should speak with her now."

Violet pressed her lips together, trying to smother a smile. She nodded.

"I think you should."

Silas closed the door behind him and went downstairs to find them a tray of food. When he returned to his room, he entered and found a heap beneath the blankets. Noting the worn gown laid out over a chair next to the hip bath, Silas guessed Clara had bathed already.

Walking toward the bed, he wondered if she was awake. Perhaps he should wait to have this discussion until they returned to Greystone... but something in him wouldn't relent. He had waited too long as it was. They needed to have this conversation without any further delay.

Moving towards the bed, he pressed his hand down to the tallest point of the mountain of blankets. It felt like her shoulder, but he couldn't be sure.

"Clara?"

At first, she didn't make a sound. Discouraged, he pulled his arm back, deciding to let her rest. He turned away, dejected and debating on taking a bath himself when a mumbled voice came from the bed.

"Yes?"

Turning back, he waited for the blankets to be pushed away as his wife emerged from beneath the sheets. She was visibly tired, with weary eyes and slightly disheveled hair but he was sure he had never seen her more beautiful.

"Silas—"

"Clara, I love you," he said, quickly, worried that he would lose his nerve if he hesitated. "I thought I was incapable. I thought I was too broken to love again, but I think that I was never heartbroken to begin with, not truly."

Clara looked at him with wide eyes.

"You weren't?"

He shook his head.

"No. Because I never knew what love truly was until I met you," he said. "The calm I feel in your presence. The happiness I feel when you say my name." He sat on the bed and reached for her hands. Pulling them to his chest, he continued. "I'm forever in awe of your patience, your ability to love someone who told you he couldn't return it." Her head dropped, but his hand came to her chin. "Your kindness and your bravery have astounded me."

"Bravery?" Clara laughed, though she didn't seem amused. "What bravery have I shown?" She shook her head. "I've never done a brave thing in my entire life."

"You have," he said. "You loved me when there was no hope for it. Don't you see? You brought me back to life."

Emotion swept over her face as her eyes shone.

"And you love me?" she asked.

Silas felt it deep in his chest. Almost as if his heart was expanding.

"Yes, I do," he said slowly, his hand coming up to her cheek.

A tear rolled down Clara's cheek before she spoke.

"I love you too."

Silas bent down to kiss her and didn't stop for quite some time.

Epilogue

One year later…

"CLARA?" SILAS CALLED throughout the foyer of Greystone, having just searched the library and dining hall for his wife. "Clara?"

"Have you checked the garden?" Violet asked, coming down the staircase. "I believe she said she was intent on going there once we left."

"No," he said coming around the back of the staircase to look up at her. "I thought you and Mother were going back to London this morning?"

"We are," Violet said, tugging on her gloves as she came down the steps. "But she insisted on staying a few more hours to play with the Augustus. I was just following her to the carriage. I'm afraid Mama has become one of those doting grandparents."

Silas smirked and leaned on the baluster. His son, Augustus Harrison Winters, had been born only two months ago and he could barely smile, let alone be played with. And yet, his mother had found that she was quite happy to be a grandmother. She was unable to help herself when it came to buying the baby presents that he wouldn't be able to use for months, and she had barely left Clara's side since their son was born.

"It was bound to happen," he said. "Are you attending the

Trembley party then?"

"Yes, but Fredrick is trying to get out of it," Violet said, shaking her head. "He wants to go to the opera instead, but Derek is quite fixated on him being there. I swear, why I ever agreed to such a long engagement is beyond me."

"A few months isn't so long."

"After a half a year of courting, and another half year of being engaged, a day is torment," she said ruefully. "At your insistence, we've waited. Even though you didn't wait more than a month."

"It was different for Clara and I."

"How so?"

"I was reckless and she was desperate."

Violet laughed, not believing a word he said.

"I should like to have our engagement over and done with by now."

"All in good time, sister," he said. "All in good time."

"Yes, I know," she said, coming down to let Silas kiss her on the cheek. She pulled back and smiled. "Tell Clara I said goodbye and that we're eager to see her in London."

"We'll be along in a few weeks."

"She did mention she might wish to travel to Bedfordshire, though." Violet frowned slightly. "It was a tragic thing, what happened to her friend, was it not? To lose a husband so quickly."

Holly had gone through with marrying the elderly baron, but had done so while he was on his deathbed. They had only been married a few days before he passed away. Now Holly was in mourning.

He nodded solemnly.

"Yes, it is."

Violet sighed.

"Be well, brother."

"You too," he said, turning down to walk out the back of the house.

A year after marrying Clara, Silas still had a problem finding his wife. She was often disappearing, though she had done so less and less the larger she had become during her pregnancy. Since giving birth, she had disappeared a handful of times with the new baby and while he wasn't particularly worried, he did prefer to be near her during her impromptu walks.

Clara's pregnancy had been a difficult one and she had been bedridden for the last few months due to the impending baby's substantial size. Augustus had been born on the first of May and her recovery had been trying. It seemed she was only ever completely content when she was outside.

He could hear a voice singing a sweet, calming song from within the maze as Silas came down the back terrace steps. He headed towards the hedgerow, following the gentle sound. After only a few moments he found his wife sat on the stone bench, feeding their young son.

Silas felt the breath catch in his chest at the sight before him. He had been sure Clara couldn't grow more beautiful, and yet she had miraculously done so. The sight of his son in her arms made his entire soul vibrate. As Silas watched them together in this one, perfect moment, he knew their future would be bright. Seemingly blissfully unaware of her husband's approach, Clara leaned her back gently against the hedge, closed her eyes and smiled with all the contentment in the world.

This image would be burned in his memory for all time. He came forward, his footsteps waking her from her daydream. Her eyes, bright and happy to see him, nearly sparkled as he approached.

"Good afternoon, husband," she said softly, before turning back to gaze at their son.

"You are a vision," he said coming to sit next to her. He kissed her head as he smiled down at this picture of love. "Your in-laws are leaving."

She lifted her eyes to meet his, slightly worried.

"Oh, I had hoped to say goodbye," she said, but Silas shook his head.

"We'll see them soon enough," he said, pulling the sleeping

baby from her arms.

Silas hadn't been able to go more than a few hours between holding his son. He was perhaps too attentive for a man of his position and overtly protective when it came to his wife and child, but then he couldn't help how he felt.

Clara looked up at him lovingly, resting her head against his shoulder.

"Are you happy, Silas?" she asked after a moment.

"Forever, my love… Forever."

The End

About the Author

Matilda Madison lives in the Pocono mountains of Pennsylvania. A history lover, she finds immense joy in knowing useless facts, exploring the woods around her home, and drinking copious amounts of tea. When she's not writing, she can be found researching obscured periods for her books, refurbishing old furniture, and baking.

Catch up with me anytime on my socials.
Website – www.matildamadison.com
Instagram – matildamadisonbooks
TikTok – @matildamadison